BEDLOE

A True Fable

BEDLOE

A True Fable

Tony Powers

Bambaz Press
Los Angeles 2020

Cover Design: Howard Puris
Author Photo: Nancy Friedman

Copyright ©2020 by Tony Powers
Printed in the United States of America

ISBN: 9798680366479

Bambaz Press
548 S Spring Street Suite 1201
Los Angeles CA 90013

bambi@bambaz.press

For Linda, who always encouraged.

"Those who can make you believe absurdities can make you commit atrocities."

–Voltaire

"Any government that waves a flag while lying to its people is an incredible tyranny—an incredible tyranny…believe me."

–President/Chairman Ransom B. Conover

"I'm

telling you, she's really dead." He coughed.

"She hasn't been killed dad. She's an actress playing a part. She hasn't been murdered. *Every time we watch this show we have the same argument. Never fails.* And you hardly even watch it, you were in the back for most of it."

John Bedloe, a tired 48, and his 16-year-old son James, were giving each other haircuts inside their rusted old broken-down unheated mobile home. Calling it mobile was a *tiny* exaggeration since its engine, transmission and wheels were stripped and sold long ago and it now rested on cinder blocks. The "mobile" home was one of two that sat in an overgrown trash-filled foul smelling lot on the corner of a run-down block in the Eastern part of the blighted New York City borough of the Bronx. The lot, like the entire borough, when it wasn't calf-high deep in dirty slush, was covered in the snow which had been falling for the last four days and which drifts were piled higher because of the rotting garbage it lay on—and which would again soon turn to the deep, dirty, brown slush by the heavy rains and occasional oppressive heat that alternated with the falling snow

"I'm concerned that whenever this thing is on that you can bring yourself to watch it. And by the way, let me thank you for the hundredth time for not making me watch those dumb cartoons anymore. So, why can't you believe it's not beyond these people to kill someone on TV?"

"And you believe the rape was real too?"

"Of course it was."

"Dad, it's a TV drama. They wouldn't do that. All due respect you're…"

"What? Crazy? Sit still James or I'll cut off your ear. It's bad enough I'm shivering."

"I'm sorry pop…I've almost got enough for that heater.

The CanTel sweat clothing they wore didn't do much to keep them warm. He was almost finished cutting his son's hair inside this wreck they called home while a horrific TV show played on TV.

I can't watch this fucking thing…I don't know how he can. They wouldn't do that. Sure. They had long stopped going to a barber because who had the money for a haircut. He'd bought a barber's scissors and, every two months or so, since his son was twelve, they'd been taking turns cutting each other's hair.

"And now you're gonna tell me that lopping off someone's head is also real."

"Yes. That's exactly what I'm—He coughed—What I'm 'gonna' tell you." *Gonna.*

"A guillotine? Real? If it is Pop, it's very cutting edge." Deadpan.

"James, please stop moving your head." *Too bad it isn't Jeffers' head on that block. Followed by his whole slimy family.*

"You know, they have murder scenes in TV shows all the time. The special effects look totally real. Holywood is filled with actors who can make you believe they're dying. That's what actors do, Dad. They're good. They can make you believe."

Holy-wood? "James, they're not that good, I'm sorry! Listen, before you were born, I saw people being killed in Iraq—I know what the real thing looks like. That's real. I know you believe these people, I know you can't bring yourself to believe they could do such a thing. They could, they do. And FYI it used to be *Holly*wood. *Holly*—not *holy*. They deleted an L for Chrissakes."

"Come on, Pop…They deleted an L. I mean, what have you got against religion? And Pop…please…again with the blasphemy?"

Oh, for the…that fucking school! One evening, when James had just begun taking an interest in FAIR News, John and his son had a short discussion about the FAIR slogan: "Truth. Not Facts." James was amazed that his father could not grasp the idea that people just make up any old facts. John soon realized that his twelve-year-old son was already propagandized beyond his reach no matter how logical were his arguments against the tyranny they were living under.

Now, as then, he was caught between trying to educate his 16-year-old son and negating many of his son's deeply held beliefs. The futility of it was almost too much to bear. So early on, for all practical purposes, he threw his arms up in surrender. There were few exceptions: the playful exchanges such as this disagreement about the TV show R!M!E! for example. What made the whole thing even worse for him, even more painful, was that since James was old enough to comprehend language his father watched that very language he so loved became perverted. And now it was beyond saving.

"James, look at all the misery they haven't done anything about. In fact, they've quintupled it. This is the ne plus ultra of bread and circus. This show is the epitome of look over there while we screw you."

As well as being upset whenever his father cursed or took the "Lord's name in vain," they had a version of this discussion—well, argument—every single time before, during, and after he watched his favorite FAIR-TV show: R!M!E! Rape! Murder! Execution!

My son can watch this fucking obscenity but he gets upset if I say "Jesus"?

In R!M!E!, sometimes the person raped was a woman, sometimes a man, sometimes even a teen, either girl or boy. The person doing the raping would then kill his victim and, in turn, would then be executed—sometimes by electrocution, sometimes by gas chamber, and sometimes, as in tonight's show, by guillotine. The show's ratings were astronomical. It was the single most-watched show in the history of television. It had franchises in over one hundred and eight countries in the world and was aired in over three thousand fifty different languages. He had been watching it since its inception on FAIR-TV in 2032 when he was eight years old. Most Associates all over the world had by now become inured to whatever horrors they saw, and they believed it was *just* a show. The few who didn't, and they *were* few, stayed silent. James believed it was a show, and he and his father had been having this argument since then. The year he was born, 2024, was the year his father dubbed the "eight-year anniversary of the fun-house mirror." *What the heck does that mean, Pop? What's a fun house mirror? What's a fun house? This isn't.*

John Bedloe did have some interesting ideas—that was for sure. But, to hear him tell it; *nothing* that the government *ever* did since 2017 was for the benefit of anyone who *wasn't* filthy rich—and, that the newly elected President back in late 2016 Ransom B. Conover should have been called Ransom B. Conjob and his chip-off-the-old-block son was worse. Ransom Conover Jr. reminded Bedloe every time that the shit doesn't fall far from the asshole.

"Practically everything that you see on FAIR is a lie—*except* this show!"
"Come on…aren't you being a bit…I dunno…"

"Angry? Bitter? I dam—sorry…I darn well am. So what? It doesn't alter the fact that this so-called Network is pure propaganda bullsh—it's all lies, James." This statement which used to be an exclamation was now offered in exhausted resignation.

He held up a small mirror for his son so he could check out his cut.

"Not bad."

"Next!

That was Bedloe's little joke every time they gave each other haircuts. As James got up, he took the towel that had seen far better days from his shoulders and handed it to his father who threw it over his own shoulders as he sat.

"A little off the top please…and the back needs some gardening. Oh man, come on… what a…how on earth can you *watch* this show? Somebody ought to throw a bomb…" *Don't give him any dumb ideas.* He stifled another cough. *But somebody ought to throw a bomb into this Network headquarters. Not that James ever would but…*

James began cutting his father's hair. *I respect him. Whatever he has to say on whatever subject comes up—I listen. Pop's the smartest person I know. Nobody at work is as smart—for sure. I'll give him that and more. But he sure has some way out theories and hypotheses. And boy, can he be dark. The new chairman is a lying bumbling criminal, nothing is ever going to get any better, in fact it's gonna get worse—if that's even possible…Nothing on FAIR is to be believed, nothing is what it appears to be, there's no way out of the servitude we're subjected to – no matter what they say on TV… And no one, no one, should be trusted. I dunno, that's pretty darn paranoid and overly suspicious. I mean, FAIR? They bring us the whole world. Why can't he see that? I think it's just like they say it is: "We bring you the world."*

His father—and his mother, Jane—had tried in vain to keep him from watching FAIR-TV when he was a very small child. But they did have the silliest cartoons that could easily occupy a restless child, and so they gave in to his insistence on watching. The boy, James, now sixteen, had been a loyal FAIR viewer since age four and learned everything he knew from the now 460 FAIR channels—world-wide—300 of which were news, which, of course, he believed. He was well and thoroughly propagandized. By his schooling and by FAIR. This fact made his father very, very sad: *it's my fault. Nothing could've been done about the schooling…But the TV? I should've been tougher. At least he's off the dumb cartoons.* Whenever he tried to turn off the TV, which was pretty much every day, it would either eventually turn itself back on, or his son, addicted to FAIR-TV, would turn it on. This was pretty much the same story in every Associate household in the country— and, in the world. *I wonder how Jane would have handled this.*

"Why do you think that TV is free?"

"So people can have free entertainment, everything else is so expensive. It helps wi—"

"No. No. Jamesy - James…my sweet son…When are you going to get it into your head, it's so everyone can be fed the lies? That's the *only* reason it's *free*."

His father was only half-right about this. He didn't know the other half of why TV was free, why governments everywhere subsidized FAIR and also provided people with free TV sets. He would soon find out. Nor could he have known how different TV was in the Elite Districts of the world's cities. Meanwhile, he was in a constant battle with his son over what*ever* FAIR News reported.

"Dad, lighten up, it's a drama. These are actors. No one is actually being raped or murdered—*or* executed. No one."

I wish I knew how to get through to him. This was a thought they shared.

Just then a siren sounded. Then a voice: "This is FAIR Sunny News. Then the pretty blonde reporter appeared standing in front of what looked like a medical clinic somewhere.

"Over 250 new free clinics will shortly open all across the country. The administration tells us that these clinics will be free to the public.

FAIR Sunny News will continue to monitor this blessing and give the locations of each of these clinics as they open. Joanne Green, FAIR News Washington. Back to you, Laurie."

"Well, we know *that's* going to happen right, James?"

"Pop...*Please*...Have a little faith. Things *will* get better. I saw where our new Chairman said that th—"

"No James, please...You *can't* believe what comes out of the mouths of FAIR or our new '*Server.*' You're smarter than that."

"Things're going to get better pop. I know it."

"Oh Chri—Sorry, son. Sorry. It's reflex. James, they've been saying the same thing for more years than you've been on this earth—have you looked around lately?"

"Pop, try. Please. Faith...okay? This new Chairman is different."

Ah yes. Faith. The answer according to James.

"You know...I *really* love you James. You know that. But you are seriously deluded. But hey...I'll tell you what. I *will* have faith. Okay? But when those clinics somehow don't open will you admit these people are liars?"

Even as John Bedloe said it he knew there would be no way to know if these clinics ever opened or not. Rather, it would just slip into the dust cloud in the sky, along with the rest of FAIR's never-ending sunny news.

James finished trimming his father's hair, combed it neatly, and held the mirror for him so he could check the back.

"Very nice. Thanks. "No proble—

His father's look brought him up short. "Um...you're welcome."

John stared at his face in the mirror and then slowly rose from the chair.

"Jesu---" *Johnny! Some respect! You have to stop doing that!*—

"Sorry kid. I haven't shaved in a week. That's another thing I have to get—disposable razors. And we need toilet paper. Toilet paper or razors? Can't get both."

"I'll give you one guess which to get. Anyway, you look ragged. I mean rugged." He laughed.

His father also laughed—mirthlessly—while slowly shaking his head.

"It's cold in here kid…Do we have any M-POW!-r?"

"I brought home a four-pak. We have seven cans."

"My *man*. Let's get wasted."

"There's a good BashBall game on tonight. The Cripplers are playing."

Bedloe shrugged.

"Sure. Why not?"

Long as I'm stoned out of my mind. He started coughing again.

One

of John Bedloe's great pleasures in life had been that every morning over breakfast he would read the sports pages of his newspaper, and then after breakfast, finish reading the rest of it in the bathroom. It was his morning routine. He was very *much* a person of routine. He didn't take a shower in the morning preferring instead to just wash his face and underarms because his work as a machinist was quite sweaty and to his way of thinking; why take a shower when he was just going to need another one an hour after he got to work? Whatever time he got home from work, he would spend a few minutes with Jane, and later with both Jane and his son James, and *then* he would take a shower. That was usually around six o'clock. And, because he was such a creature of habit, his friends all knew not to call him at six because they all knew at that time he'd be luxuriating under that nice warm shower. He called this routine "washing off the day." He also did not like to hang out after work. He wanted to be home and got really antsy if he wasn't home by…at the latest six-thirty. He equated his need to get home anywhere between five-thirty to six-thirty as akin to a salmon needing to swim upstream to spawn —it was deeply embedded in his DNA. Also, they liked to begin their preparation of dinner around seven—his specialties, seafood, pastas, Caesar salad, were pretty good. Jane's dishes were top-drawer. Everything she cooked was delicious. She was a foodie and could have been a chef and, since she was an adventurous eater—as was he—they enjoyed many exotic dishes together. She liked his favorites such as trippa alla Romana and octopus—and she prepared them skillfully and sublimely. Done together, this ritual of prep, dining, and doing the dishes was usually reserved for between seven and nine. The grocery shopping was done by whichever one of them had the time, but they were serious about dinner together and planned the shopping list for the next dinner *as* they were eating that dinner. All those happy days, all those comforting routines, and all those delicious meals remained only in memories. Many other families had similar histories and they both wondered why there weren't more people who were indignant at being robbed of this. And, for the last twenty-years, being robbed of *whatever* family life they once had.

He missed being able to talk with his mother. His father? He might have spoken with him twice in his adult life. His parents were working-class progressives, and had pictures of all the Progressive People's Party Presidents on their walls—and two Loyalists who they also admired—men of the opposition who could now never fit into the New Populist formerly Loyalist mold.

There were five of them in a one-bedroom apartment in the East Bronx. His parents, Ervin and May, Marvin, his younger brother by three years, and Roberta, his younger sister by five years. His father, judging from the pictures in their apartment, was a young dandy, and his mother was quite a beauty. He recalled seeing a violin in their closet when he was about four years old and knew from what they called "affairs," weddings, Christenings, Bar Mitzvahs, etc. that his father was very musical, with a beautiful baritone voice, but had to put any desire he may have had for an artistic life aside to support a family. Bedloe was in his late teens when he realized that this was the genesis of his father's anger and resentment. He also realized his father had no idea what having three children would mean. He remembered that up until he was five, or six—his father would take him everywhere and, after five years and two more children came, the seeds of his father's anger and resentment sprouted. He became short-tempered, distant, called everyone a "moron," and hardly ever took him anywhere anymore. *I used to look at the pictures I had of him and me and I wonder why it is we look happy—because it's not the way I remember it. What I remember is that he yelled a lot and when he was really angry with me actually beat me with a razor strop. A strop, for those important times in any child abuser's life when the hand just isn't good enough.* He tried, but for the life of him couldn't remember what he could have possibly done to deserve it. *I do remember that he used to, on occasion, call me a "boob." It was many years before I understood that I didn't do anything and could forgive him for taking all his anger out on me. On all of us.* He had to try to understand his father in order to heal whatever scars all of it may have left. *I'm not so sure the healing is complete. I'm also angry. But I've never taken my anger out on my son.* As things grew tougher he saw the demands of having a family making his father angrier...more short-tempered. *I've always thought he shouldn't have had children.*

His friends always looked at him funny when he said that out loud. *But John just wasn't cut out to be a father. Maybe he had the three of us because it was what you did. For all I know it was what my mother wanted and he went along. I'll never know, and none of us ever talked about anything that ever meant anything. I want to believe he did want us and did love us once. I suspect that having to get up at five AM to get to his job at a hat factory downtown couldn't have helped his disposition either.*

These were the kinds of thoughts that caromed off the walls of Bedloe's skull whenever he thought about his father and his home life in his formative years. Importantly, in later years John discovered that the expression "mad as a hatter" had a sound basis in fact. People who blocked felt hats for a living, as Bedloe's father did, were subject to asbestos poisoning due to that mineral being present in the cloth facing of the hat felt. John came to realize, too late, that his father, being unknowingly exposed as he was over so many years to this toxin, might have had a damn good excuse for increasingly flying off the handle. He so wished he could have had a civilized conversation with him about all these things. Would his father cop to any of it? All of it? *Too late now.*

His mother, on the other hand, had always encouraged him, even telling him when he was very young—around six—he was like a duck, in that everything just "rolls off your back." He wished. Oh, how he wished. That he would not stand for petty shit was evident from the very first day he ever went to school. The teacher told him his shoes weren't shined. He promptly rose, walked out and when he got home his mother told him he was right in doing so, buffed up his shoes a bit, and took him back to school. The teacher didn't say a word when he walked back into the classroom and sat down in his seat. He was quite a cut-up in public school and a good artist. Once, in fourth grade, he was caught drawing obscene pictures and passing them to girls in his classroom. They called his mother to school and showed her the pictures. She looked at them, took him home, sat him down and made him promise, on her life, to always respect women. A promise he kept.

Even without much money she always managed to put a well-balanced delicious meal on the dinner table. She worked catering on the week-ends and in his early teens he worked alongside her and saw how hard she worked. How efficient she was. He was smiling now: *man, was she a huge baseball fan. She used to go to Yankee Stadium and took me with her so many times before Marvin and Roberta came along. I remember she had that favorite seat in the first row down the right-field line because the fence was waist-high and the ball players who knew her by name—because she was there so often — would come over to say hello. The great Derek Jeter, who was her favorite always came over. I wish I knew what happened to the autographed ball he gave me.*

Since all Associates no longer had phones or computers, and the postal service only operated within every city's elite districts, he could no longer stay in touch with his sister who lived in Chicago or his brother who lived in Boston. He tried visiting his brother once, in vain, and he had been cut off from his parents who had moved to Detroit. Separations that existed now for almost twenty years. He kept thinking he would jump on a train one day and make the long trip to see his parents. Of course, there was the matter of the fare to consider and since it meant a forty plus hour round trip he'd need two days off from work for a very brief hello. It was a total pipe dream. The only free trains were the inner-city subways that took Associates to their jobs in order that they could service the ten percent. Or, to be accurate, since their old trains didn't run into the better neighborhoods, to their connections to the newer, faster trains—the Centipedes. As to the Associates who serviced the ten per cent; the Associate class was divided into three tiers, encrypted into their transi-passes. The A Class—the Upper Associates, the A Minus Class—the Middle Associates, and the B Class—the lowest of the Associate classes. What defined the Associate classes was not money—since all Associates earned pretty much the same amount, give or take ten or twenty dollars a week—it was health. Only, twenty-five per cent of the Associate class was considered healthy enough to come in contact with the ten per cent. The people who worked in the Financial District for example. People like James who was in the A Class. John Bedloe, because of his persistent cough, was in the A Minus Class.

The A Minus and B Class Socees were only permitted to work in Socee for Socee businesses. Businesses operating in Socee neighborhoods such as a grocery, a laundromat, a diner, a bowling alley, and so on. Anyway, he hoped his parents were well and coping with the new reality of the way things now were. He had no way of knowing that his father had passed away a year before and his mother, now ill, had moved in with her sister Agnes, and so was no longer even living in the state he *thought* she was living in. People were now torn apart by two tyrannies, the tyranny of distance as well.

It

wasn't that she was beautiful because he really couldn't say that about her. But there was something undeniably lovely and feminine about Lacey which drew young James to her. That, and the shy way she smiled. Oh, and her eyes. Her striking green eyes. The Socee girls he had come in contact before at work were dour. And they hardly ever let a smile ruin that dourness. And, on the rare occasions when a smile managed to escape from them it was…sad. Forced. With the cheeks, not with the eyes. Her smile, though it wasn't *always* a full beam, was…it was a communion. It was genuine. Eyes, cheeks, mouth…her whole face lit up. And it lit *him* up every time she directed it at him. Also, it appeared easily whenever she said hello or goodbye to any of her co-workers—which was practically every time they passed each other. The fact that it was rarely returned didn't deter her from offering a friendly smile either. He found this so appealing and wanted to get to know her better. He soon learned that behind that smile she was a bit shy. But, as their friendship progressed and she found him quite easy to talk with, that shyness slowly dissipated. Today would be the eighth day in the last two weeks they'd be having lunch together.

"I just…um…I wanted to come over and say hello because you're new here and…you know…maybe I can tell you a few things about the neighborhood. Um…where to eat…"

That was how it began two weeks before. For three days all the way down to work on the ancient train James had thought about how he would approach her. On that third day, by the time the train came to its last screeching halt in the last Socee neighborhood it covered and he had to transfer to the soldier protected Centipede —which then entered the Server areas and which took him to the Financial District —he had decided on exactly what he would say to her. And, after making two deliveries, he worked up his courage to finally approach her and that was what he said. Her smile told him that what he said was okay.

What James didn't realize was that for the same three days she had been watching him from the corner of her eye as he came and went. *I wonder if he's smart. Or nice. He's very good looking. Probably has a girlfriend.* She wished she wasn't so plain, wasn't wearing camos and maybe had a little lip gloss on—the only real make-up she *ever* bothered to wear. *And maybe Mom's eye shadow?* So she was quite surprised when he came over and offered to tell her about the neighborhood. Specifically, about a place to eat in the area.

"Thank you, James. It's very nice of you. My name is Lacey."

She found it strange saying the name, but it was what it was. She wasn't yet sure of why her father got her this particular job but, all the same, she felt she could be friends with this boy who she could tell was kind. This made it even harder for her to begin their friendship with a lie. Still, it was the way it had to be. And on that day just before she had to go out on a run they made a plan to eat lunch together. That was the way it started.

Now, two weeks later, and for last eight days straight, they had been taking walks together after work. Usually on the promenade down by the river at the edge of the Financial District. He noticed that she had also begun to use some eye shadow. Not much, but her green eyes, which needed no help to be beautiful, were now even more striking. On one such walk, out of the blue, he mentioned that his father thought that FAIR was pretty much all propaganda.

"Your father sounds like an intelligent man."

He was shocked that she seemed to agree. And that she was willing to say so—however cryptically though...

"He is. But...I dunno, I think sometimes people need to have a point driven home for their own good."

"What if it's not for their own good?"

"I guess we're talking about *our* own good."

"Yes, James, *our* own good."

"Well, of course that's...it's *not* good." They looked at each other. And then they both burst out laughing. They finally stopped laughing and continued walking.

"But...Seriously James, what then? What if it's not for their own good?"

"Then I don't see what chance these people have. Do you?"

"No...No, I don't, James." They walked on a little more.

"Lacey...You think FAIR tells us things that aren't for our own good. Like my pop?"

"I don't know, James, maybe we don't know what's good for us anyway."

He thought this over for a bit before he spoke.

"I think I know what's good for me, Lacey. And I also think FAIR does a fairly competent job in keeping us informed about what's going on in the world."

"I'm not sure about that."

"You're not?"

"Do you think all these wars they report on are real?"

"I think they are. My father sure doesn't."

They were down by the river. It was twilight and the snow wasn't coming down as hard as it had been. They stood at the railing overlooking the water which was half frozen.

"So, your father…he thinks a lot of it is what…lies?"

He looked down at her as she looked out over the water. She looked troubled. As if there was a lot on her mind that she wasn't saying. His father had always told him not to talk politics or *anything* to do with what they thought about *anything* with *anyone*—because you never really know who's who and what's what. But there was something about this girl that drew him in. She was the first girl he ever had a serious conversation with. She could see both sides of a question and he liked that about her. He liked that she was serious. For her part, she thought James was the exact opposite of all the teenage jerks she had been around her whole life. There was something very comforting about him. A kind of quiet strength that didn't call attention to itself. An ease. He might have been propagandized, but it was no fault of his own, and he was still willing to question. She was comfortable being with him. It didn't hurt that he was tall and good looking either. She might have been somewhat of an introvert…A thinker. But she was also quite ready to come out of herself.

"He comes from another time, Lacey. Like yours I'm sure."

"Sometimes I wish I could have lived then."

"From what my pop tells me it was very different than it is now."

They stood gazing out over the water. The snow began to fall a little harder again and it was getting darker.

"Should we go?"

She nodded yes. He held his bent right elbow out and she took his arm. They began walking back towards the Centipede which would take them to the train that would then carry each of them home.

"My pop says there was no such thing as the Associate class then and people voted, and there were a lot of different newspapers. I mean, I wonder…"

"People voted? For Chairman?"

"For something called President he says. Oh, and the weather was different. It had begun to get bad then but it didn't always snow or hail, or snain, or whatever like now, and there were lots of sunny days."

She had heard this about the weather too. Still, she couldn't imagine how this could be. And people voted? We didn't appoint a Chairman? If this was true why hadn't her father mentioned it to her? Of course, the answer to this is that she had been indoctrinated as well. And, as far as the weather was concerned, ever since she was old enough to be aware of her surroundings it either snowed, or rained, or snained. Sunny days were very rare.

"And he says the food he ate was far better than what we eat now. But you know, he had a wife in those days…My mother was alive then. So maybe everything just seems like it used to be better because he wasn't alone then. I mean, he has me but…"

"I hope you don't mind my asking what happened. Did she get sick?"

"She was in a car accident. A hit and run."

She pressed herself closer to him.

"Oh God James…I'm so sorry." *Why do some people have all the luck?* She reached her other arm across her body and placed her hand on his right arm as they walked. They continued on through the snow to the Centipede station. He shivered slightly—but it wasn't because he was cold.

"James, are you warm enough?

"Yes. You?"

They had walked about a block along the promenade and were just about to turn into the street which would take them to the Centipede that would then carry each of them to the train home when James saw a small fluffy white dog about twenty yards from them just sitting by the railing. He looked around and saw that, except for some soldiers way off down the promenade, there was no one else around. He turned to her.

"Lacey, that dog doesn't look feral to me. He's too clean. Can we just check on him…or her?"

She immediately agreed and they quickly walked over to the small dog who sat shivering in the cold. They could now see there was a pink ribbon behind the dog's ear and a collar.

"She's a girl. And we don't keep pets, unless they're big guard dogs, so the odds are she has a good home. I'm pretty sure anyone who owns her wouldn't abandon her."

They knelt down next to her and began stroking her. She rolled over on her back as she stroked her ears and he rubbed her belly.

"James, This puppy is so sweet. She's a Maltese."

And as soon as she said it she wondered; *Should I have said that about her being a Maltese?*

There was a tag on her collar and he held it still and read it.

"Her name is…Lulu and…hey, her owner lives three blocks from here. There's a phone number too. Let's go."

He scooped up the tiny white creature, opened his coat, and nestled her in in his arms.

"Lace, would you please close my coat?"

Lacey was quite touched by his kindness. She couldn't imagine any of the boys she'd ever come in contact with doing such a thing. She closed his coat, placed her arm over his arms as he held the pup, and stroked Lulu's tiny head which peeked out from under his coat.

"It's alright Lulu, you'll soon be home. Man, something like this makes me angry that we don't have cell phones to call this person. Lace, How do you know she's a, what did you say? A Maltese?"

"I saw a picture once in a book on dogs."

It upset her that she just couldn't call whoever the owner was also, but it was simply out of the question. They headed for the address on the pup's tag.

"James, is she still shivering?"

"Yeah, let's hurry and get her home."

"The owner is probably frantic."

"Unless they abandoned her. And if I thought that someone just abandoned this innocent creature…I don't know…I mean how could someone well-off do such a thing?"

They hurried up the street.

"People can be cruel."

"My pop likes animals more than most people."

What she said next surprised even her:

"I like you."

Over the days he had grown to like her a lot, and to hear her say this was too good to be true.

"God, I…I like you so much Lacey." *I just took the lord's name. Forgive me but…*

She snuggled closer to him "Hear that Lulu? He likes me so much." *I hope you like Alex too.*

He looked diagonally across the street.

"That's the building."

They crossed the street and walked up to the doorman.

"Excuse me, we found this dog on the promenade and her tag says she lives in this building."

"Lulu! You found her on the promenade?"

The doorman turned to go into the building motioning for the two teens to follow him. He picked up the building's phone and called the owner, who sounded as if she was crying, and said she'd be right down. The doorman stroked Lulu's head while they waited for the woman to come down to the lobby. Finally, one of the maglevators opened and the woman came rushing out to them.

"Lulu, Lulu, where were you?"

James handed the little Maltese over to the woman who nuzzled the dog's head before she held her to her chest. He didn't want to ask how she lost her dog fearing that the answer would make him angry. *Probably some variation on "that stupid maid."*

"Thank you so much for finding her. I don't know how she wandered away from my housekeeper, but I am so grateful to you for bringing her home. Please take this." She pressed a twenty dollar bill into James' hand. *The housekeeper. How did I know?*

"We don't use…It's all the cash I have. Take it, please. And thank you so much."

James knew how much he could use twenty dollars. At the same time he didn't think it was right to take money for something any decent person should do as a matter of merely being human. Lacey watched him. *He's not going to take it…He's uncomfortable about it.* James handed the bill back to the lady.

"There's no need. Thank you is enough. I would expect someone to return my pup if it happened to me."

"Are you sure?"

James nodded. Lacey looked at him admiringly. *I like him. Even more than I thought I did.*

"But I think Lulu can use a cool drink of water and a warm blanket."

"Yes, you're right. You're a special young man. He's a keeper, Miss. Thank you again. Both of you."

She turned and she and Lulu disappeared into the maglevator. James and Lacey left the building and walked in silence to the Centipede. She was thinking; *he's a keeper alright.* He was thinking; *she said she likes me.* They reached the Centipede and she turned to him.

"James, what you did was so wonderful."

"What *we* did."

She stood looking up at him with those glorious green cat's eyes wanting him to kiss her.

Does she want me to kiss her? Should I? But he didn't. *So kiss him.* She kissed him, not on the lips as they both wanted, but on the cheek—and turned to the Centipede entrance.

"See you tomorrow? For lunch?"

"Safe home."

He watched her descend out of sight to the platform below before he moved. *Why didn't I kiss her? Why didn't…Next time.*

James

woke at the crack of seven and lurched to the small bathroom. After their puppy rescue, and Lacey had descended to the Centipede platform, he had to rush back to the District to see three as he now called them—clients. And, because he was so late, two of them had qwik-linqed him to cancel. *Well, that was ten bucks.* And, he was groggy from then staying up late to watch some of last night's FAIR-TV Dillyman and Gloober cartoon marathon. *I must be an idiot for watching even an hour of it. Pop's right, they're stupid. I can't believe I watched them a couple of years ago. Well, they are on every channel so, if the TV's on...Anyway, if they make him laugh... well... after a couple or three cans of M-POW!-r, then what's the harm? He doesn't laugh enough. He had a good rant with the laugh though. It's good to get him stoned, it lets him get it out. People can't watch News all the time. Praise God, the cartoons do lift some people's spirits. We can use that.*

He began his ablutions. *Water isn't too bad today. Gotta leave some toothpaste for Pop.*

FAIR-TV constantly reminded everyone that watching the news was crucial to learning since there were no longer any public high schools for young people in their economic strata—Socees—like them. His father told him that because of this he had wanted to home-school him, but since he had to go to work he couldn't—though he tried to do what he could at night after he came home from work. At first James remembered being left with a kindly neighbor, but then she moved away and his father told him he reluctantly had to put him into one of the Young Evangelical Literate Learning Schools that were in every Socee neighborhood. In larger neighborhoods there were sometimes two, three, or even four such schools. His father said he regretted having to put him in one of those schools. But, since he had to work there was no alternative. *He's way off on this. They poisoned my mind? Pop, they gave me a great education!* He washed carefully in the murky water. Dried himself, combed his hair, and because maybe he might soon have his first girlfriend, he decided to put on a small dab of the Bay rum his father kept in the medicine chest but had stopped using years ago. *Still smells good.*

Ever since he was old enough to care about the news, James watched FAIR News. And, of course, it contradicted everything John tried to tell his son. The boy also never thought the designation "Associate" was an insult, which so galled his father. And that it was great for *all* young Socee kids from three to twelve years old that—even though there were none of these "high schools" his father had told him about—they were able to go to Evangelical Schools and graduate with honors from eighth grade. *If kids had to go to these "high schools" how could they also go to a job? Earn some money? I dunno...I like it better this way. I still got an education. I think FAIR is right; the Evangelicals who run the Young Learning Schools are pretty good teachers. Mine were. Though I have to agree that Pop's right; it is really funny that the acronym for the Young Evangelical Literate Learning Schools is YELLS.* He checked himself out in the medicine chest mirror. *Maybe we should find a different lunch place today. She hasn't been eating much.*

He put on his sweatshirt, slipped into his jeans, checked to see that his socks were dry, sat down on the toilet, put them on and then, picking up his boots, he tip-toed back to their closet. He did this all as quietly as he could every morning so as not to wake his father. But especially so on this morning since he noticed John had downed twice as many cans of M as he had while they watched some of the D & G marathon. It was one of his dad's late shift days and he was surely sleeping off his speed-induced anti-government word-into-word rant. *No wonder the military makes M standard issue in all the boots-on-the-ground theaters of war. Funny, even calling war zones "theaters" ticks him off. I dunno, ConRan World-Wide has some goldmine in M-POW!-r. What genius thought up a synthetic Methamphetamine drink? It's good we have a connection to get it cheaper. Sweet. I wonder if Lacey drinks M?* At the closet, he took out his jacket and his CanTel hoody, a gift from a client. *It ain't wool or cotton but like they say; "Nobody Can't Tell."* He laughed quietly. *I love this thing. Makes me sweat but...Man, today's cold. We were shivering' last night... Cripes, the other day it was over ninety. I still gotta score a heater. When it's freezing not having a heater is a total drag.* He heard his father coughing from the back of the mobile home. Carrying his boots, his jacket and the hoody, he slowly closed the squeaky door separating its two halves and softly moved up to its front.

Everything bothers him, but the front door and that door doesn't? I gotta put some oil on those hinges again. I have to get some oil. He set his jacket and hoody over the back of his chair and his boots down by the front door. *I need some coffee.* He began to brew up a pot of Kaw-Fee. *That cough isn't getting' any better. I gotta make him go to the clinic.* He clicked the TV on, careful to quickly lower the volume so as not to wake his father. He wanted to watch his favorite news program which played across all the FAIR News channels. He tore open an Ultra-Nutri-shus Twin-keez Pluss Ten-Pak and slowly ate breakfast while watching the early morning show "The Real News."

Is that blonde news lady the same one who was on yesterday? They are for sure good looking, I dunno, I think Lacey is way more real than any of them though —blonde or no blonde... I haven't seen Pop as happy in a long time as when I told him about her. The usual hourly message filled the screen; "If You See Something or Hear Something - You'd BETTER Say Something." *I guess I would but....* A siren sounded.

The new Chairman, Server Colonel Jack Jeffers Jr., war hero and the face of M-POW!-r was about to speak at a coal miner's rally. He, and his father, ex-Chairman Server Jack Jeffers Sr., were both great businessmen and had ties to ex-Chairman Ransom B. Conover Jr.'s family and M-POW!-r, and a large number of other businesses in United Europe and PanAsia. Jeffers Jr. was the logical successor to Chairman General Jack "Big Jock" Jeffers Sr. Also, FAIR News constantly showed a tape which they said was from 2021 in which ex-Chairman Ransom B. Conover Sr., speaking from Conover Tower, vouched for Jeffers Sr. saying that the General was a "brilliant military man—as am I—and an incredibly tremendous businessman, incredibly tremendous —like me. I'm not bragging but…And I am sure his son Jack "Little Jock" Jeffers Jr. is as well. Believe me. And, don't let the nickname "Little Jock" fool you, take my word for it, there's nothing little about anything there…Nothing little. Take my word, nothing.

What James couldn't know was that this "interview"—which never happened—was created by digital manipulation in 2023, a year before he was born. Absent that knowledge, there was little doubt in his mind that the board had appointed the correct choice.

The K-F's pretty good this morning. Even their slogan "Virtually Real" upsets Pop. I love how he thinks the words "virtual" and "virtually" were invented for con men…And if someone needs that explained to them than they're the ones these words work on? Is he hinting he thinks I'm dumb? I know exactly what he means…But I mean, virtually real is…it's real, isn't it? Anyway, the coffee tastes pretty good so…As long as the water's boiled… He poured another cup. On TV "Little Jock" Jeffers was facing the large crowd assembled in this huge mine pit. He was, of course, coatless—with about a dozen flags waving behind him—and looking oh so heroically earnest.

"First and most importantly, my fellow Servers and I must express our sincere gratitude to all of you—our Associates—for your generous, and may I say, patriotic contributions which continues to keep our great United Federation of Workers strong in the face of many dangers in the world today. Many dangers." This was met with prolonged applause. He waved them quiet.

"I have to tell you all that as of four AM this morning we are in a cyberwar with PanAsia." *What?* A murmur of surprise rippled through the crowd. "Now, you all know that, like my father, I know how to fight. And when the fight is for our freedom, well… I'm your man." The crowd erupted in cheers. Jeffers yelled over the cheers. "Every man here *knows* that I will fight for him. You have my word on this. Believe me. My word. And my word is good. We will win this war and continue to make America tremendous… it will be incredibly tremendous! As always, the job creators will be working for you. And, we will never…*never* allow anything as costly, as unreliable and as wasteful as solar energy, or that cancer causing windmill energy crap, to destroy your jobs—and the great industry of clean coal mining which we all know powers America." The cheers and applause were deafening. "We have your back. You, incredible Associates are the ones who power America…You! Men! Power! America! Never, never forget it. Never!" The cheering and applause was deafening. "And, *big* news…*Huge* news. Are you ready? Are you? Huh? C'mon" Another full throated roar; "YES!" He smiled as he waited for the crowd to quiet. "We are working on a plan to lift you great Americans up out of the Associate class. As well as that promised new better health plan *and* - wait for it - raising your take-home! Yes, that's right! We will be raising your take home!" The place exploded. Jeffers waited grinning broadly and giving the thumbs up until finally they calmed down. "Never, never forget this. We Servers have your backs. You will soon have higher pay. It will be tremendous. You'll see. Tremendous. God bless you all and God bless America." *Boy, do I hope so.* The crowd, each and every one of them with a can of M-POW!-r in their hands, and many others holding supportive signs, erupted in another huge roar of approval. Then that disembodied voice that you always hear on the league pro BashBall films intoned from off-screen somewhere; "Chairmen Jack "Little Jock" Jeffers Jr., and Ransom B. Conover Jr., giants in the long line of great New Populist Party Servers for the people - and M-POW!-r - the preferred drink of our fighting men and women everywhere in the world…Three on a perfect match. Remember the New Populist Servers will always keep our democracy strong - and working." And then that great martial music played.

Raise our take-home! Blessed Mother! Wait 'til pop hears. And they were all drinking M-POW!-r too. Was that a tribute to Jeffers' grandfather who invented it? A trillionaire…Sheesh. I don't need to be that rich, but wow, more pay! Man, it would be nice to be a little better off…Maybe even use DigiCurr. I could maybe take her to a nice restaurant. We're in a cyberwar with PanAsia?

The Servers—the "job creators," and the people in the high income brackets never carried cash. They used digital money or DigiCurr. He, and the rest of the ninety per cent of the population, the 390 million Associates, still used cash coupled with government issued credit card readers, and free TransiPasses, which also tracked their movements and whereabouts for law enforcement—should it be necessary. Certain businesses in the Financial District, such as the one where he worked, held cash for the express purpose of paying Associate's salaries. The messenger service where he worked used DigiCurr. The diner his father worked in, was "Socee—only." It was cash only in exchange for goods and services. All Socee classes were paid in cash. Taxes were easy to compute since all Associates made ten dollars an hour taxed at thirty-five per cent. Which brought the government 3.4 trillion dollars—the "generous contributions" Chairman Jeffers alluded to in his speech to the miners. Ninety per cent of this "generous contribution" was spent on the military, the National Security apparatuses, FAIR-TV, two national newspapers and the infrastructure of the well-off ten per cent. This encompassed the neighborhood streets and utilities and especially the roads, bridges and tunnels, for those older people who were well-off and who still preferred to travel by Andro-car as opposed to Heli-Vee—and to maintain their airports. A mere ten per cent of their "contribution" went back to Socee infrastructure, and those monies were allocated to the maintenance of those roads, bridges and tunnels which, unavoidably, *had* to be used to take those Elites through any Associate neighborhoods. An extra ten dollars a week was also deducted to fund the one Associate-only medical clinic in each of the city's boroughs. In every Socee-only business district a computerized track of hours worked was kept for the purpose of collecting these "contributions"—under harsh penalty of law.

He was grateful for his job, and though most business-to-business packages in the Financial District were sent by PneumaTube, which connected every business in the District, there were still some packages that had to go to specific people within a business, and, if not available, could not be left at the business, and needed eye recognition and signature. He was glad these parcels had to be delivered by hand and glad that the air smelled far better where he worked than where he lived. Where he lived the air stank of a mixture of rotting garbage and the waste matter of all the feral dogs, cats and homeless humans. In fact, every Elite neighborhood in the city voted on the prevailing scent in their air. The air in the Financial District smelled of a combination of Vetiver and bourbon. The city's vast underground AirFresh system, which was installed in every Elite neighborhood in 2031, and paid for by Socee taxes, made that possible.

Suddenly, a promo for one of the most popular FAIR-TV programs The SooperToons Squad, came on. *I watched that too, and it's even dumber than Dillyman and Gloober.* He finished his Kaw-Fee and wolfed down the last of the Twin-keez. *Man, these're really soft – I gotta score a heater, an' I gotta save up for a mini-fridge like the ones I've seen on TV. It would be way better than having to keep buying ice for our cooler every few days. Ten dollars a bag is gettin' way too expensive. Good thing the Twin-keez stay fresh without one*

He put on his boots, opened the creaky front door, went outside and quickly washed his cup in the cold water from the rain barrel gravity hose his father had jerry rigged to save on their water bills – and have water that wasn't as foul smelling. *Man, it's crazy cold* – and hurried back inside careful to wipe his boots on the old towel. *We need to buy soap…another expense. It's getting colder earlier. Showering under the hose is a bi…a bear. The water bill – another problem. We'll get by—Jeffers Jr. and the Servers'll have to do what they've promised. They'll get us this raise.* Again, he heard his father coughing. It seemed it was getting worse. *I gotta get that heater.*

Besides his regular special bonded messenger job he had two clients to see—the usual older Wall Street types, then he'd see their connection, get on home and open a couple cans of RanCo MmmEat Stew. *I dunno about the claim that it's fabulously delicious and incredibly healthy…I know pop doesn't think it "tastes better than anything." I know he hates it 'cause it's RanCo. But it's no worse than stewed Norwegian. I mean, I get why pop calls the Conover family the "Conjobs" 'n "Conoverallofus." Okay, maybe that's fair. But he's smart. So why doesn't he get that when you're in such a powerful position there are times you're forced to…you have to stretch the truth? You have to! And you have to be evasive. National security is a tough one but…* John, out of principle, refused to eat the stew for months. He finally gave in after he'd lost twenty-five precious pounds and they couldn't afford anything else. *I hope he'll eat tonight, and drink some M and watch the BashBall game with me. He might speed-rant up the wazoo but so what. I know life could be better. And soon as we get that raise I can stop having to turn these tricks, and life will be better.* He put on his hoody—hood up—and his coat, opened the front door, and stepped out into the deep snow that was still falling; *I have to get new boots. And kiss her.*

There

was blood everywhere. On the floor, the walls…the chair on which he was sitting, on his shoes, which were sliding back and forth beneath him … He was floating high above the room, then way up high clinging to a railing on a stairs that rose up above a chasm far below. He was scared he would lose his grip on the blood-soaked railing and fall into the nothingness below. Jane was speaking to him - from where he couldn't tell - but he could hear her. *John, I'm here…don't worry. It's alright. I understand…It happens…It happens…You tried…*He looked around searching frantically for her throughout every room in the house. Room after room upon room. Every room bare. Every room dark.

In the gas station the assembled judges were waiting—ready and eager to hear his poetry. He knew they would be impressed and that he would finally get the recognition he so richly deserved. He had labored in anonymity for so long and now here they were alerted to the groundbreaking work they were now about to be witness to. He reached for his reading glasses. He thought he had put them in the breast pocket of his jacket, but they weren't there. He checked his inside pocket…He felt his shirt pockets, his trouser pockets…where were they? Where were his eyeglasses? No matter…He would read his poems without them. He picked up his book on which pages he had scrawled the most brilliant lines of poetry. They would surely agree. The judges, who were sitting on milk crates eating hero sandwiches, leaned forward. They stared at him in anticipation of this event. This was his long-awaited debut performance. He opened his book. They were there…His earth-shattering word images waiting…Waiting to be uttered by the author himself. Waiting to be heard by the people who would soon be rising to their feet applauding. By the judges who would soon be his peers…The judges waited in keen anticipation. He looked at his book…No! No! Not now…not tonight! Was every page an unreadable blur? He frantically turned the pages. Every page - page after page - was an unreadable blur. He would recite from memory. He cleared his throat and began:

Andine mllhb mkihf dpoy

sjfgcfrw nfkiluljtryt

rthxisi ykfywvdk

Ymkcccddj…sighuggnyt.

The judges stared at him as they chewed.

He was running up the street…Running, running. *Johnny, I love your poetry.* He looked around for her. *I always have. Where are you Jane? I can't see you? I'm here John…I'm here…where you left me. No…no…I…There was…Where you left me…JANE…JANE…Here John here…*He looked in every corner of every dark room…*Here…In the blood…Look in the blood Johnny…In the—*

A violent spate of coughing suddenly woke him. Reflexively, he glanced over to his left at his son's own single bed a little more than a body length away. No doubt James was already up and at work. He was covered in a fine sheen of sweat. *What time is it? Christ…That dream. Jane was there…That same fucking dream.* He lay there trying to remember a little more of where he just was. *I'm up. It's cold. It's my late day and I don't have to get up early. So why the fuck am I up? Did I stay up and watch the game with James last night?*

You're an idiot. But what? I'm going to go to bed at nine? I need some of that gunk we call coffee. It's cold and I'm sweating...

He lay there staring at the discolored ceiling. *It was the blood again. It had to be pretty bad to funk up the bed like this - again...We have to do a laundry. Can't keep putting it off.* He closed his eyes, determined to get back to sleep again. Two, three, four minutes, but his mind was now irreversibly awake. *Shit! Why the fuck am I up?* He coughed, sat up, and concentrated on trying to remember the exact events of his nightmare. *It was that same lousy dream again. The anxiety thing again.* He struggled to remember. *I can't.* He sat up. *Jeez, I have to take a wicked piss.* With some effort he slowly lifted himself out of bed in sections. *Christ...*He quietly wobbled the five paces to the small bathroom. He slowly slid the balky accordion door closed behind him, moved to the toilet and tried, with some success, to steady himself as he stood there urinating. *My head...I can't keep drinking that piss. I'm addicted - and it's unhealthy. I have to - we have to stop it. What kind of an example...Some father. Why do I...*He flushed the toilet and looked at himself in the mirror. *Holy Christ on a clamshell.* He tried, and failed, to stifle a cough. *This damn coughing is getting worse. I could pack for a long trip with these bags. Jeez...*

Even though the volume was low he couldn't help but hear the TV... *Yeah... God bless us all and God bless America. Let's all pray for a way better day.* A ravaged, sourish face stared back at him. *Pure poetry. I should be writing their slogans. Where do I apply?* Bedloe kept staring at his reflection in the part of the mirror that still passed for a mirror. *It had to be the same dream. At least I was with Jane.* He stood there searching his face. *It was that not being "able" shit again. I was in a sweat...must've been. You weakling. Couldn't you have put your foot down? Just fucking once? Mister nice guy. Mister perfect husband. Mister equality. Fuck you, you fucking prick!* He stared at his ravaged face for a few more seconds then; *Wash and get dressed idiot... You're up.* He squeezed a tiny bit of toothpaste onto his toothbrush, leaned over the small sink, and began to brush his teeth in the brackish water. In the last year he'd lost two teeth, one from the upper right and one from the lower left. He freaked out when the first loose tooth hit the sink basin and was even more shaken when the second one clanked onto the stainless. The M was exacting its price for the high. After each tooth bid him bye-bye he swore that he would stop drinking it...he rinsed his mouth careful not to swallow any of the water, slipped his undershirt off, placed it over the towel bar and began to wash his face. *Why couldn't it be my mind that was going instead of my body? Then I could just be a drooling idiot and I wouldn't give a shit about it. Or anything.* Of course every time he had that thought, which was far too often, he knew that even if he could make such a choice the fact that he had a son would take that choice away from him also. He rinsed the soap off of his face and began to wet his underarms with one of the small slivers of soap stacked in a chipped saucer on the sink. He soaped his armpits and, leaning over the sink, rinsed them. He reached out to the small towel bar and grabbed the same tattered towel they used when they cut their hair. *Still damp...and we have to do a laundry.* He threw the towel over his shoulder and began to wet his hair to comb the sleep out of it. *Thank whatever I still have a head of hair to comb...fat lot of good that is.* He finished combing his hair, patted his face, underarms and hands dry and placed the towel back on the bar. He looked at himself for a few seconds - *as good as it gets* - grabbed his undershirt from the bar, turned and, with some effort, slid open the bathroom door. He moved to the closet, took his clothes from the hook and then, still in slight wobble mode, went back to his narrow bed and plopped himself down on it. After a few minutes he rose, put on his work shirt, stepped into his overalls and sat back down on his bed. *I failed her and I've failed him.* He sat there. *I have to stop drinking that shit.* He sat there feeling as shitty as he did the day before - and the day before that.

He finally made his way up front and was thankful to see that his sweet son who already left for work had made a pot of K-F. He switched on the TV to see the time. *Hey, it's the new puke Jeffers festooned with all the trappings. Yep...everything's going to be great...Yada yada yada and God bless America - and a fucking network to give it the Great Homemaker's seal of crap.* He spit on Jeffers face on the TV screen and shut it down.

As

they had done for the better part of the previous two weeks they were again walking down the snowless heated and drained sidewalk of the Financial District to the Androbus station. In the restaurant today when he held her coat for her to step into she again thought he smelled nice. What was it? It was a faint whiff of a familiar scent. *That scent...It's...it's my father's bay rum.* She zipped up her coat and watched him as he put his hoody on. *I love the way he looks at me. He's...He's so not preppy. Maybe he wants to go to a movie sometime.*

"Lacey...should we go to a movie sometime?"

What am I saying? I can't afford a movie.

"James, I...you'll never believe that I was just thinking the exact same thing!"

They stopped and turned to each other laughing. They fell silent and stood for a brief moment looking into each other's eyes. Then a smile - which grew broader - and then they stopped smiling and leaned in towards each other hesitantly and *almost* shared a first awkward kiss. They stood that way holding hands and looking into each other's eyes before, still holding hands, they continued on down the heated sidewalk to the bus stop. After about a half of a block he broke the silence.

"You're right…That food in Greasy Lee's sure is mediocre."

"Maybe we can find someplace better?"

You haffta tell her. "Lacey, I'm sorry, I don't know why I said that about a movie. I guess I'd like to, but I can't spend any money that way…I got a little carried away."

Don't embarrass him: "Believe me James, I know how tight things are."

They continued walking.

"There's a place called the auto-café. We'll try it tomorrow. Yeah…my father is always talking about when he was able to eat fresh fish."

They reached the bus stop and sat down protected from the falling snow. *Should I tell her stuff? Why not? Shouldn't I be honest? I mean, if we're gonna be boyfriend and girlfriend? Or, I dunno…maybe even more?*

"My pop says the Conover and Jeffers' families eat like kings while we eat crap. But it's…I…I think we have to tighten our belts to support all the wars we're fighting. I mean, that takes money. Right? So maybe that's why there's no money for better food."

"That *is* a reason, yes."

"It's why he doesn't eat much. And I have to get him to a clinic."

"What's wrong?"

"He's got this terrible cough an' it's getting worse. I'm a little worried. And I feel bad that I haven't been able to get him any cough medicine. But what with work and all…This weather huh? My pop says it's something called global warming. What do you think?"

"Well…You know scientists *do* say that we have screwed up our weather."

"You and my pop would get along nicely. You know I'm…I'm not supposed to say stuff like that about Conover and Jeffers, but I feel like I can talk to you."

Alex, change the subject. "So, how long have you been at the messenger service?"

"Um…a couple years now. I mean, we have to give these new leaders a chance Lacey…don't we? I would love a good steak but…"

"Yes, I *would* love a steak."

"I mean, if tightening our belt is part of doing our part—well…Yeah, I'd love some better food but… Mostly we eat food outta cans. But every day on the news I hear that we'll soon have better jobs, more money—even free healthcare. I hope it's all true because all that would be great—my father could use a doctor. That's for sure. He thinks Jeffers is a liar. Actually, he despises him. I shouldn't say this but--- *Then don't James…don't. Please. Please James….I like you. I like you so much*—He wishes Jeffers and Cletus would die in a Heli-Vee crash." *No. No! Oh God…He didn't just say that, did he? I don't want to hear that. I am so liking him.*

"I mean you're not gonna repeat any of this to anyone anyway. Right?

She was in a bit of shock. "What do you mean? I'm telling everyone."

He laughed. She smiled. Her eyes didn't.

"He thinks Jeffers and them are dangerous criminals. I dunno… I think Jeffers seems like he really wants to make things better for everyone."

She heard herself respond from somewhere off in the distance.

"Well…No offense but…We really do need to be careful about what we say."

"Yeah, my pop says the same thing. Enough said. Never mind."

Now you have to Alex. You have to. "So uh…He didn't really say that… about wishing Jeffers would die in a Heli-Vee crash?"

"We were walking home and…yeah."

Walking home…Maybe it's not on the holo-vid…But the surveillance cams…But still, he said it…

"So…Does he work?"

"He washes dishes in a greasy spoon on Simpson Street in the Bronx."

"Ahh…Does he like it?"

"Are you kidding? He was a skilled machinist once."

"Really? What happened?"

"His factory got shut down…Moved to what he said used to be called China—a long time ago."

"That's a lousy break."

Should I say anything more about pop? It does feel good to talk with someone about all this. She was the first girl he ever felt this way about, or whoever felt like this about him, and he couldn't keep himself from confiding in her.

"Well… Oh, the heck with it. I trust you—"

More? No, don't James. Please don't. I do not want to hear this.

"He says it was the first Conover who did it…Hates him with a passion. He's even got a bunch of nicknames for him: Conniver, Conoverallofus, Conjob, Conovereveryone. Oh, wanna hear something funny---*No James, I don't*—he calls Jeffers…um… jerk-off."

Well…that's not so bad. "Well…sometimes he *can* be a jerk."

"I guess it's funny. I guess a lot of what he says is…Except if the wrong person hears it."

Is this why I have this messenger job? Because they've already checked? If they have then…then there's nothing I can do. I have to pursue this.

"And his hatred for the first Conover…It's beyond obsessive. He says he lied his behind off about making us great and taking care of working people and then he turned around and closed hundreds of plants, his included…and…you know, he's bitter. He's angry and he's bitter and he thinks everything they say is a lie—and Conover II was just as dangerous and the Jeffers are just as bad. We have these…I dunno…I guess they're disagreements. An' I didn't say any of this."

Oh, God James…They might have already looked. It's impossible I…I can't ignore this. Oh, James…James. Why? Again, she stared blankly ahead. *Maybe it's just talk.* Again, barely heard the words that came out of her mouth.

"Any of what?"

He couldn't help but notice that her mood had darkened. "You okay?"

"Oh…yeah…I think it's the food in that place."

Maybe I shouldn't have said all this stuff?

"We'll try that auto-cafe tomorrow. Okay?"

She nodded weakly.

"It's pretty horrible that we can't even say what's on our minds these days." Now, as her spirit was slowly sinking, her brain was on pure automatic.

"I know. We have to be careful. It stinks. I mean…I watch the news, James, and to *me* I think Jeffers' Jr. *can* make things better….Aren't we getting a raise soon?"

"Yeah. That is so great! I think he's on the case too. Seems like it."

"Your father sounds like he has a lot in common with mine. What's he like?" She was now irreversibly on auto.

"He's…He's actually pretty cool. He used to be a musician. Saxophone."

"Wow…how great. Use to be? No more?"

James…I really like you…You can't…Why are you making me do this?

"No. there's no live music anymore, anywhere…at least not jazz. That's part of why he's so ticked off. He's been a doorman at a swanky building in mid-town for the last - oh, I don't know…going on twelve years. He has to hold doors for rich people as they go in and out every day and he hates it. It's a miracle he hasn't been replaced by a droid."

"And your mom?"

"She's a breakfast and lunch waitress in a corporate dining room."

"Good tips at least."

In for a penny…"Are you kidding? These rich jerks don't part with a nickel. Last Christmas one of the partners gave her a picture of his family as her gift. We burnt it."

"Yeah, some people can be *real* jerks."

They sat in silence looking at the falling snow.

"Yeah…I fight with my dad too. I think your father sounds interesting."
"He does have a lot of opinions. He's mostly angry, that's for sure."

"How old is he?"

"Um…Forty-eight."

"Mine's forty-seven---*In for a pound*---Maybe someday I can meet your father."

"You want to meet my *pop*?"

"Well…I don't know…Like I said, he sounds like an interesting man. We learn a lot from older people. I've learned a lot from my father."*At least that much is true.*

"I guess he is interesting but…he knows a lot about a lotta things but…he's not the easiest…like I say he's really *very* angry. He doesn't believe anything - or anybody. I mean, I love the man and I am truly sorry he lost his wife - hey, I lost my mother, but it's been years and… I disagree with a lot…well, most of what he thinks, but I still try to cut him a lot of slack. I think he deserves that much."

"Very" angry…Oh no, James, this is not good.

"I know…Like my father. My father would be in the underground if he could."

"There's an underground? My pop probably would too if he had energy. You wanna hear something crazy? Some evenings I get home and there's a big glob of spit on the TV screen. He spits at the TV. It could be the image of Conover I or II, or either Jeffers that set him off. That's how much he hates our Chairmen - or *any* Server. I'm not sure that hate is a strong enough word even."

"Why does he even put the set on then?"

"Sometimes it goes on by itself. Does yours? And anyway, that's how we check the time. And when he does and one of these people are on the screen he spits at their face on the TV before he turns it off. I just wish he would wipe it off though."

For a little while they sat in silence watching the swirling snow melt as it hit the heated sidewalk. "I'm glad I've met you James, but I don't know about this job."

"I know what you mean."

"How long have you been working there?"

"Umm…Since I was almost thirteen. I guess right after I graduated Evangelical school. But I also learn a lot from TV so…"

"Ours goes on by itself too. But, it's great that it's free."

"My pop says it's free so they can brainwash us."

"You know James—I think I like having my brain washed every now and then."

They both laughed. She couldn't help that hers was half-hearted.

"Lacey...Do you think R!M!E! is real?"

"I don't know. Sometimes."

"You think *sometimes* it's real?"

"Well...What do you think?"

"I think it's actors. My father thinks it's real."

"My father also thinks it's real."

"They should have a beer together."

"You're right—they should."

They laughed again. He didn't notice hers was forced. "Well...they do seem to have a lot in common."

"Anyway, I really did mean it when I said I hope I meet your father."

"I...I don't know why you would he's...I told you, he's pretty angry."

"So's my dad. I'm used to it. It's like I said, I think we have a lot to learn from older people. You know - they remember history. They've been through way more than we have—well, *that's* obvious. They also have a lot of valuable insight."

"I suppose."

"And...I like his son."

This was real. And it made her sad that it was.

"I really like you too, Lacey."

"I'm glad."

They sat side by side watching the falling snow. *She likes me.*

"Does he work Sundays?"

"Huh? Oh, um…No…Every day but. Noon to early evening."

"Our Socee life eh?"

"Our Socee life. I mean, it's work…Gotta pay the rent and all. So…"
"We do what we have to."

"And we have what we do."

This time the chuckle they shared was equally rueful.

"Maybe I can come over and we can all watch a BashBall game together one night."

"I dunno Lacey…I mean, I'd like that but…He's not the easiest person to be around."

"I want to meet him because I like you. I'll bring a six-pak of M-POW!-r."

"Well…I *know* he'd like that."

"I can't wait to meet him. I've been meaning to ask; where do you guys live anyway?"

"Um, in an old mobile home in a junkyard in the south Bronx. Another thing he hates."

"You can move around?"

"Nah…it's pretty un-mobile. No engine. Or wheels. You?"

On auto, she replied in a voice far off from her thoughts.

"Uh huh. The landlord of the building my dad works in owns the building we live in. And because my dad's job only pays in tips and gratuities he lets us live in the Chinatown building rent free. A one bedroom. My sister and I sleep in the living room."

"Wow, lucky."

"That's why I usually have extra money, I don't need to chip in for rent."

"I think we're pretty lucky too. Just the two of us live where we do and, you know, we don't have heat so the rent is real cheap. I dunno what my pop would do if we had to live minimum ten to an apartment like everyone else. And what they pay in rent—eight thousand a month minimum? It's crazy. Is your sister younger? Older?"

It took her a few seconds to realize he was asking her a question.

"Oh…Younger. She's eight.

"I had no idea they hired people for just the afternoon."

"I guess my uncle pulled some strings. He's the janitor in the owner's building. And, it's a good thing too, this way I can watch my kid sister 'til my mom gets home."

"Speaking of home, I should be getting there. I'll walk you to the Centipede."

"James, it's sweet, but there are soldiers in this neighborhood. You've walked me every day."

"Yes, and I'm walking you today too. I'd be really bummed if, somehow, anything happened to you because I let you walk to the train by yourself."

They began walking to the Centipede. After just a few steps she smiled at him, moved closer and put her arm through his. *You're being stupid about him Alex.* He felt like a champ. This sweet girl on his arm. Though it *was* an upscale neighborhood and the sidewalks were heated, it was snowing hard and trying to accumulate and his feet were still getting soaked through the holes in his boots but he didn't care.

"You're a gentleman."

"It's no big deal…and anyway…" *Tell her.*

"…Anyway what?"

Tell her! "I…I really do like you…A lot."

They continued to walk in silence until they reached the Centipede station. *This is so lousy. To meet someone this sweet, this kind, who likes me. Who I like.*

"This is me. If we miss each other at work then Greasy Lee's tomorrow. At one? And I also know a movie theater that is so easy to sneak into. You want to?"

Sneak into a movie? "Um… sure, yeah."

"We'll pick a date."

"Great."

She moved in close to him leaned forward on her toes with her hands resting lightly on his biceps and kissed him on each cheek. Each kiss lingering just a little. *Bay rum.* He wanted so to kiss her. She couldn't help hoping he would. She waited, looking up at him. And…he did! Finally. It was her first kiss. It was his first kiss. It was wonderful. They had sealed their love - and she never felt so miserable. After a few seconds they parted and she headed for the entrance to the Centipede.

"Safe home. See you tomorrow."

"You too. Tomorrow."

He watched her descend to the Centipede platform. *Man, she is…I have a girlfriend!* Then he turned to walk back to the bus station. He could hear his socks squishing. *I gotta get new boots. 'N I still have to get us a heater. Sneak into a movie? She's done it before? What if we're caught?* He reached the station just as the bus was approaching. He moved to where the driverless AndroBus would read him. It stopped and he got on and waved his TransiPass at the eye. He found a seat in the back and sat down. *We kissed!* He sat there thinking how much he liked her. He was glad he walked her—what kind of a man would let a lady walk to the train alone? She was all he could think about—for the entire trip home. He hoped he wouldn't have to wait too long for the train he still had to get. He couldn't wait to tell his father that he was pretty sure he had a girlfriend. *And,* one who said he sounded interesting—*and* wanted to meet him. *Pop's gonna love her…no doubt. But sneaking into a movie?*

What *she* was thinking was how bummed she was that this boy, the first boy she ever really liked, ever seriously kissed, had a father who might… might be…well, dangerous. *But was it on the record?*

On

the Centipede platform Alexandra Winstead took out her flexi-card and called for her Andro-car to meet her three stations down. The car was there when she emerged from the subterranean train stop. *Do I tell daddy about today?*

It was still snowing when her android doorman greeted her as he helped her from the car. She stepped out into the Mr. Lincoln Rose-scented air that the neighborhood had voted on, almost unanimously, and made her way across the heated sidewalk, on which the snow immediately melted, to the front of her building, a grand limestone-fronted masterpiece. The doorman hurried in front ahead to hold the building's massive bronze framed glass door open for her.

She entered the grey marble lobby and walked to the maglevator that would take her up to the sixty-fourth floor, where she would change to her family's private maglevator which then went up one floor to the sixty-fifth floor and PH-A. As she did she felt for her key card in the pocket of her cargos, fished it out, slipped it into the slot, looked into the iris scanner and unlocked the maglevator allowing her access. On the way up to their sixty fifth floor three story penthouse she was thinking that she would wait before she told her father about her day. *God, I like this boy.* She watched the floor numbers swiftly change until the door opened on sixty-four where she boarded their private maglevator. On sixty-five the door opened on the spacious entry of her parent's apartment. She could hear the strains of Mozart's Piano Sonata No. 16 in C Major softly playing. She took off her coat and scarf, hung them in the hall's triple wide walk-in closet, removed her scuffed boots and placed them in the basket on the mat beside the maglevator door. The seductive aromas of a prime rib roast—with its potato and root vegetable side dishes—perfumed the air. It should have mattered more to her that her mother had hired such a good chef this time—but it didn't. She padded down the art and flower-bedecked hallway, past the oak and mahogany-paneled library and peeked into her father's main floor office. His gestures told her he was interacting with his eyeglasses computer. She could see he was dealing with something important and moved on, glad that for the moment she didn't have to tell him about the day's events.

Alexandra Winstead, aka Lacey, was her father's daughter. She adored him. From as far back as she could remember she looked up to this large smiling man. Arthur Winstead was that warm broad-shouldered man smelling of coffee, sweet pipe tobacco, and Bay rum, who swooped her up in his strong arms and perched her on his shoulders to watch the flags of the many holiday military parades go by. The one who it seemed rarely, if ever, failed to make her the focus of his attention no matter how busy he was at the moment. She'd laughed at the holo-vids showing how he taught her to walk at ten months. And the ones showing him and her mother lovingly hovering over her shoulder helping her blow out her birthday candles every birthday before she was six.

He was the proud beaming father at all her Lacrosse matches, even though she wasn't very good, at her swimming meets, where she was doggedly competitive, her class debates, where she excelled, *and* he helped her with her homework.

Her father was an important man, Head of Internal Security for sector one - the entire northeast. It was he who coined the phrase; "Dissent

Equals Descent." He was a war hero and her hero, and as far back as she could remember her dream was to follow in his footsteps. He was a many times decorated national hero as well and a respected figure in all the halls of power. Recognizing her keen intelligence, and allegiance to the ideals he stood for, he had been teaching her surveillance and interrogation techniques since she was seven years of age. She remembered her first visit to his office way downtown in that nondescript windowless building. He showed her the vast rooms lined with OLED FF's—Flexi-Follow TVs —and filled with holograms. He explained the importance of the mission he and his staff were charged with. Everywhere the sign "Dissent Equals Descent." He explained how much the country depended upon the sacrifice and vigilance of all the dedicated people in the building, and the corrosive effect that *any* dissent, even the *smallest*, had on the fabric of the democracy they were entrusted to protect. Their family had served in the highest levels of government security for three generations. He had followed his father and grandfather into Yale, and then into the NSB, where, via his many important arrests, convictions and success against the Socee underground, he rose steadily up through the ranks to his current position.

She had started in CyScenSec, the cyber-scenario sector, after school at the tender age of eight. She had learned how to create the news of the cyberwars the country had to be in, as well as the techniques of holo-film and vidi-mani—the digital creation of holograms and videos that were useful in posi-prop—positive propaganda. This included the simulated terrorist bombings that reinforced the need for protective surveillance and security. Since 2022 every major power in the world had agreed to partner in the necessary global cyber-conflict story line. Her father had explained to her when she was very young that this agreement among the combined world Plutocracies and Oligarchies was implemented by clearer minds among them so that their country's power grids and economies would not suffer any more damage in the protracted destructive cyberwars of the past. As he explained it, these cyberwars began to be a serious problem in the early part of the century and no one profited by any one of them. As an ancillary benefit, the NCA agreement—the Non-Cyber Aggression pact

—was an effective way of keeping the smartest and best educated people in charge of running things. They should be honored, he told her, that they were among these people and she should never feel ashamed of all they had since they were using it in the service of keeping the world a safe place. It was nothing more than their duty as being among the very best. He explained that it is indeed a world plutocracy run by the privileged. But the alternative—leaving everything to the Associates of the world—the uneducated and unsophisticated, would surely result in world chaos and the destruction of all the good work that governments had done through the years. He also explained how important it was to continually flush out the Socee underground, fanatics bent on murdering the leaders of Governments all over the world. She had always sincerely believed all he told her. He pointed out that as far back as when the country was formed the founders did not trust the populace at large to make the right choice of leaders so they created The Electoral College. And when they realized that the vote couldn't be trusted to elect the best and brightest they amended the Constitution and created a Board to appoint the leaders. He explained that this provided the necessary insurance against the unqualified gaining office. He made it abundantly clear to her that the boots-on-the-ground wars were real wars - planned, but confined to bleak areas in deserts all over the world and what remained of the third world. And that they were necessary. So she grew up believing from an early age that these wars were necessary in order to maintain a healthy degree of Nationalistic pride. And that they were invaluable in keeping every government in the capable hands of the most qualified and most educated among us. And, of course, the Associates fighting these wars received a paycheck which benefited them greatly.

She learned from an early age that actual rebel insurrections in any form, usually Socee underground fomented, were met immediately with warranted force by The United Oligarchy's Special Elite Troops. Of course, the federation known to all in the topmost echelons of the world order as "The United Oligarchy" was never called by this name other than between themselves. To the Associates of the world the world government was always referred to as it was on FAIR TV; The United Federation of Workers. Also, her father never mentioned the fact that, like her, these troops were indoctrinated from a young age to believe to a man in their mission to protect democracy and the stability of world order. He never mentioned it because he didn't believe that it *was* indoctrination in any form. It was duty, plain and simple. The wars were musically scored, and shown in ten languages on FAIR Worldwide Television. What he did mention, and what she knew to be true, was that it was unfortunate that these conflicts had to sometimes be encouraged by infiltrating the Socee rebel's cause because doing so served a greater good. These victories, losses, sacrifices and heroism, they agreed, fanned a healthy nationalism.

Since there were ongoing rebellions all over the world there was never a shortage of real battle footage. Every week or two, gruesome beheadings carried out against our troops were created and shown on TV—reinforcing the need for these wars. And they certainly justified the need for continual surveillance and hyper- security. And, as a member of CyScenSec, she was duty-bound - and honored - to be able to serve in this important protection of her country. She learned from a very early age that all these procedures, though sometimes manipulative, were vital to keeping the world order.

Even so, on those trips downtown through some of the Associate neighborhoods when she was seven, and then all along on the way to her early teen age years, she became increasingly aware of the terrible iniquities that existed in her city. At first it was only the beggars and the ragged people sleeping in the doorways. And then the air she breathed, and the garbage and roaming feral dogs and cats she saw whenever she had to travel anywhere outside her own clean neighborhood. Outside any of the neighborhoods of the Elite. She smelled the fecal matter and the urine. She saw the snow piled high on the garbage on the unheated sidewalks, the deep slush left over after days of rain. These occasions, however rare, revealed a world she saw that was filled with deprivation. Filled with a need she found hard to ignore. While the food she and her family ate was varied, nutritious, in the main healthy, and most importantly organic and real, she became aware that most of the class she knew as Associates had little more than canned food, much of it highly processed and ersatz. And too much of that was rodent and insect based. Now, she had the pleasure of experiencing this Socee "food" first hand. Most of all she saw that these people were filled with a hopeless sadness. A tired resignation. Moreover, where *she* began to see all these desperate conditions as the petri dish for the toxic brew that *created* these threats, her *father* only saw, and only dealt with, the *results* of their desperation. She soon realized that these iniquities existed everywhere in the world and couldn't help but feeling guilty at all she had when so many she saw had nothing. She wasn't sure how all this came about but she was still sure that people of her class were *all* that stood between civility and chaos. She could be saddened by it all, but she still could not escape from the iron bubble of her indoctrination. And, what would it do to her father if she ever did?

Her mornings were spent at the nearby ultra-exclusive Briarleigh School for Young Women, where she was in her junior year. She was an above average student who never did blend in with the school's inner circle finding most of the girls there to be vapid, clique-ish, casually cruel, and obsessed with the trappings of wealth. She knew she was plain and actually thought of herself as unattractive. She never had a boyfriend and at the co-ed dances with boy's schools she was mostly a wallflower whom - no surprise to her - the boys did not find as attractive as the other, more extroverted, girls. For her part she thought the preppy boys she'd been in contact with immature and stupid, and only interested in showing off and "making out."

Her father had asked her if she thought she would like to begin her career in Cyber-Security at the bottom, as it were, in a random placement and only wanting to both be part of the solution, as well as making him proud, of course she eagerly said yes. This was her very first trial in the field which is how she found herself in the position of being a messenger and among those of the Associate class for four hours a day. And, most distressing, in love with a Socee boy.

She padded one flight up the wide staircase to her brother's room. Her eight-year-old brother was on his device. She gave him a kiss and laughed when he tried unsuccessfully to avoid it.

"What are you playing?"

"Trap."

"So…have you?"

"Give me a break…*Lacey*."

"I've asked you to please not call me by that name. Telling you anything is a mistake. Where's Mom?"

"I think she's in her office. Go away. Hey—wait, wait. I have a great idea for a security Bot. Can you show me how to write the *algorithm* for it later?"

"I can…I even will. If you stop calling me by my code name."

She padded out of the room and down the hall to see her mother. She loved that her parents had made it a point to always sit down to dinner as a family. She softly rapped twice on the open door and stepped into her mother's office. She was at her desk writing. No doubt penning by hand the personal invitations for their annual dinner and ball. Her mother was a former Prima Ballerina of the Ballet de Monte Carlo, and presently was The International Affairs Strategic Relationships Liaison in the Mayor's office, a position she had held for the last nine years. She looked up from her writing;

"Bonjour chérie."

"You look as if you've been sleeping better, Maman."

"I have been. The new prescription knocks me right out."

"I wish you didn't need sleeping pills."

"C'est la vie ma fille. Will you please choose a nice red for dinner?

Maybe the Domaine Faury Saint-Joseph Rouge '29? I'll be done in a few minutes."

"Oui mère. See you in a few"

"Alex, I like that you're wearing a little eye shadow. It's pretty."

She turned and continued on down the hall to the wide staircase to go up one flight to her bedroom.

Once there she took off her camo cargo pants and sweatshirt. James, who had been a blur in her mind all through the conversation with her mother, now came into sharp focus. *Why James? Why? You're real. You're sweet...kind. Not like any of those smug jerks.*

She stood under the jets of a warm shower. *An unheated un-mobile home in the Bronx. In this weather.* Toweling off she checked herself out in the full length mirror. She was, at sixteen, a full five inches shorter than her five foot ten mother and, though, as noted, she was rather plain looking, she had her mother's striking green eyes. Her hair was brown and cut short. Studying herself she wished her breasts weren't so small. She brushed her teeth, re-applied the eye shadow and finished up in her bathroom. She walked into her bedroom and padded to the bureau that stretched almost across the entirety of one of its walls. Since she had never given much thought to clothing she dressed simply and quickly in a grey sweater and black slacks. Cashmere...her mother had insisted. All the while feeling a heavy sadness which she knew she would need to hide at the dinner table.

She brushed her hair, returned her gray pearl earrings to her ear lobes, one of her two indulgences, and dabbed the tiniest bit of Amour Fou No 5, her other indulgence, on the pulse points inside of each wrist and in the hollow at the base of her throat. *Amour Fou...perfect.* She took a last look at herself in her Cheval mirror. *Smile girl.* She turned and proceeded downstairs to the wine room to pick out the wine and decant it.

While

he loved his son James unconditionally, John Bedloe abhorred the James' mindset. Sadly, he understood the why of it. His son, like so many very young people had grown up on a steady diet of FAIR-TV coupled with no available public schooling per se. Their classroom was FAIR-TV and, possessing that capability intrinsic to all young minds, they absorbed what was fed to them like greedy sponges. They did, however, lack the filter of experience, and by the time that filter might have been in place and able to protect them from deciphering cleverly disguised falsehoods from actual fact it was too late - they were indoctrinated.

Try as he may he was, up to now, only mildly successful in dissuading his son from believing in these monsters that were acting in direct opposition to his welfare. This was the case with many Socees. *These people turned us into something called Associates. It's nice to know we're their partners. I guess we all work in "Mall-Wart" now. People actually believe that the New Populists are going to make their lives better… Pull them up out of this horrendous Associate class. Who the fuck can believe such shit? My son…My own son does!* And, hardly anyone ever stopped and thought about how laughable the designation "Associate" was. At least not anyone he *now* knew. The magnitude of the cynicism attached to the designation seemed to have completely eluded them. *And I'm a B class Associate to boot. The lowest of the low. People just go to their ten dollar an hour service sector jobs like robotic ants. How could we have let this happen? I had a good well-paying job once...a lot of us did.* In the situation they now found themselves in he had to carefully draw a fine line between continually bumming his son out with the reality of their lives and letting some stuff go by so as not to deflate his son James' fantastical aspirations. His own were long gone.

He thought about his grandparents who had come to this country from Czechoslovakia in the 1950's and whose original last name was Cvrtnyk. One thing his father had told him was that his grandfather, realizing this last name would be quite difficult, if not completely impossible, for American tongues to deal with and feeling proud to now be a citizen of this country, knew he wanted to change the name. He wanted something patriotic, so he did some research in the library—of which there used to be such a thing that had books with facts in them—and found out that the island on which the Statue of Liberty stood, was then called Bedloe's Island. So he changed the family name to Bedloe. His grandfather took every opportunity to say his full name; Jánoš Bedloe. People called him John, and his parents named him after his grandfather. To him, his name, John Bedloe, a name that once carried so much meaning, had now become a dark joke. A name that had meant *so* much to his grandfather—freedom, the American dream—now meant nothing. *Less* than nothing. Bedloe told his son this story of his last name when James was only nine years old. Even at that tender age, James couldn't help but feel the emotion comingfrom his father as he told his son this piece of family history. The only person, who ever caught what John's surname represented was his dear wife Jane, who had remarked on it when they were in high school.

And now his son James, who bore that once proud last name, and for whom they had envisioned good, if not great things, was a ten dollar an hour messenger with *no* chance ever at anything more. In 2023, while they were finally pregnant, and in spite of what was happening in the country and to the economy, he and Jane had talked optimistically—and in hindsight unrealistically—about starting a college fund for their child.

They would insist their child study hard and get grades good enough to earn a scholarship. By hook or crook, he or she, would get a good education, grow up to be a professional. Perhaps a doctor or lawyer. Something that would give their child a good life, with the means to have a family and do the same for their children—their grandchildren. They knew that whatever their child aspired to they would encourage. And, for a while they were putting aside what they could for the baby's future. This dream was a possibility for exactly two years. What he foresaw with the 2016 election of Loyalist Ransom B. Conover was made manifest with the inevitable 2024 "appointment" of Ransom B. Conover Jr. to the Chairmanship succeeding the eight year Presidency of his father. *Now they called themselves Servers. Great, so bring me a mid-rare bone-in ribeye muthafucka.* In 2025, Conover Jr. and the "Servers" created the three tiered "Associate" class, the "Socees." This finally finished what Conover Sr. started. Along with putting the finishing touches to The People's Progressive Party or PEEPS, they killed whatever plans the Bedloes and millions of others had. Sixteen years of what the Conovers—both of them front men for the real power—had wrought. Years of lies, accusations of fake news, propaganda, blatant in-your-face self-serving profiteering on the backs of the public at large, and destroying free secular public education, had completely eradicated any pretext of democracy. Years during which the world's working middle class was drained of what little they had left and those monies shifted over to the pockets of the ten-percent. He had health insurance through the Veteran's Administration. But Conover Jr., had that privatized and he was then unable to afford the exorbitant premiums. During that time the hilariously named Servers, as the ex-Loyalists newly christened New Populists were fond of calling themselves, had deported eleven million immigrants. And they replaced their lost jobs in agriculture, construction, industry, and leisure and hospitality by creating history's largest population of uneducated minimum wage workers—three hundred and ninety million people—*all* working for ten dollars an hour. It was the same in every industrialized country in the world. Yet, people still believed things would get better. *I understand how people under the age of twenty could be completely propagandized and can't think critically or have the mental acuity to connect the dots. My own sixteen year old son, who was born a year before the Associate class was created, included. The Department of Evangelical Schooling and FAIR News took care of that. And the rest of us —the people my age and older—are all just overwhelmed by the sheer weight of merely getting through every day… the forces arrayed against us. I can't even join the resistance. What happens to James if I get killed? Most of us have lost the will to fight, the ability to question.* All his adult life Bedloe knew that question is the answer. Now, people were either too uneducated, too propagandized, or just too exhausted by surviving to question anything. They only had strength enough to plod straight ahead to their minimum wage jobs, return home, eat garbage and watch TV. FAIR-TV of course. Go to bed exhausted, physically and mentally, wake up, and do it all over again. Day after soul-crushing unchanging day. Metropolis realized.

The rot was set deep in diamond. Not only was he an Associate, he was part of a minority within the Soccee class, since the world population was now only 12.5% Caucasian. The Money, or rather The State—the super-rich who controlled the world respected only one color. Black, brown, tan, yellow, white—it hardly mattered. If one was super-rich one shared *one* common skin color; Green. The Money, 48% of which was white, all saw each other as green. And the Green People, The Money, fiddled together while the rest of us burned.

No matter how hard he tried, how much he explained, he could not convince his son to understand all this. As far as his son was concerned things would get better. He was a TV junkie and TV was FAIR-TV. Worldwide. Mostly FAIR News. The rest was basically ridiculous ads and commercials, cartoons, sitcoms, sports and B movies. In every country. In every language. Except in the elite neighborhoods, where one could watch many business channels, cooking shows, and movies made before 2016. FAIR, in the Socee neighborhoods, besides keeping everybody dumb and diverted, said everything was just peachy-keen and, thanks to our Servers, getting *even* better. Yippee! *The well-developed Fascist's wet dream.* Didn't the newly appointed Chairman also promise that he would create well-paying jobs? Bring back manufacturing, and Social Security and Medicare - for

Associates old enough to remember those two programs. Why would he say these things if they weren't going to be acted upon? How could the most powerful trusted media outlet in the world broadcast the news that the economy was getting better if it wasn't true? *It hurts my heart knowing that my own son believes all these blatant fucking lies.*

Though he himself had never gone to college he had a voracious appetite for knowledge and was a learned man, the irony of which was that at a young age he began accumulating his vast store of knowledge from, of all places, the same thing he had now come to despise—television. As a youth he had an insatiable curiosity about science, world history, politics, current events, the arts, and spent hours absorbing what was then a medium that contained shows that could inform people who wished to be informed on all those subjects. At any hour, on any day of the week, besides the usual bread and circus, the silly sitcoms, the burgeoning right-wing propaganda spewing news, and talk shows, there was *always* many hours of something highly informative. And most importantly it was factual. So one had in one's remote-held fingers a vehicle to learn from if one so desired. And desire he did. That was television from the early nineties—when he was born— right up to the middle of the second decade of the twenty-first century. Before he was seven he began to use the internet almost exclusively, and he liked to joke that he had a masters in Wikipedia and Google. Conover's election in 2016—courtesy of another superpower—began the corruption of the internet. By the end of his first term that great no-holds- barred font of knowledge became censored. During that time he often became enraged whenever the TV news people and pundits laughed off Conover's lies and gaffs and sheer breathtaking incompetence. He could understand the late-night comics making fun of this clown but not the news people. It infuriated him that some of these TV news people were treating this man as a joke. He wanted them to *always* take this monster very, very, seriously. He knew that Conover was as serious, and as lethal, as lung cancer.

How serious? Conover and the Loyalist Senate *amended the Constitution* to change elections to "appointments." This, they explained, was far more convenient then having to spend the better part of a day standing in line to vote. And people bought it! This made it possible for the Loyalists to choose Conover's son in 2024 and, by extent, choose *him* also.

John Bedloe was a New Yorker. Born and dragged up as he liked to say and, like all New Yorkers, painfully aware of the stink Ransom B. Conover left wherever he went. He, like them, was witness to forty-five years of Conover's lying, conning, womanizing, mob ties, and refusal to pay his debts. Debts that were mostly the salaries owed to the people who worked on his projects. So, Bedloe never could understand why the seemingly independent and savvy New York media, knowing what an amoral crook Conover was could say; "he doesn't understand," or "he just doesn't get it," whenever Conover did something blatantly in violation of the norms of governance. It made him want to scream; "Yes he does! He knows *exactly* what he's doing! He's trolling us! He understands alright! He's trying to make us all crazy. It's not that he doesn't get it, he just doesn't give a fuck! He's the king. We are peasants!" In late 2023, while they were pregnant, the internet went dark for good.. And then he stopped all mail delivery.. Bedloe now imagined that if Conover were still around, and there was still such a quaint thing as the mail, he'd go on TV and exclaim; "well, the post office motto is; neither snow nor rain nor heat nor gloom of night stays these couriers from the swift completion of their appointed rounds...right? I'm right, right? But they never mentioned snain. Snain makes it impossible for them to deliver the mail on time. Many people have said this. Many people. So I have to discontinue this for the American pwopie." Bedloe imagined this right down to the last slurred brain-damaged word. Oh, of course these two restrictions only applied to the Associate neighborhoods, not to the elite districts. Information, in any form, was like bleach to the state.

As president, the first thing Conover did was to begin to pack the country's courts with Loyalist judges. Most damaging, he packed what Bedloe called the "Supreme Whores" with activist judges who, to the delight of Evangelicals, immediately voted to ban abortion while voting to reinstate the death penalty. Then, Conover's newly appointed *federal* judges dismissed *all* the convictions of Conover's cronies for their many various crimes. All this, in one glorious flag-hugging month. In these signs of impending incipient Authoritarianism cum Fascism, the Conover years began. *Missus est alea*, the die was cast. And "die" was what freedom, or the illusion of same, did. Bedloe never told any of this to James fearing his son would think him well and truly gone if he told him what seemed so impossibly unreal and straight out of a bad movie. And anyway, the opposite of all this appeared in James' text books and on FAIR News "documentaries." This was the "society Bedloe was now an unwilling but unavoidable part of.

To no longer be able to enjoy the simplest of life's pleasures - things his son seldom, if ever, had in his life…real coffee…eggs…a steak…fish… or any food that Bedloe himself grew up eating? To be unable to afford clean water? A bath? A hot shower? A warm shower? Not if one couldn't afford a large water bill. Or *any* water bill. It was a good thing that the electricity used by the TV was never included in the utility bill. Bedloe always wondered about that.

Now, he missed many things that in the past had gone unnoticed in the ordinary day-to-day. The simple things that made up a life. Things like cooking a real meal. It took a while, but after Jane was gone he could do nothing. Then gradually he finally continued cooking. It was his meditation. His oasis of sanity. It was climbing a mountain - you could not think of anything else but what you were doing or you'd fall - or at least your soufflé would - and, at this summit you had something good to eat. He cooked for himself and James until buying real food was put out of his reach. Seeing these plump, uncaring, well-fed, rosy-cheeked New Populist Servers, and the fawning FAIR news anchors infuriated him. They were all thriving at the same time, in the same world, on the same continent, in the same country, where he, and every other Socee, ate something called "Bredd." A product containing nothing that resembled wheat. All of it triggered in him an anger he'd only approached once before in his entire life - and an abiding hatred for Ransom B. Conover. A rage which was later stoked even higher. *Jane, we couldn't know; but I am so sorry we ever brought a child into this.*

What the world once was - *his* world - that was another story entirely. He and Jane were idealists, protestors in the streets. He wrote his blog with the hope that the possibility of something better always existed. People still worked together for a cause that would benefit all.

He held tight to a memory of an evening when they watched a televised concert. It was The New York City Philharmonic Orchestra from Lincoln Center led by the brilliant conductor Lorin Maazel, and the guest pianist was the great Herbie Hancock. He remembered it as if it were yesterday because it was an all Gershwin program. An American in Paris, and his favorite, Rhapsody in Blue. The earliest music he could remember was Gershwin. It was embedded in his psyche. Either it was always on the CD player, or it was playing on their record player because his parents actually had what were called 78 vinyl records since they liked the warm sound of a record on a turntable. He recalled that as the strains of the Rhapsody, played by this most marvelous orchestra, washed over him, he was immediately connected on a very visceral level to his childhood…to perhaps when he was in his crib. These melodies had always done this to him. They resided deep in his subconscious …they always brought tears to his eyes. He sat there listening, watching, tears rolling down his cheeks, marveling that such beauty could actually come from such creatures as we. It was as if what was in front of him at that moment was all the possibility of human beings realized - the huge orchestra all together as one, in perfect harmony, making this joyful sound. He was completely overcome by it and afterward he and Jane had talked long into the night about the emotions that had overtaken him. He explained that part of the reason for his tears was in experiencing through this powerful musical ensemble playing this transformative music the demonstrable gulf that lay between what humankind *could* achieve, and what, in reality, we were *actually doing*. Now, certainly. But even back then. The overpowering majesty of that man-made moment, that example of what is possible, that zenith of human potential, of humans unselfishly working together for a noble purpose - in that case to make that glorious music - was us at our *very* best. It was a confusing flood of emotions in that it also made him very angry. Angry that we, as a people, could not understand how great we are when we play together - that we could not grasp the idea that, like a great symphony orchestra, when we work unselfishly as one we make beautiful music for the common good of all - and we are all better for it. At the time he remembered thinking that to *not* be able to understand this *could* be to our everlasting detriment. And now it *was*. And it was so, *so* too late.

He was aware that all this looking back only served to make him angrier. He knew that dwelling on what brought us, him, to this point impinged on his health. A nice way of saying it made him sick. And what...he was going to stop thinking about Jane? Re-living the life they shared? The only part of this life really worth anything to him? Yes, he had his son, but the boy was so brainwashed that it physically hurt him to see it. Thinking of his sweet Jane, and better times, was the only thing that was keeping him from screaming, or crying uncontrollably, every lousy day of what had become a lousy existence.

He looked up in time to see that the ancient train was screeching to his stop. The mix of snow and rain called snain was coming down. He stepped out of the train, mindful of the large gap between the car and the platform, and carefully made his way down the slippery, litter-filled old metal stairs onto the slushy sidewalk piled high with soaking wet stinking trash. *Of course the garbage hasn't been collected, or the snow plowed. And, of course they'll be putting in solar heated sidewalks in our neighborhood - and this one too. Count on it. And if they ever do they'll leave the heat on when it's ninety-five out. And that could be tomorrow.* He had a soaking three block walk to the diner. *That there climate change stuff is fer sure some hoax, yuk yuk. The fact that it's snowing again in New York in late September and it was eighty-nine two days ago, hey - what does that prove? I can't wait to hear how FAIR is going to report today's weather tonight? They'll have a perfectly reasonable sounding explanation for it too...Especially if you're just too fucking exhausted by life to even care to parse it. James likes slogans? Theirs ought to be "We shine shit." James...I don't know...he's gotten a bit more willing to question but...*He slowly shook his head trying to concentrate on not slipping...*How can my son buy the FAIR line that we can't be experiencing global warming because it's* *snowing? Or snaining? The weather will soon be improving? Snain? There was no fucking snain when I was a kid!*

He coughed. *Damn it, I can't shake this lousy cough.* He'd been coughing for the last three weeks and it was starting to worry him. And that was another thing; Going to a doctor necessitated having the one hundred dollar deductible. *I don't know how we can afford it and still make the rent - and buy even the basic things we need. I wonder what some over-the-counter cough medicine would cost. Probably far too much.*

She

took James' arm as they walked to a nearby auto-restaurant in the upscale neighborhood.

"I'm hungry. Are you at all hungry? My idea, my treat. I insist. Just this once. James, I don't chip in for rent, right?"

She tapped the table for two menus.

"Hmm…what looks good? Let's see…Umm…Split a burger?"

I'd love a burger. He'd had half of one about over a year ago. A leftover his father brought home. *Holy…it's thirty-two bucks?*

"It's thirty-two dollars" he whispered.

Don't embarrass him. "Yes…it's way too expensive. Maybe next time. Let's get the fresh grub fries."

"I'm good with the fries."

She tapped the table for an order of grub fries.

Next time…I Dunno… How the heck am I gonna pay the next time. It's not right. I can't let her. Tell her…be up front…

"Lacey...I...I really can't afford pay my half of a burger. I'm...I'm ashamed I have to say this but...There's no way I can return this favor. It's just way too rich for me. And with all the things my pop needs..." *Why are you using your father as an excuse?* "Um...that's not... It's me. I just can't spend that kind of money."

She looked across the table at this boy who was not only nice... sweet...but painfully honest. He looked so earnest. She reached across the table and took his hand.

"I'm with you James. It's crazy. It really costs way too much."

She looked at him. She wished they could fly away to the picture in her head. She meant what she said next.

"Wouldn't it be nice if we could just go away somewhere?"

"Yeah...that would be something. If I had the money I'd buy you, your family and me and my pop the tickets to that place."

He squeezed her hand tightly. "Where should we go, Lace?"

"Someplace warm...An island with a beach...and clear blue water. Someplace far from all this...these problems." *If only we could.*

"It would be great."

They held hands and stared into each other's eyes. "Lacey...I'm...I think I love you."

Tell him. "James...You're the sweetest boy I've ever met. And I love you too." *It's true. How can I do this?*

They sat holding hands for a while.

"We'll share something. Okay? You have to eat."

"I'm good with the fries."

The table alerted them that the fries were ready. He went to get them, returned and sat back down, putting the fries between them.

"And after these, let's go buy our plane tickets to that island."

"We'll just take our bathing suits and our toothbrushes."

"I'll fish for us."

"Hey, I may be small but I can fish buddy!"

"Okay…You'll fish."

He smiled broadly and then he grew serious.

"And we'll…We'll fall asleep together?"

Now she squeezed his hand tightly. "Yes…Yes, I'd like that."

They sat for a while that way. After a while, he began to eat the fries. And, as much as she wanted to, she really couldn't eat more than two.

"I guess my stomach is…I'll be okay tomorrow." She smiled.

When they rose from the table he held her coat for her to slip into and brushed her ear with his lips as he did.

I can't possibly love this boy. How did this happen? How can I do this?

On her way home, she decided she was going to ask her father if this messenger placement was because they had information on someone specific, and if so, on who? She knew he might have to be evasive but it was the only way she could know if CyScenSec was on to James' father. She also knew that if indeed it was just a fishing expedition he would want to know why she was asking, and she wasn't sure she could obfuscate—or flat out lie to him. She might be tripping an alarm that wasn't set in the first place. This was the danger in even asking.

# # #

At the same time James was falling even more deeply in love in the auto-café his father, who had already shut the TV off twice, was thinking about his wife. It was his late day and he was sitting and drinking Kaw-Fee.

From the moment he met Jane in high school they knew they'd be married one day. That day was just after he came home from Iraq. His raven haired beauty; level-headed, kind and, for that brief time, a wonderful mother—until she wasn't. And then, he had a one-year-old son to raise and to whom he eventually lied as to the reason for his mother's death. *We were so in love. Remember how we tried for years unsuccessfully to get pregnant and then, suddenly, finally, you were pregnant.*

Bedloe couldn't stop beating himself up for going along with her choice of having an abortion. *Why didn't I stop her? Go against her wishes? In my heart of hearts I knew she was right - one child was enough. Bringing another life into the mess this country had become by late 2025 was crazy. I knew that an illegal abortion in a back room somewhere was a risk we shouldn't take. God fucking damn it—I knew it!* This thought haunted him. *I should have manned up and put my fucking foot down!*

The abortionist fled past him as he sat and waited to take her home. He yelled at her as she ran past him and out the door, then hurried into the back room—and found the lifeless body of his wife—blood pooled beneath her. He knew he couldn't call the cops. The one thing the government still cared about relative to Socees was abortion. *Muthafuckas need worker bees and soldiers.* It took him at least an hour to decide that he might have to do something unthinkable. He couldn't be arrested for aiding and abetting an abortion—and no less one ending in a murder. He'd be put to death, as the law now mandated, and his son would then be left without either parent.

Panicked, he couldn't believe the crazy thoughts ricocheting through his mind; making certain his wife had no ID on her and using the abortionist's tools to cut off his wife's fingers at the top joints, and pulling out all her teeth so they couldn't check what dental records there may have been. He couldn't believe he was even *considering* doing any of this. He must have sat there for the better part of an hour thinking about what he should do…his mind reeling from crazy to insane. *Would pulling her teeth be enough? Do I have to sever her head from her body? How do I dispose of her head, her parts? There were surveillance cameras everywhere…what am I thinking? What am I—Oh, God—you fucking lousy motherfucking piece of shit! Karma? Fuck you!* After what seemed like an eternity he decided that the only thing he could do was to risk just leaving her there since the authorities cared less than a little about whatever mugging, or accident, or murder, befell any Associate. They would probably just chalk this up as another Socee murder to do nothing about. He sat there staring through tear-filled eyes at his wife's lifeless body so ashamed of what he was about to do. *How can I just leave you here? What kind of a man would do such a thing? But, our son…You would want me to get home safely Jane.* The terrible fact was that his beloved wife was dead…*Nothing that I can do will change this horrible fact.* Still churning everything over in his racing mind; he knew that if they cared to do anything at all about the incident that their cameras, their drones, would have seen them both enter the building, and he knew that their cameras would show him leaving alone. He had to risk it. *There's no other way.* He would leave her there and hope his calculations were correct. *Oh, my sweet girl…My love…My heart…Goodbye…Goodbye.* Her lips were already cold. He had to stop crying before he got home.

He remembered trying to be as calm as possible under the circumstances as he left the building and walked to the subway hoping he was doing the right thing. *There is nothing you…It's all you can do. Just get home. Be calm.* And all the way home he kept repeating to himself what they both thought about the reality, and the concept, of death. *Death is birth. Death is birth. Death is birth.* And then; *I hope they don't, but if they come for me, fuck them.*

The next day he tearfully told his son his mother had been run over crossing the street and because of how damaged she was he thought it best to have her immediately cremated. He never heard about it from the authorities, but from that day on Bedloe's hatred for Conover, The Money, The New Populists, Servers, *or whatever the fuck these criminals want to call themselves,* burned fiercely. And from that *night* on he had the same nightmare at *least* once a week. And on many other nights that were sleepless he lay there examining his obsessive hatred for all of them. Thoughts he did not like came at him relentlessly and he was powerless when it came to trying to hold them back. Yes, Conover was responsible for killing his wife—whether indirectly or not. *But, do I bear some responsibility for your death by not fighting harder against your decision knowing that it would not be performed by an accredited medical person? Is my own guilt at having gone along with your choice to terminate the pregnancy under those back-room conditions fueling my obsession? Is this all-consuming loathing I have for Conover magnified out of all proportion because—in this terrible event—I see something in myself that I hate?* He wrestled with, and lost to, these dark questions—the answers to which kept changing.

He clicked the TV on again. It was 12:18 PM, and the day's propaganda was flying in full bullshit mode. He spit on the screen, shut the set off, and shuffled back to the closet to get ready to go wash some dishes.

Bedloe

was feeling worse than shit. He'd had one of those terrible nights where he was again visited by the nightmare of his wife's death. And earlier in the day, of course, the diner was slammed; so as fast as he could clean them the dirty plates, glasses, and cups, were still stacking up.

He was coughing. One more hour to go. *Just keep your head down and do your job. I have to do something about my hands. Rubber gloves. What do they cost? And why don't they have them here already?* Every time he'd meant to do so something, another thing that he knew was more important came up. The rent, the water bill, the laundry, food, for crying out loud... *Sentenced to life at a deep sink.* And, what would his son face in the coming years? *This girl can't save him but at least he'd have someone.* In light of the present he couldn't imagine a future that held any promise. If anything, it would get meaner, harsher, and even more cannibalistic. He had to stifle his cough. The owner had warned him that it was getting annoying and although he was way in the back of the small kitchen some of the staff had complained that maybe it was something catching. He tried to reassure them that it wasn't, but he himself wasn't certain about that. *Do I have some kind of a virus? All the shit we've put into the air, the crappy water, the food. I have to get to that clinic. Can I leave early one day? Can I even ask? Maybe I ca—Holy sh—is that half an order of meatloaf left on that plate?* Of course, he knew that the menu said meat loaf—and he knew what that meant—but he didn't care. Whatever "meat" it was he knew that they ground it fresh and, no matter what "meat" it might have been; *it's fresh and better than anything that comes out of any can.* All meat leftovers of any kind were supposed to be set aside in a big pot to be later ground and re-made into hashes or loaves or burgers. Whenever he took a left-over he knew he was risking losing his job. He quickly looked around. Everyone was occupied in this dinner rush. He grabbed one of the small dish rags, quickly scooped the meatloaf up with it and jammed the whole thing into his overalls pocket. He looked around again. *No one saw.* He immediately continued washing and stacking cleaned dishes in the racks. And a minute later he felt a tap on his shoulder:

"Boss wantsa see ya."

"Me?"

"He's in the office?"

Oh shit…did someone see me cop this meatloaf? I could've sworn I was out of camera range. Did I just lose my fucking job? He wiped his hands and slowly walked to the office where his boss sat going over some orders. He paused at the door, his heart was pounding with the fear that he might have blown his job for some leftover mystery meatloaf. He knocked softly on the door frame.

"Gus?"

His boss kept working on the order sheet:

"What's in ya pocket?"

Oh God, I've blown it! He felt an immediate wave of nausea.

"Please Gus, I am so sorry, I swear it'll never happen again I swear. It's just my kid so seldom gets fresh meat because we can't afford—

"So? Stealing from me is the answer?"

"Don't fire me, Gus, please. I...we...*we* need this job. It won't happen again. I swear to you. It won't."

His boss finally raised his narrowed eyes from the order sheet and stared straight at him for what *seemed* like a full minute; *please don't fire me...please. Please.*

"Make sure. Don't make me an idiot—put it in the pot and go back to work."

He walked back to his deep sink shaking and put what was in his pocket into the leftovers bowl. *Christ, that was close... the fuck have I come to? I just groveled for my shitty fucking ten dollar an hour crap job over a piece of leftover probably pre-chewed meatloaf in quotes that isn't even any meat I'd enjoy eating.* He felt emasculated... Impotent...Again.

On the train going home he sat there fighting all the lousy thoughts in his head; *no more leftovers that's for sure. Fuck! I'm almost glad you're not here to see what the hell I've become. No, no...I do wish you were still—we were still... Two miscarries...how the fuck did we ever get pregnant the second time anyway? What if we'd never got pregnant? Was it my fault? You didn't want another child. I could swear I pulled out in time. Did I subconsciously do this? Could I have done such a thing because...because I wanted my son to have a brother—a sister? Did I cause the pregnancy that led to your death?* This was a new tangent and he couldn't stop his mind. *Wait a minute...I couldn't... didn't. I didn't do any of that...It wasn't my fault and definitely not your fault. That cocksucking crypto-fascist Conover and his bullshit Supreme Whores who made abortion illegal again. The religious fucking right. They all...all of you killed her. You fucking bastards...you killed my sweet wife!*

She was the prettiest girl he'd ever seen. She had creamy white skin and short raven hair exposing the most graceful neck. Try as he might he couldn't help staring at the nape of her neck from his desk in the rear of the room diagonally across from where she sat. And though at age thirteen he would not have described it as such, he realized later that the nape of her neck was the most sensual thing he'd ever seen. It was 2005, and it was the first day of his freshman year in high school. The homeroom teacher, Mrs. Kraus, was saying something about organizing their lockers and showing them a diagram of where the other important rooms were like the library and the gym, the cafeteria, the nurse's office, the main office etc. He knew at once that he wanted to get to know her and he hadn't the faintest clue of how to go about doing this. While he was mulling this over the bell rang for them to go to their first class. His was English - he got up quickly and managed to time it so he could be next to her as they filed into the hall. He hoped they would be walking in the same direction, and wondered what her first class would be - if they would even have any classes together. Their eyes met and, in that brief instant, he managed to muster a smile. *And*, she smiled back!

"So…um…what's your first class?"

Those halting words were the very first he ever spoke to her. And it was as if he was taken over by some strange force and the words weren't even coming out of his mouth.

"English. Yours?"

Her voice was the only voice that could have possibly come out of such a creature.

"English also."

"Mr. Graddis?"

He looked at his class list.

"Um, *yeah* —Mr. Graddis."

She smiled again.

"I'm Jane."

He remembered saying, "Nice to see a friendly face," which encouraged him. He knew at once that the expression "love at first sight" was a real thing. He was instantly madly in love with this girl. They fell silent as they walked, him trying desperately, and failing, to come up with something to say to her. *Say something...Anything...*Nothing.

"Do you live around here?"

To this day he was thankful she said those words.

"Uh huh." He managed.

"We just moved to this neighborhood...I like it - it's okay...and this school is supposed to be a good one too."

That killer smile.

"There's a really good movie theater in the neighborhood also.

"I'm a foreign film nerd."

So was he. "Have you seen *Children of Paradise?*"

"That's the best film I've ever seen."

He couldn't believe she said that. "And how about the way it was made."

"Yes, yes. A film this ambitious made right under the Nazis' nose in occupied Paris. It's amazing."

He couldn't believe it. He was blown away by everything about her. And he couldn't believe he was actually having a conversation with her *and* finding things to say. She made it easy. By the time they'd reached their English class he'd told her about a good pizza parlor nearby and before they entered the classroom they had made a date for a movie and pizza. He couldn't believe it. He sat next to her, and all through English class the only thing he could concentrate on was that he had a date with this gorgeous girl with whom he was already hopelessly in love. She was also, it seemed, quite a good student, answering a few of Mr. Graddis' questions about books like *The Great Gatsby* and *Metamorphosis.* She'd read them and was able to discuss them intelligently. He was impressed. After English class they stood in the hallway and quickly compared schedules. It turned out that they also both had third period Geography with Ms. Modica, as well as sixth period Algebra with Mr. Cohen and later, in the cafeteria, in-between those two classes, they chose seats at the same table. He was crazy with joy. He walked her home on that first day —and almost every day after that.

The date was amazing. What was amazing about it—besides her— was that it was the very *first* date either of them had ever had. They saw Woody Allen's *Match Point*. They were both struck by the film's message that luck rules all our fates, which they agreed could very well apply to them, and did bode well for their future. Plus, as he recalled, the pizza they shared in The Sterling *never* tasted so good. As for the luck part, well... By their sophomore year in high school their friends were calling them "Jay-Jay." Outside of the classroom, rarely did anyone see one of them without the other. By their junior year they knew that one day they would be married and have three children. She wanted two boys and a girl. In that year they both worked in a phone bank making phone calls on behalf of the Prog presidential candidate. *When he won we thought that the country had no place to go but up. Everything would get better. More good jobs, less war, the infrastructure would be rebuilt...it was all going to be great. That's what we thought. What did we know?* They graduated high school in 2009, and in late 2009 though the economy had improved after being put in a tailspin by the eight year term of the new President's predecessor, he found it difficult to get a good decent paying job. So, over Jane's objections, he enlisted in the army. He figured he could learn a trade and earn a paycheck and in the army and when he got out he would be able to then get a good job and he and Jane could then get married. *And,* he reasoned, they would both have health insurance through the VA. She finally relented. He was shortly deployed to Iraq. She got a job as a secretary, and for the next two years she prayed to the universe for his safe return while living in dread of the arrival of a green-clad soldier at her door bearing a folded flag and terrible news. Thankfully, her prayers answered, he made it through and, after one tour of duty, was discharged in 2012, angry, as others were, at learning he'd fought in a liar's war.

In late 2012, they voted for the first time for the incumbent, the first African-American President. In 2013, at 21 years of age, they were married and took a modest one bedroom apartment near his new job as a machinist. And then came 2016, the year the unthinkable happened. The "maybe" millionaire grifter conned enough people out of their vote and the joke called the Electoral College, Team Tyranny's great goalkeeper, did the rest. *Had she won instead of him there wouldn't be any such thing as an Associate class.* Nor would there be the twenty terrible years of deprivation that ninety per cent of the people of his country—of the world—had now endured. He had long wanted a woman to lead this country and this particular woman was eminently qualified. Smart, tough, fair—a woman who had fought for people's rights for thirty years. Rights? We don't need no stinkin' rights! So they smeared the hell out of her.

In general, he believed women were far from being the "weaker sex." And, as far as who the real boss is, he took his cues from nature. In most of nature the male is the brighter-colored one, this is for the purpose of attracting a female. In short, the males do the dance and the females sit there and decide, hmmm...yeah, you'll do big boy, impregnate me, you big gorilla you. He proposes, she disposes. And as far as who is tougher, again he relied on nature as the ultimate arbiter—throughout nature the female is the deadlier of the species. He used to say, "I've never heard of a black widower." He knew women were far more resilient than men. He also believed that the *men* who knew this were far more removed from our cave-men ancestors than the ones who thought men were stronger. In his mind, men weren't even *physically* stronger. In his experience, he'd observed that most women possessed the ability to bear great pain—great difficulty. More so than men. Women—for the most part, he believed—have a way of getting on with it. When a woman gets a cold she goes about her day as usual. When a man gets a sniffle he takes to his bed for a week—and *she* brings *him* soup. And these somewhat frivolous examples do not at all *begin* to approach all the many ways in which he believed women were stronger than men. Men, in general, also complain far more than women do. And let us not forget —women give birth. These were just some of the thousand reasons that he believed this country would have been far better off had they voted this woman into the white house. Of course, he didn't think that merely because a person *happens* to be a woman they automatically deserve anyone's approbation —man *or* woman. *There are too far many men and women who would get no respect from me, whose opinion does not matter to me in the least, and who I would no sooner listen to than I would listen to an avocado.*

He was fortunate that he'd had a good number of male friends when younger who he would say were "women's men." They were men who he had rarely, if ever, heard complain about the hand they were playing and who possessed a well-developed feminine side. They recognized how much better they were as people owing to the marvelous women in their life. They were not afraid to appear vulnerable—*and*, in that willingness to be open and unguarded he knew there lay strength.

So he was drawn to women like Jane who, while possessing feminine beauty, exhibited whatever we thought of as a masculine side—and men who exhibited the same ideal in a well-developed feminine side. *I always thought it quite revealing if, while driving a car, a man couldn't accept directions from a woman. Or couldn't take suggestions from a woman, or who would discount a woman's opinion out of hand, or who feel threatened by a strong woman. I always thought of them as the men who won't wash a dish. Hey, have another shot of irony Johnny boy.*

The woman who should have been our President—if the popular vote had counted, was a prime example of the best of both sides. Instead, we chose a knuckle-dragging Neanderthal criminal as our leader. His Supreme Whore appointment sealed the eventual repeal of Roe v. Wade and made him John Bedloe's sworn enemy for life. Women lost their right to choose. Jane Catriona Stewart-Bedloe lost her life.

In 2018 due to a second miscarriage, they lost another child. Though they debated whether or not to try to get pregnant again—especially in light of what the New Populists were doing to the country—they decided, since the pandemic was over, they would try to become pregnant and finally had James in early 2024. A month after their son was born Conover Sr. decided to move the factory Bedloe worked at to what was then still China —and his machinist job was gone with it. Then the Veteran's Administration was abolished—and there went their healthcare. Their best laid plans had been destroyed by the President of the United States. He was unemployed. The three of them now had to make do on her meager secretarial salary, which they had been planning on her quitting when the baby came. But, now with him out of work she had to keep it. He searched in vain for a decent job. Very few, if any, existed. Despite all her reassurances he felt less and less a man and grew angrier by the day. Now, he had to stay at home and take care of their infant boy, his white-hot anger directed at Conover and his minions.

Their lovemaking, once such a source of power for him, became a mirror held up to the impotence he could not now help but feel. That lasted a full year. During that time he heard the two worst words a man can hear when he's in bed with his lover; "it's okay." *No, it's not! It's not fucking okay!* Finally, through a friend's connection he got news of a job he was qualified for. It was a hen's tooth. He couldn't believe it. He took his one year old to the interview and, miracle of miracles, he was hired. He was overjoyed. He hit an ATM and went home with fifty dollars' worth of food, wine and flowers for his wife. *She'll understand, we need the money, but we need this more.* He bathed their son, laid him in his crib, and couldn't wait to tell her the good news as soon as she came home from her job. The smile—*that* smile—back on her face once more made him glad beyond description. They toasted his new job, and then made love, both of them giggling in the beginning, *"I'm workin' here babe,"* as if they were teenagers —until it became seriously, seriously passionate. She gave herself over to him completely. He was himself again and she was relieved. Then, together they cooked a beautiful dinner. After dinner they stood at their sleeping son's crib sipping a pretty fine Pinot and rejoicing in the return of the good fortune they had allowed others to temporarily take from them. *The most memorable night of my life. And a minute later she was gone.*

He was totally unaware that he was sitting there on the train shaking violently until that moment—so deep into the past had he transported himself. The loss he felt in that moment was staggering in its enormity. His anger equaled by its rage. *Bastards took everything from me. Everything! I wish I could have had my hands around Ransom B. Conover's neck. Stared into his eyes as the light died, heard him gurgling as the last foul breath left his soulless body. I know you'd tell me that such thoughts are a waste of energy, but sweetheart, you...you just don't know what this life has become.* He realized his fists were clenched tight, and had been for he didn't know how long, his nails drawing small dots of blood in his palm.

His son wasn't there yet when he got home. He was relieved because he wasn't ready to talk anyway. He was in a dark place. He'd have a little bit of sorely needed alone time without FAIR News—*or any of their filthy 460 channels fouling up the air.*

Lately his moods had become extreme. Up and down. Very down. Now he was once again mired in the gloom of his life. It being the end of the month had something to do with it. *Always comes too soon. Always kills us.* The rent, the water bill, the laundry—*if* they even *did it* that month. And the food they needed in order to have the strength to go to work and then come home to sleep in this opulence, and then wake and go to work again - and then do it all over again. Joyless hamsters. What surcease there was existed only in his mind. So he existed in his memories—and *they* were bittersweet. The TV turned itself on. It was the Kaw-Fee commercial featuring Caw-Fee the Krow. "Caw, Caw Kaw-Fee, It's virtu—" He had fairly leapt for the remote and turned the TV off in mid caw.

"GO FUCK YOURSELF! You fucking asshole Morons."

He wasn't exactly sure why he found himself going to the hidden compartment in the bottom of their closet to look at the M1911.45 sidearm he'd brought back from Iraq, but there it was in his hand...oiled, chambered, ever ready.

There were too many fitful nights made blacker by the nightmarish unending surreal loop engendered by his wife's death playing in his mind. Too many mornings. This morning, after one such tortured night, as he sat with his Kaw-Fee fighting feeling sorry for himself and feeling sorry for everything in general, his thoughts were pelting him like stones. Now, here he was—once again alone with uninvited leaden thoughts. Thoughts he could not hold back. Thoughts he never expected he would ever have…Yet, there they were clawing at him. And he powerless to repel them. *Fucking lousy life…demeaning job…groveling to save it. There's nothing. Nothing. I should…just fucking end it.* For the first time in his life the thought of suicide entered his mind. Suicide. It had come to this. He had gone so many years putting up with what he was now reduced to - what his existence was — that the surprise was it had taken this long for this thought to crawl on all fours into his mind. It would end the contempt and the hate that ate him up from within. End the insult that slapped him in the face day after day. End the guilt he could not help but feel and which weight was unbearably heavy. *Jane. Jane. I could have stopped you. I should have—Stop! Stop you… How selfish is this? To condemn you to this…this torture. Why would I wish such a thing on you?* The sadness he felt covered him like a shroud. He was damned without her, but were she now here wouldn't she be just as damned? Thoughts which later shamed him now entered his mind; *were you lucky? Had death rescued you? Did your very goodness save you from this miserable existence? Oh God in whom I do not believe…what the fuck am I thinking?* He couldn't shut his mind off. He wondered how many others in his situation had this same thought of suicide.

He looked at the gun. *And if I do blow my brains out what will become of my son? He's sixteen. I can't leave him alone in this mess.* He stared at the gun. *Even this way out is shut to me. I can't kill myself and I can't join the underground. But this girl James has met. He says he really likes her… Says she likes him. Maybe she's his Jane. Maybe…this girl could be my son's life partner… my boy wouldn't be left alone if I…if I do it. He'll have someone to grieve with, someone to comfort and support him…She works, they could split the rent and everything.* He couldn't believe he was thinking these morbid thoughts weirdly mixed with this pragmatism. Today was a *very* bad day—so much so that for the first time in his life he felt like he wanted out. *Death is nothing. It's living like this that's unbearable. No way can I ever leave my son alone. Is this girl the way out? I was a grown man when Jane was taken. He's a kid…He'd be even more paralyzed than I was. He needs to have someone.* He was rooting hard for this new relationship to grow into something real. *I need to meet this girl Lacey to get a feeling for who she is. Gauge her feelings for James. They need time while they grow closer. Are they going to grow closer? I need to know.* From what James had told him there was a good chance of this happening. *He'll know pretty soon.*

It's a miracle that more people aren't killing themselves…Who knows, maybe they are. They sure don't report it. They don't report anything about the underground either. Wouldn't look good. Everybody's happy. No Problem. I wouldn't want James to find me like that… I do it either at work, or a couple blocks from here…or on the train station. Anywhere but here. So many other ways his life could have gone. A different outcome in the 2016 election— and all the ensuing events set in motion by that outcome. Chiefly, his wife not being butchered because of it. The Associate class never happening. *Match Point* indeed. Why did some of the worst people succeed in life? *Why do they seem to go on forever while kinder, younger, worthwhile people die? Is it down to luck? Fate? Do these things even exist? Is it all pre-ordained? How do I deserve this? How did I offend the universe? I must have. Is it because I'm really not such a paragon of goodness that life has overstayed its shitty visit and kind death hasn't come knocking?* He looked at the gun in his hand. *I am good. I am. Why am I being punished by having to endure this last twenty years of hell?*

His thoughts had never been so dark—and it freaked him out. Until he could take matters in his own hands and end this life sentence he'd better just man up and stop feeling so sorry for himself. He still had a son to take care of. To set an example for. *Stop fucking whining!* Mercifully, a Zen koan found its way into an empty space between these thoughts; *when you can do nothing, what can you do?* He kept staring at his pistol. Finally, he wrapped it in its chamois and put it back where it lived. How many others had actually done it? He came back up front and turned the TV on to check the hour just in time to hear Natasha Conover saying; "Jeffers Two, like Conover One, is the focal point of the great—He spit on her and shut the TV off. *Cunt! More like fecal point. When you can do nothing, you can get good and wasted. Please kid…bring some M home tonight.*

October...

and it was like a sauna outside. *Yesterday it was snowing in the morning and raining in the afternoon and then snain and now this…It's gotta be pushin' a hundred. An' muggy as heck to boot.* He stepped away from the small window and clicked on the TV. *I dunno about this weather. Maybe the both of them're right.* He began to put up a pot of Kaw-Fee. *Lacey's been looking a little green around the gills with the fries. We have to find another place for lunch. I have to.*

As James spooned the Kaw-Fee into the pot he watched Chairman Jeffers with Vladimir and Connie on Mornin' All Y'all, one of the most influential news show on TV and where he, and most of the country, got their news first. He reached into the cooler and insta-zipped open a cold can of M- POW!-r and took a long chug. It was a terrific energy drink. He sat back feeling the almost instant intense overpowering warm rush. He took another swig from the can. The ice kept it really cold but the synth-meth made him feel warm. It was electric. He was invincible. *I got a girlfriend! And she's great! And so am I!* He ran the cold can across his forehead, behind his neck, and on his wrist. *This wrist is killin' me. I gotta get another bag of ice soon. Eleven bucks—the same bag was ten a week ago. They were right. They said it on all the talk shows—prices would rise, but it's just temporary. We just have to tighten it up until the Servers straighten all of this out. An' we're gettin' a raise soon.*

He knew things would get better. *We have to have faith. Faith can move mountains. They're right about these regulations. They obviously make it really difficult on the job creators to increase the work force. No wonder we haven't been able to get better jobs…It's no wonder I can't make more money. But we're gettin' a raise soon so… Conovomics is workin'… Why does pop call it Conovomit? What does it have to do with that old President's "Trickle Down" economics? Why does he say that it was a flat out disaster? I never saw that in any of my history books. In fact, from what I read it was exactly the opposite. It is funny though that—*He laughed, *"Trickle Down" makes him think of some old man urinating on his head from above.* He took another swig of M. *I can't believe we were so messed up last night we must've clicked the TV remote on the offer box on one of those commercials that come on every five minutes. Now we have to pony up sixty bucks for two Dillyman and Gloober Forever T-Shirts. How stupid…How stoned. I can't even remember we bought 'em—but the message on the TV says we did so…And the money was for finally buying the heater—well, not for today but… Oh damn, that money could've gone to a clinic visit for him.* He knew how his father, who also wouldn't remember their doing this, would take this news. *At least the water color isn't as dark brown as it was the other day. I wouldn't mind a drink of cold water…* He was searching through his pockets for the $19.99 he would need to buy a gallon of pure water. *I'll make Kaw-Fee with this brownish crap but there's no way I'm drinkin' it straight. That guy at work got paralyzed drinking this water without boiling it. I could boil it on the hot plate. But, by the time it got cold…An' there's hardly any snow out there to get it cold anyway. 'N even if there was who wants to wait that long.* He saw he only had $14.45. *I'm gonna have to get another five and change before I can have a drink. At least I have a full slate of clients today. I'll get some clean refrigerated water in the Financial District. Praise God for that!*

I wonder if he'll be up to going to work today. His cough seems to be getting worse. No sooner did that thought leave his mind than he heard his father shuffling towards the tiny bathroom, coughing as he went; *He's gonna go to work…This heat, it'll be deep puddles… Oceans…totally slushy and dirty as heck. He should be staying home but…We can scrounge up the hundred bucks for the visit pop! What a stubborn… Man, it's hellish hot! Maybe I won't have to buy a heater so soon. Anyway, they wanted sixty bucks for that one on sale the other day from PanAsia 'n I dunno how 'cause we're in a cyberwar with them. I gotta ask pop how they can do this. There's gotta be a good reason. Sixty bucks… 'N that was a sale. Why the heck did we buy those tee shirts? Damn M! Maybe I'll make some of it back today.*

The Kaw-Fee was ready and he poured himself a half of a cup. *I'm pretty lucky to have these clients.* He was doing his messenger job and this man had asked him his name…this investment banker. After a few minutes of small talk the banker offered him ten bucks if he would masturbate him. At first he was taken aback…shocked actually. But the banker said that ten bucks was nothing to sneer at these days - and then he thought; *what the heck - for a hand job?* The more he thought about it the more he told himself that this money would help his father and would therefore actually be Godly. *Ten bucks is ten bucks.* Besides needing the rent, they needed the usual—soap, toothpaste, toilet paper—and they *had* to do a laundry. And, after all, it was just some skin—so he did it. And that first man turned him on to a few other men, and even a couple of women bankers. They all wanted the same thing, and the money was a Godsend because, just as now, they were barely scraping by then. And, even though the New Populists had defunded the clinics that, among other services, provided free Aids testing - saying there was just no money for it anymore—he felt, as far as Aids went, faith would protect him. And there was no danger in just masturbating people anyway.

On Good Mornin' All Y'all they were informing the country of the latest greatest successful surge in the Twenty-Two United Arab Federated Countries war. They were saying that not only was it a shame that it had cost us 46,250 lives to date, but in their humble opinion the worst thing was that it had cost us *far* too much money. *Two Trillion* dollars and counting. Money that could have been used to help the Associates they said. Chairman Jeffers agreed, adding that "nothing great ever came cheap, so as true patriots always do we'll all tighten our belts and make a few more sacrifices." *Well…we're this close to ultimate* *victory - an' maybe bringing our troops home. So...*Vladimir and Connie congratulated the Chairman on all of it, and they all gave a thumbs up and smiled into the camera. *They're right though, two trillion dollars could be used to extend the Centipede Train to us, or build an upper roadway for some Straddling Buses to run here. I know we'll never have a Heli- Vee. 'N if we can't fly over the streets at least provide snow plows to clean them the way they do in the Financial District. Hey, stop complainin' jerk. At least we have a home. An' we're getting' a raise.*

His face wet, Bedloe coughed and stared at himself in the bathroom mirror. *Christ, he's in there listening to that crap again. No big deal. Only 46,250 lives—to date. We're insane. We are the fucking virus. Civilized? Conover put children in cages? People now being "disappeared?" Nazi soldiers walked people into gas chambers? They bayonetted children? How could one human do such things to another? Brain-dead desperate-for-a-paycheck kids whose only out is to become soldiers who carry out deranged orders from insane criminals? If they could somehow bring themselves to say no then what?* He opened the tap; *Fuck man! Even darker.* He shook his head as he began to brush his teeth - and shoved the toothbrush up his nostril. *Jesus fucking...Should water smell like rotted fish? Another lovely day. Earth's infection...that's us. The damage we've done. Still have to buy toothpaste.* He rinsed his mouth, careful not to swallow any of the putrid water. *What, you don't want an enema?* He looked at himself in what was left of the medicine chest mirror. *Louis Vüitton would love those bags Johnny ...*He washed his face. *Careful.* He grabbed the towel from the rack. *Cancer in the air, sea life dead, constant rain and snow—and today this heat...Jesus Christ.* He dried his face. *Wonderful—now I smell fishy and musty.* He began to wash his armpits. *We've given the planet a fever. Can't even afford deodorant. Should I shave today? To wash dishes? Almost lost my job. Need razors. I need some Kaw-Fee. Kaw-Fee? Unreal. Literally. Shit, we need toilet paper...funny. A laugh a minute. Laundry, toothpaste, toilet paper, razors. We need... We need more money is what we need.* He combed his hair. *We must do a laundry—soon. Everything's musty. The kid's got a girlfriend... we have to.* He stared at himself in the small mirror...*this is you Johnny* *boy—get used to it.* He coughed a couple of times and spit up some ugly phlegm into the toilet. *Celadon, my favorite color.* He flushed the toilet and walked out of the small bathroom into the back sleeping area. He took a shirt off the door hook, smelled it, and made a face before he slipped it on. *That's it, laundry —tomorrow!* He slipped it over his head. *Shit, ninety-nine per-cent of all the species that have ever existed are now extinct. That'll be us... soon. Survival of the fittest baby...We are the missing link, and we are not fit.* He stepped into his musty overalls.

#

James poured another half of a cup of Kaw-Fee, careful to leave his father his usual three cups and watched raptly as the subject turned to Chairman Jeffers' most pressing issues; the issues he said we should all be most concerned with; "the latest terrorist bombings - *I think I'm more concerned about the raise guys*—"which means the pressing need for even more tightened security. There is also the lingering imminent threat of invasion by Canada which means the possible need for more young men and women to be drafted." *Huh? This could be serious.* A new slogan appeared on the screen: "Our Children, Our Warriors." *I don't know if I'm ready for this. I mean, I have a girlfriend...* Vladimir and Connie heartily agreed that security was of the utmost importance. *That's why they can't tell us where the terrorist bombings happened. Should we invade Canada before they invade us? Pop said Canada is sandwiched between us and Alaska—so why the heck would Canada even think about starting a war with us? I guess - but they said Canada's leader is crazy. I dunno...On this I have to think pop's right.*

His stomach was now beginning to growl. He hated hearing his father's persistent coughing. *I should score that heater anyway. That's why he's got this lousy cough. Why on earth did we spend all that money on those t-shirts? We can still get the hundred for the visit and he's gotta go. It's somewhere here in the Bronx, but it probably closes before either of us get off work. We have to work that out.*

He checked the time on the TV. *An hour to get to work...And Lacey.*

He sipped his Kaw-Fee. *I hope she feels better today. That new slogan: "Our Children, our Warriors" is pretty cool. I could be a warrior. What about that raise guys? No mention of it?* He sat sipping his Kaw-Fee; *that President we had many, many, years before with that funny name—he wasn't even a citizen. How did a foreigner swindle his way into the Presidency? That guy completely ruined our economy. It was the worst it had ever been because of that guy.*

His father tried to explain to him that in 2021, during the first Chairman Conover's second term as Chairman, he incorporated the country and passed the perversely named New Order American Corporations Helping Economy act or No-Ache, which, his father said, drove the working class to the poor-house. He didn't believe it. And, the next day after that his father told him the New Populist Board of Directors, in a unanimous vote, re-wrote The Good Start program to only cover people making over $500,000 a year. They called the new program Here's Your Job. *There was nothing like that on FAIR or in my school's history books either. It was just the opposite. What is he talking about? Why does he always say that the Servers just create slogans and misery? The job creators need the help most of all so they can create jobs. It's logical. What, are we supposed to create jobs ourselves?*

He knew from a FAIR-TV documentary called "Great Moments in America," that, in 2021, on the first day of his second term in office, President Conover One, as he was always referred to on FAIR, with the approval of Congress, decided to change the method by which the country chose its leaders to a more convenient one, explaining that manufacturers stood to lose a valuable day of production while people voted. He learned, and FAIR explained this in very clear terms, that it was better left to the Board of Federated America Corp to appoint a Chairman. Someone vetted "extremely" who had the best interests of all the people at heart. His father insisted it was unconstitutional. Criminal. *Pop said the vote no longer worked for Conover because most people, especially women, hated him. I dunno, I learned it was the exact opposite. And, to me, it's obviously better that we don't have to take a Tuesday off from work and lose a valuable day's pay…And, it was convenient. Why should we trudge through the snow, or get wet in the rain, or sweat in the heat just to vote?* He disagreed with his father and agreed with

FAIR that the Constitution *was* outdated having been drawn up centuries ago. And, having a Board of Directors appoint a Chairman was easier on us and *way* more convenient.

He'd also had a few heated arguments with his father about whether it was better to have the internet or not. *Sheesh…he's apoplectic about it. Why is he so upset that Conover created the New Information Act? This is way safer. It's easier for terrorists, and all our enemies, to propagandize and radicalize people through the internet. I'd make the internet off-limits to most people too if I was in charge.*

The FAIR Siren sounded: "This is a special FAIR News report." An attractive blonde anchorwoman was standing in front of an Evangelical School. "Schoolchildren will now be issued assault weapons. A move that will undoubtedly save many lives. This new mandate has been unanimously praised by teachers everywhere. Fair News will have more on this later. This is Laura Simmons Fair News Indianapolis, Indiana. *Wow, I only had a pistol in school?*

He switched the channel to the popular morning soap "Our Socee Life." Joey had just landed a managerial position at FuturaBot which came with an annual salary of a million dollars and had instantly propelled him and Angie into the Elite class. It was interrupted by the FAIR Sunny News coverage of a heroic rescue in Iowa. They were showing an interview with an elderly couple who earlier had been lifted out of a huge sink-hole by a teen-ager on his way to Evangelical School. "It just opened up right under us." The reporter was saying: "we've been advised that the sink hole will be immediately filled and the street, will be made better than—what's that? Ah, *far* better than before." The survivors then thanked God "in His most merciful greatness" for sparing their life. *Wow. Amen brothers…Amen.*

Darn, my wrist is really killing me. An' all those clients today. Seven jobs yesterday an' that guy who took just forever. An' that last client of the day, that banker Charles. Every client should be so quick. Guy came in my hand in maybe two minutes…I can't believe he talked me down from my usual fee.

He's loaded—ten bucks is too much for him? Still, he knew Charles was right when he said: "hey, I can go to anybody else out here—there're lots of kids your age out ready to do what you're doing and they would welcome the money. Be a smart kid and take the five bucks." And he did. He knew that he couldn't afford to lose a good client—and the banker knew it too. It was a Godsend that these rich people used their set-aside traceless cash to pay him - and, the bonus for him was that it was tax-free. It was a little risky but so far so good.

This hurts. I'm gonna go lefty…Screw how many complaints I get…an' it's a heavy schedule tomorrow too. If we had a mini-fridge I'd have some ice to press on it whenever this happens. I gotta spend another eleven bucks for an extra bag of ice if it becomes worse. I'll be glad for the raise. The FAIR siren sounded.

Reverend Cletus was live from his church announcing that they had to close thirty clinics for security reasons. And, to remind everyone that in an emergency prayer *never* failed. Then the jingle played:

God, Jeffers 'n Cletus,

Them 'n the Servers'll lead us.

Cripes! I hope ours is still open. More bad news. But…if it's for security… Then from the TV: "This is a special FAIR-TV program note. Another four hour FAIR-TV cartoon marathon tonight - a special event; The Very, Very, Very Best of Dillyman and Gloober, along with the Complete History of the D&G Cartoons! Followed by a special showing of your favorite reality show, Rape! Murder! Execution!" *We're gonna need some M for R!M!E! Most merciful Father, please let the ache in my wrist stop so I can get through today. Amen. And let her feel better today too.*

Getting

out of bed each morning was becoming a real effort. Something else, somewhere else, on his body either ached or was bruised but Bedloe knew he had to get downtown to work—they badly needed the eighty dollars. The cough was getting worse, but heat, rain, snow, snain, he was stuffing himself onto that train and bringing home a few dollars. *Fuck this shit.* He looked out the small window and it was…snowing? *Yesterday was ninety something… Jesus.* He heard his son in the tiny galley making Kaw-Fee— and for the thousandth time his mind was playing the same thoughts: *it wasn't fair, that this kid lost his mother at such a young age. Jane, why did I ever agree? You were right. There was no way on earth the way things were we should have another child but…I'd gladly struggle with two children to have you here. And what if I was making a decent living then? What if that criminal schmuck hadn't moved so many factories to countries all over the globe? What if that fat bastard hadn't appointed a religious nut Supreme Court judge who lusted to overturn long-time settled law in the first place? That alone validates everything I still think about The Money and the New Populists. To nominate and prop up an amoral cocksucker so enamored with the sound of his own voice…A mean piece of shit who needed praise and applause so badly. Who used fucking up the world as a shield—and took great delight in it! Our future-tense President; "I will, we will, it will be, you will have. And his go-to bullshit; "We'll see what happens." Did I really once think his insane actions would destroy him - and the craven bunch that thought him fit to be President? Would finally turn The Money against him? Stupid me. He pitted us against each other. Pitted wives against husbands. He emboldened the rise of those populists all across the globe. Control; they craved it and he cemented it. All these liars are his spawn. Servers! My son actually believes he's going to get a raise.*

He had a fond remembrance of an evening when he was in his teens and he saw a wonderful documentary on a man named Henry Rainey aka Groovy Smoovy. Rainey was a founding member of the Phurst Church of Phun, a secret society of comics and clowns dedicated to ending the Vietnam War through the use of political theater. It got him to questioning as to why, at such a young age, he harbored such an animosity against the right-wing of this country. He knew now for certain that after being exposed to the way Groovy Smoovy lived his life of "protesting" for world peace and sanity that he, John Bedloe, was *far* from enlightened, and *far* from wise. *If I were, even after what happened to Jane, I wouldn't have this abiding, debilitating animosity towards this political party.*

While he was an idealist who could easily imagine what John Lennon imagined, he knew that any Utopian vision was unrealistic and merely something to aspire to. Yet, The Money—and their current hand puppets the New Populists—steadfastly refused to provide even a modicum of training, or education, or needed assistance necessary to buoy a drowning people. What they did do, as Jesus would have no doubt done, was put children in cages. And while they "aspired" *only* to control, and to amass wealth beyond anything anyone would ever need, they were breeding a class of illiterates which suited their purposes perfectly. *"Idealism"...for suckers... "Socialism"..."Ooh...Comumunism." And that's against the "spirit" of laissez-faire Capitalism. Against the "spirit" of the free market. Why on earth would you want us to spend your tax money on you? Their world's a zero sum game. They re-wrote the expression to; "I've got mine—and it used to be yours." These were ghouls; quite comfortable going about their selfish pursuits while blithely ignoring the sufferings of others. And, professing to religiosity...I feel bad for you Jesus...Dying for these parasites.* He viewed all this as convincing evidence that they were the most worthless humans among us and worthy of his abject contempt. *At least the hand puppets for The Money on the PEEP side were inclined to do some things on behalf of the working class.* Against strong Loyalist opposition The Progs had managed to give us Social Security and Medicare and the New Deal, which dug us out of the Depression. Now all gone. He was not naïve, he knew The Money operated much the way bookies did. They played the middle; backing both sides but risking a little more money on the party they thought more represented their interests. Usually, that was not The Progressives. In the long run The Money was ahead. Far ahead. *The mere act of trying to get dressed is becoming more difficult every day. I'm forty-fucking-eight and I feel double that. It's a fucking effort to bend to tie my shoes. God, I'm outa breath.*

"Dad, I'm leaving—there's Kaw-Fee on the hot plate, I'll see you tonight...I'll try to score something good for dinner, so don't worry about it...okay? And dress warm." *Yeah, I'll put on my chinchilla.* Bedloe heard the front door creak to a close and continued dressing. *He's so totally fucked and doesn't even know it. I only hope this girl he's met is for real. He'll need someone to help him get through this mean existence. They'll need each other.*

He shuffled into the tiny bathroom and, as was his habit of late, stared at himself in the mirror above the sink. After a minute he opened the tap. *Jeez, it's the color of a taupe fedora I used to have. Careful Johnny—the shits are shitty.* Done with his ablutions, he left the bathroom, threw on his clothes and went up front. *I have to take the laundry in. Thirty-five to forty dollars. It can't be put off too much longer. The bedding's got to be cleaned. Can't do it myself in this water. Even doing the fucking laundry...*

He sat over a cup of Kaw-Fee; *twenty-four years...I've gone from a twenty-five dollar an hour skilled machinist to washing dishes in a greasy spoon for ten bucks an hour. And thankful for the job. My son will never be anything but a messenger. I suppose it could be worse...so many people are in the street pissing, shitting, begging...sleeping in doorways, on subway grates, we step over them in the middle of sidewalks...with the feral animals and rats.* He had a fit of coughing.

*I went to a phony war for this country. I believed. What a sucker I was...
me, and every dumb kid who ever picked up a rifle to protect the property of all
the world's well-fed fucks.*

He never could explain to his son how his mother had died beyond just
saying that she was killed in a traffic accident. He had, however, tried many
times to explain to his son that the world was a far different place when he
grew up. *It was far from perfect, but...at least we felt free. It might have been
a grand illusion, but it seemed as if we had some say in some things. We finished
high school—a lot of us. We voted—some of us. Went to college—not enough of
us. Now ignorant thugs roam the streets beating people up...Nobody in charge
gives a flat-out fuck as long as the crimes are confined to the great unwashed.
We could rob and kill each other. They practically encourage it. Try attacking
anyone in the wealthy class—or their property—try it if you're an "Associate."
It happens...now and then. And the great elephant's foot of The Money comes
down and crushes whoever like bugs. They've brought back the fucking guillotine
for Christ's sake! Funny, how they finally made having any kind of firearm
illegal when they created the Associate class. What an amazing coincidence!*

*I don't even have what to read on the john anymore. The Daily Fare? The
National Truth?* He would spit on them whenever he saw either one of
them laying there on the train. *Of course, they're free.* Those two, and FAIR
fact-filled news...that was it. *There must be people in the world as angry as I
am. Good thing the M fogs me up pretty good. Or maybe it isn't...I don't know
anymore.*

He sat sipping his Kaw-Fee. After a while he switched the TV on to
check the time. 9:21 a.m. A promo for tonight's "Live from the Front"
came on. "Tonight's two hour show would be live from the United Arab
Federated Countries w---" He spit on the screen and shut it off. *That's why
TV is free.* Well...once again, he was half right.

He hated it that back in 2010 he'd fought in Iraq. He was eighteen, and
joining the Military was the only recourse he had at the time if he wanted
to make some money. At least he'd learned the machinist trade in the Army.

He was discharged in 2012 and in 2013 he and Jane were married. They had two miscarries, and finally got pregnant in 2023. But, by then Conover had been hard at work destroying the country. And by 2025 he had a one-year-old son and was unemployed, thanks to Ransom Conover Junior who, following his father's lead, moved hundreds of factories to what was now PanAsia. And, by late 2025, thanks to the Conover Supreme Court, his beloved wife was dead—and for all practical purposes so was he.

He remembered how they talked about karma when Conover I, who was by then Chairman Conover, was assassinated by a White House secretary in 2023. The woman had said that he had been groping her for the better part of two years until she could no longer live with herself. So, knowing - hoping - that she'd be guillotined for it, she stabbed Conover to death with a scissors to the neck. *Goddamn*, it made Bedloe happy. The official news on FAIR at the time said Conover was killed saving a beggar's life. So, he became a martyr and his son Ransom B. Conover Jr. was quickly appointed to the Chairmanship. Of course, no one thought to question how on earth Conover I would have even been near enough to anyone even *remotely* resembling a beggar since the man always moved around in a bulletproof limousine with darkened windows, or in his private jumbo jet, and *never* went anywhere that smacked of any Associates. *We didn't play much golf.* The future, which once seemed so bright, was now dismal. Twenty-four years ago a black man was President! And a woman had been an inch within the Presidency. Moreover—and this was hard for him to even think about—women had a right to choose when it came to reproductive matters.

He poured another cup of Kaw-Fee. *Karma? God? Oh, there's a God alright. James thinks so. Prayer will deliver...Praise the Lord and pass the can of rat meat.* Given this climate of hand-to-mouth existence was it selfish of him to wish his wife was still here with him? *Is it better that you've been spared this life and the spectacle of seeing your son become a tool of the state? That's what he is Jane. I love him, but he is what he is and I can't seem to be able to do anything about it. Would you have been able to get through to him?*

#

Alex, aka Lacey, was dealing with her own turmoil. *Should I tell him? Should I warn James of the danger his father might be in? Do I basically renounce my entire life? Can I? Can I tell him and disgrace my father? That's what it will do. He's in danger of being without a parent. This will destroy him. And...I don't know if he and I can ever make a life together. If I do tell him I can never go back to the work I...I thought I wanted to do. Can he ever do anything to earn a decent liv—what am I thinking, he's a Socee...of course he can't. Can I? If I were to warn him what would it do to me? Would it, in the end, be for nothing? Would I be sacrificing everything my entire family has always stood for just for a boy's love? Won't there be another? I'm sixteen. Surely I'll forget this boy in time. Surely I will.*

Of late her nights were sleepless as kinds of these thoughts played over and over in her mind. She kept asking herself why this had to happen to her. Why, in a life that was mapped out for her ever since she was old enough to understand, had this yawning chasm opened on her otherwise clear runway to take-off. She had been on the glide path she always wanted to be on - and now this. *Maman...she doesn't sleep well herself...What will this do to her? But I know how I feel when I'm with him. How happy I am to see him. If I do what I've been tasked to do, and his father does incriminate himself, it will wound James deeply. It will break his heart. And...I think—I know he'll be beyond repair. Can I ask to be taken off of this? What will that accomplish? It might still go badly for James, and maybe if I'm close to him I can help him through whatever this turns out to be.*

Though when she thought about it at length she couldn't exactly see how her presence could help James after the eventual outcome. *How can I be with him after I do this?* Her heart was breaking because she couldn't see any way out of this terrible situation. *I'll be hurting people either way.* Again, and for more times than she could remember, she began to cry. *We could have had a life together. What kind of a world have we made where two people who love each other can never be together?* She was now fighting the painful thought that her life had been a mistake. Were the things her father had told her far from true? Was what she had always believed a monstrous lie? But her father was a good man. She knew this to be a fact. She saw how devoted he was to his wife, his children. *But was he really concerned with the well-being of people less fortunate than himself?* Were they really the only people fit to be in charge of everything? She couldn't bear thinking about the answers to those questions. And yet, those questions persisted. Sometime in the early hours of each of these nights, with the uncomfortable answers to those questions ringing in her head, sleep would finally find her.

She

hadn't as yet ruled out either telling James everything or asking her father to tell her why she was placed in the messenger office. She was still wrestling with what she had to do. She knew she wanted to meet James' father. She reasoned it was safer to find out for herself if what she felt for him was in vain. However, she still wasn't even certain about this decision. She was thinking about all this as they walked.

They had gone straight from work. The movie theater was in an upscale neighborhood uptown on a street patrolled by soldiers. He was amazed at how easy it was for them to sneak in without paying. They left work together and took a Straddling Bus to the Centipede to within three blocks from the theater. Lacey had planned it out so they would be inside just as the film was beginning. She led him inside and instructed him to pretend they were looking at the glass covered holo-poster cases lining the walls which showed the upcoming films. She said that as soon as the android ticket-taker was preoccupied, or left its post at the door, they would make their move - and to follow her quickly when she did move. It worked. In a matter of less than a minute they were inside and had found two seats. *Sheesh…she is so…calm.* They sat down just as the message "If You See Something or Hear Something—You'd BETTER Say Something," appeared on the screen. It was the first time in his life he was ever in a movie theater. She had leaned close to him and whispered that she thought that the warning was a bit much. He whispered back that he thought it was necessary, but that his father would agree with her. The movie was about federal agents infiltrating a cell of violent revolutionaries and he wasn't prepared for the fact that when the airships in the movie dove and banked so did his seat. And whenever there was gunfire the armrests on his seat became assault weapons and jets of air whizzed past his head. During one scene it was raining and drops fell on him. Most surprising was that in the fight scenes his seat would punch him in the back. TV was never this exciting. The 4dx holography was way better than anything on TV. *Even Pop would enjoy this.* She sat as close to him as she could. *Her body is so warm.* During one particularly suspenseful scene she clutched his arm and pressed herself against him until the scene was over. She suggested they go for a soda after saying that she saved a little money, and would he mind just this *one* time if it was her treat since the date *was* pretty much her idea.

"Did you like the movie?"

Should I tell her this was my first time ever in a movie theater?

"Yeah, it was great. I had no idea that...I mean, do all the seats do those things?"

"First time?"

"I bet my dad would like it. I'd be surprised if he's been to a movie in twenty years. Yeah, this *was* my first time. Did you know it was like this?"

"I guess. Yes." *Don't ask me how James. Please.*

She was thankful he didn't. And they continued walking to a nearby restaurant.

"So...Is your father improving?"

"Um...not really...thanks. And I still need to find out where the clinic is and how much it'll cost."

"It's terrible when someone you love gets sick."

"Really sucks."

They reached the restaurant and went inside. *Should I tell her about my side job?* He mulled it over as she pretended to study the menu.

"Lacey, if I tell you something do you promise not to tell anyone?"

"Who am I going to tell?"

"And will you still be...my friend?"

"This sounds very mysterious."

"I'm serious, will you?

"Of course I will. What could you possibly tell me that would *ever* make me dislike you?"

Should I tell her?

After maybe 15 seconds in which he stared at her as she studied the menu.

"Um...I uh...I have another job."

"So...so what? I wish I did." *Or a different case.*

"Yeah, but...It's not exactly something I'm particularly proud of. But... it gives me extra cash and it's tax-free."

Not proud of—Oh God...What is this going to be?

"This wealthy finance guy thought...He thought... He thought I was...you know...cute."

Cute? Her brow furrowed.

"And he asked me if I wanted to make a few extra dollars."

Occupy yourself. Order something. Ketchup. She tapped the menu. The robot voice said: "One more dollar."

"One more—? No. Lacey, I don't need ketchup."

The server brought their scarab fries. She slowly placed a small piece of a fry into her mouth.

Should I tell her? What the heck. She's cool.

"He asked me if I would…do something to…for him."

She looked at him quizzically. He bit the bullet.

"Masturbate him."

Oh my God… Don't react. Don't look shocked. But…

He shrugged. "Crazy huh? A lot of kids do it."

What? Is this the lengths they have to go to just to…? She couldn't believe it. But she managed weakly:

"James, please…don't feel you need any extra money because of me."

He stared into her eyes. Behind the two green gems that returned his gaze he saw a strange mixture of pain, shock, and despair. She held his gaze and nodded in understanding.

"No, sweetheart…it's not for you."

He reached across the table and took her hand.

"No. I've been doing it for a while. Long before we met. A lot of kids do it. To help with our bills and stuff…And I've made you sad."

"Oh James…I'm so sorry you have to do that."

"You're not…Does it turn you off…what I just told you?"

Of course she had no idea that Socee kids had to resort to this sort of thing. Somewhat sickened, she managed:

"I wonder…I wonder if I had to, could I do it too."

She was shocked at herself because she was actually debating if she could bring herself to do such a thing. *Is this how impoverished these people are?*

"I mean, if I had to bring home some extra cash for my parents…I don't know…it's a tough one." *Would I? Could I?* "I don't know if I could. But I do know you're only doing what you have to."

He stared across the table and could see how sad he'd made her.

"Lacey, I'm so sorry I told you and I only pray you never have to do such a thing. But it's the only way I can get him the money so he can go to the clinic.

"No James. I'm glad you told me. And I think under those circumstances…I *would* do the same. For my father or mother I would." *I would…But how horrible.*

"And I still have to ask the boss to let me have the time to get him there." She couldn't help asking if all his clients were men. He felt even more uncomfortable telling her that some of his clients were women. And this made her feel even more terrible than she already did. She squeezed his hand.

"James, I understand. I do."

She did…but she felt so very sad, and that night she cried herself to sleep.

The

next morning James was slopping through the slush to the el. *This is becoming serious. Two blocks and my socks are soaked. This is...I can't keep putting off getting new boots. What the heck is this gonna cost?*

He had decided he was going to ask his boss today. If he knew what a pinball machine was then, he would have been able to describe what was going on in his mind as he stood on the train platform among his fellow Socees. They were waiting for the ancient train that would transport them all to their labors. Thoughts were caroming off of its walls. *How should I appeal to him? I gotta make him see that I need the extra time it would take to help pop?* Should he flatter the man by ascribing to him the quality of empathy - something he had no idea if his boss possessed? Would it be better to just cut to the chase, lay out the gravity of the situation, not mention the clinic at all, and wait to see if the man—on his own—suggests he go there? He was churning through scenarios in his mind as he waited for his train. *And where was the clinic anyway? I have to somehow get this done, his cough isn't getting any better.*

Now crushed in among the bad breath of the unkempt, mostly un-showered throng standing on the train he was running through all the ways he could ask his boss for what he needed. He decided that the best approach would be an appeal to the man's understanding of a son's love for his father. *He's got a father, he'll relate. He must love and respect his father. He'll understand how serious my father's condition could be. Maybe he'll even bring up our need to get to the clinic himself.* He was being jostled as the train got even more impossibly crowded. *I should change cars... Something smells in here... That guy's got no front teeth.* He couldn't move even if he decided to. *I'll let him know my mom's gone and I can't also lose my father. I still have to finesse the day off to go with him to the clinic - but one step at a time. I mean, I'll beg if I have to.*

At work, on the few times their paths crossed in the course of the day before he went to his manager's office, Lacey encouraged him.

It was with great trepidation that he approached the boss's office. This was the moment of truth. He *had* to do this. His father was a relatively young man but his health was getting worse. Maybe it was just a cough, maybe it was something far more serious. All he could think about on the train to work was the best way to appeal to his office manager. Having decided that his approach would be to bank on the man's ability to put himself in the same situation, having his own love for his own father, he ultimately came to the conclusion that he couldn't ask for more than an hour besides his twenty minute lunch break. He figured—he hoped—that an hour would do, but that would only be the half of it. All he could do in this visit was find out the days and hours that the clinic was open and the best day to go, if there even *was* a best day, and maybe make an appointment—if they even did such a thing. He suspected there'd be no way his manager would also give him the entire other day it would take to spend at the clinic with his father. He'd learned from a co-worker where the Bronx clinic was located. *Twenty minutes on the Centipede train, twenty on this train and a five block walk in the slush. An hour and a half... maybe two. Cripes! Why the heck doesn't the Centipede go anywhere near the Bronx? They promised they'd be extending it... but when?* He knocked twice softly on the office manager's door.

"Yes? Open."

He opened the door and peeked in "Can I help you?"

The man didn't look up at him but continued whatever he was doing.

"I hope so."

"So?"

"Do you have a minute?"

"Speak."

"I need to ask a favor."

"Oh?"

"It's my father's health. May I?"

The man finally looked up, stared at him for a few seconds and then nodded for him to come in.

"I'm pretty busy so make it quick."

"My father has a very bad cough and needs to go to the clinic in the Bronx."

"And...?"

And? I... He forced himself to press on. *Say it!* He blurted the words out quickly before he had any chance of losing the courage to do so.

"In the condition he's in I just can't let him go before I find out if there's a best time, a best day...if...if they make appointments. And, even if I knew the phone number, we don't have phones to call them. I can find out the information if I had an extra hour off to go there. Please."

The man continued to look at him.

"An extra hour's impossible. In fact you were just about to be sent out with a delivery."

James stood there crushed. Then:

"I know you would do the same for your father. Please."

"You do?"

He stared at the boy.

"Look…I shouldn't do this, but… how 'bout I get you the phone number and you call on one of our MorPhos later?"

"Oh…That would be…Thank you. I would really appreciate it, thank you."

"Go back to making your deliveries and I'll let you know when I have the number. Go."

James backed out of the office relieved at this outcome. It would save him the trip and, he hoped, signaled that when the time came his manager would be inclined to give him the time off to go with his father to the clinic. Lacey, noticing his relief smiled, blew him a kiss and gave him a thumbs up on her way out to a delivery.

As the day wore on, and he delivered his packages to the people they needed to go to, all he could think about was when he would get this number—and when he could call this clinic. He also realized with some apprehension that he had never before used a MorPho or telephonic device of any kind, and hoped doing so wouldn't prove to be too complicated. With his mind on this, and this alone, he almost botched a delivery. *That would have put an end to this whole thing. Concentrate, concentrate!*

When he got back to the office after his third delivery he was given a slip of paper with a twelve digit number on it and shown to a desk that had on it a MorPho bracelet. He sat down, stared at the number, took a deep breath, and slowly pressed the corresponding numbers on the bracelet's flexipad. The tiny phone rang…and rang…and rang. He was panicked. Would the clinic not answer? Was this a wrong number? Was it clo—a robotic voice intoned; "You have reached the South Bronx People's

Associate's Clinic. If this is a life threatening emergency please hang up and dial 1211. If you know your party's extension please dial it now. Our clinic hours are from 8 AM to 7 PM Monday to Saturday. Please listen carefully as our menu has recently changed. If you would like to leave a message for the office staff please press one now. However, your message will not be picked up until tomorrow. If you wish to speak with billing please press two now. If you wish to speak with pediatric press three now. If you wish to speak with the gynecological department please press four now…" As the message droned on he was getting more and more nervous. *Give me an effing live person!* Then; "If you wish to speak with the operator please press zero now. *Why don't they say that right away?* He pressed zero and after anxiously waiting through four rings an unmistakably human voice answered the phone.

"People's Associate's Clinic. Rita speaking, may I help you?"

He was almost unprepared to speak.

"May I help you?"

"Yes, yes…Rita… Rita, thank you. I need to know if there's a best time or day to bring my father in to see a doctor?"

"What is his problem?"

"He has a terrible cough, and it seems to be getting worse."

"Has he been here before?"

"Um…maybe a few years ago."

"What is his name and last six digits of his number?"

"John Bedloe, 837493."

"And your name?"

"James, James Bedloe. His son."

He waited as she entered the information.

"Is there a best time to come there?"

"I'm afraid not."

"Well…Um, can we make an appointment?"

"The visit will be two hundred fifty dollars."

"Huh? Excuse me…two hundred and fifty dollars?"

"No cards or checks."

As if he had either of them.

"But…this is a clinic… I don't--- Why? My father said the visit is one hundred dollars. How can it be two hundred fifty dollars just to see a doctor?"

"I'm sorry, but the cost has gone up four times since Mr. Bedloe was last here. This is the new federal guideline cost. I'm afraid we have nothing to do with it."

He sat there stunned at this turn of events. *How long's it gonna take to get two hundred and fifty dollars?*

"If I get the money, can we make an appointment?"

"I am sorry, but we only see patients on a first come first served basis."

What? This is crazy. His mind was stumbling around for some kind of something he could ask.

"Sir?"

"Um…sorry…I uh…and if we get there at eight, how long will we wait?"

"Usually at that hour the line is already halfway down the next block. My advice is you need to get here around five AM."

"Five AM?"

"People camp out overnight in sleeping bags or heavy blankets." A head popped into the room.

"Boss says to get a move on."

He waved an "okay." For a moment he was rendered speechless at what he'd just now learned about the "People's" Associate's Free Clinic. "

"Rita, you're telling me all those people have two hundred and fifty bucks?"

"I suppose. Is there anything else?""

"Is it the same at every Associate clinic?"

"I believe it is. It's a law. Will there be anything else?"

"So, there's no appointment possible?"

"Unfortunately, no. I *am* sorry. Cough medicine might help. Will there be anything else?"

He sat there numbed by this turn of events.

"Sir?"

"Um...I uh... I don't think so."

"We sincerely thank you for your call and invite you to please stay on the line for a telephone survey regarding th---"

By the middle of her sentence he'd already slammed the bracelet down. *Go...eff yourself Rita!*

He couldn't believe it. So much for getting his father to a doctor.

The

prevailing wisdom is that anger never got anyone anywhere. While Bedloe knew it was true that in time all things pass, and that in the great scheme of things getting a good anger on doesn't mean too much, and the universe that birthed us will eventually swallow, digest, and disgorge all of us in a different form anyway, he and Jane still believed that working up a good case of anger could be quite healthy. Especially at what was happening to their country. It worked for the Lemon Party didn't it? They talked with their friends about how all of us who are still somewhat sane ought to be good and stinking pissed off fuming irate at the misguided, uninformed, downright ignorant yahoos who were controlling the country's debate. And since perception seemed to be everything, their thought was to just replace the word anger with the word indignation.

In that light they wondered why more people weren't the least bit "indignant" over the carnival sideshow barker whose handshake probably would leave one looking for an industrial strength de-greaser. A man who had the nerve to bray, "I will be the greatest jobs president that God ever created." And; "I'm really rich! I'll show you that in a second. And by the way: I'm not even saying that in a brag." And this bit of intelligent banter about his wife on a radio talk show; He and wife Brandi went on the show and shared intimate details of their life. "Brandi looks best when she wears only a very small thong." The host asked what would happen to their romance if she was disfigured. Conover replied: "How would the breasts look?"

I'd have rather been hung up by my scrotum than live among the imbeciles who thought this monster was fit to lead us. Or, among these upright "Christians," who lack the gene for shame which would keep them from showing up to support this oaf without a mask covering their face. Even such notorious lowlifes as the Ku Klux Klan had the decency to at least attempt the impossible and try to cover their ugliness with a bed sheet.

One day, even before the botched abortion Bedloe asked himself; *why do I take his very existence as a personal insult? Why do I have such a hatred for him?* He gave the question some thought. *Because I'm unemployed and bitter and this man is a huge success despite the absence of everything we prize in people; honesty, humility, intelligence, empathy, integrity, self-control, and the courage to be emotionally open. This grotesque buffoon is the waddling opposite.*

Of course the people who couldn't work up a good case of anger—indignation—whatever you care to call it, didn't know, or didn't care enough about what would eventually happen to our food, our schools, air traffic, our environment, our healthcare, etc. with a weakened government and a bunch who hated regulations because it would regulate how much money they could steal. *We cared, and many others we knew cared and had this burning anger at what we saw was happening to our country and we had the vote. But they had the Electoral College.*

The relentless attack on the media, which began during his campaign and continued until Conover successfully shut down all the newspapers and the objective TV news, slowly but surely eroded the people's confidence in whatever factual news they were reporting. Whatever the news reported that was in any way a negative about his administration was called fake. *We watched it happen and were mad as hell that the informed people of the country ended up being held hostage by the vote of the propagandized uninformed. They amended the fucking Constitution for Chrissakes! And we watched them do it!*

In the second term of his Presidency Conover I and his partners created the PBBL—which fans called The Pebble. The Professional BashBall League, formed to compete with the National Football League and which, in 2021, began showing a FAIR game every other night and four games on Sunday. Ultimately, because of its ridiculously low player's salaries and extreme violence, the PBBL drove the NFL out of business. The former owners of the now defunct NFL did not care to own a BashBall team because BashBall lost money. It was just bread and circus subsidized by the government. But the owners did not go easily and, being Conover's cronies in the trillionaire club, bargained with him and were ultimately given important positions in the administration along with large salaries and perks in return for their unquestioning fawning fealty. Also in his second term, along with banning the internet to all but the ten per cent, he mandated that every citizen be given a free TV—*and* free FAIR-TV service. People were thrilled. FAIR-TV was given an annual budget of over 750 billion dollars to provide this service. This covered all FAIR-TV America production costs including round-the-clock news programming *and* the creation of an animated series to be shown every evening after the game. Thus, Dillyman and Gloober was born. FAIR News preceded all BashBall games and was the lead-in to Dillyman and Gloober after every game.

It was left to Conover's son and successor Chairman Ransom B. Conover Jr. to finish taking FAIR world-wide and propose the creation of R!M!E! Rape! Murder! Execution! The insanely popular show—and crowning glory of FAIR-TV, currently airing everywhere in the world once a week, with plans to add a night or two…or three. BashBall, cartoons and dumb sitcoms, were some of the major amusements facilitating the relentless dumbing down of the world's populace.

Prior to these demented diversions he and Jane saw the gradual erosion of the elegant and nuanced English language as a harbinger of the terrible things to come. The meanings of words was being lost. The adulteration of our language was accelerated. All of a sudden around 2014 many people responded to anything that was quite ordinary as "awesome."

"Paper or plastic?"

"Plastic."

"Awesome."

That, and "no problem" annoyed the hell out of him. As a student of language—and a lover of the English language in particular—Bedloe couldn't help but wonder what word might we then possibly utter in response to the knowledge that in just our Milky Way galaxy alone there are some four hundred billion stars, the closest one—not counting the sun—Alpha Centauri, being twenty four trillion eight hundred and ninety billion miles from us? He wondered that if the answer to the question "what did you think of the last episode of The Real Housewives of Beverly Hills" is "awesome," then what on earth could anyone say of the vast seemingly unending mystery that is the cosmos? When he discussed this disturbing situation with Jane her dead-pan remark was that she had the "distinct feeling that even after Mr. Alexander Fleming told Mrs. Alexander Fleming over the Sunday roast that he'd just discovered penicillin she did not say *awesome*."

They laughed as they riffed on Alexander the Great, Katherine the Great, Peter the Great, and all of the other "Greats," and decided that all of them could not have been all *that* "Great" or they would have been called Alexander the Awesome, Peter the Awesome, Katherine the...and so on. And having thought that, it further occurred to Jane that Alexander the Great's elders, especially his crotchety old grandfather probably muttered something under his breath like "Great? What's great is a good bowl of česnečka!"

They knew they were *maybe* taking this a *li–ttle* too far. But...to his way of thinking, linguistic skills, a person's ability to use as much of the full range of tools available in any vocabulary in order to express oneself concisely, was always the gold standard measurement of intelligence. The elegance of a well-constructed, carefully nuanced sentence had, for him, forever been the hallmark of a well-read, well-educated, and cultured individual. John and Jane Bedloe could both easily see that, because there existed such a climate of anti-education, anti-intellectualism and anti-cultural values, these linguistic skills had deteriorated to the point where too much of what had become the current idiom was made up of hyperbole. The new president being a prime example of this phenomena of the meaningless repeated word. Everything was "tremendous," or "unbelievable," or better yet, "incredible." His language exposed his ignorance. Ignorance and intransigence was so rampant that one congressman who fell sick during the terrible pandemic back in '21 actually speculated that the mask he had to wear might have caused him to contract the virus. In one speech Conover called Gettysburg "hollowed" ground. This knowledge that an uneducated un-read public which had left itself ripe for exploitation by those who would capitalize on their ignorance of others greatly disturbed him. He saw this debasing of the language as the inexorable crawl to the robotic stupidity that was happening before his eyes and which, of course —aside from what he soon realized were his futile attempts to shed light on this in his writings—he was powerless to do anything about. It tore at him every time he heard someone exclaim "incredible," "unbelievable," fantastic," "tremendous," as this new President constantly blathered. He cringed upon hearing these words, and couldn't help but wonder if the people who said them actually read. If they ever talk about ideas as opposed to gossip, and if they could be trusted to think critically. He knew this joke of a President couldn't—and didn't—and it frightened him to think that many of these people actually had been able to find their way into a booth to vote for him.

Sometimes Bedloe agreed with his friends that he was carrying things a *bit* too far solely from hearing someone say something was "awesome." But, all he was hearing them say was "I haven't a clue as to what's going on in the world, in my country, even in my city, I don't read, I couldn't answer even one question on Jeopardy, and what's more I really don't care, could you pass the ketchup." And then not even a please or thank you—and, also of course, to which the passing of same they would respond: "awesome."

Jane, an intelligent, artistic, lovely woman of Scottish/English descent reserved the remark "it's okay" for anything she deemed praiseworthy; a Magritte, the poetry of Rilke, the Taj Mahal...*whenever she said it's "okay" about something I'd written or hypothesized I knew I was right in suspecting that perhaps whatever it was I was on about really didn't suck too badly after all. I'm certain her response to hearing someone say "awesome" to anything less than a bolt of lightning shooting down from the sky and leveling a skyscraper would turn out to be Scottish for "moron."*

He and Jane *loved* the word extraordinary. They both thought it a perfect word for the time since so much had begun to be *out* of the *ordinary*. It wasn't awesome, it wasn't unbelievable, it certainly was not incredible, which meant the exact opposite of what you wanted it to mean, and yet it was so much more than just plain vanilla ordinary. It is, and was, *extra* ordinary. Why, they wondered, had this lovely most accurately descriptive word been forsaken by most of us?

Granted, he was a curmudgeon. His thinking was always a bit esoteric, pedantic, and, back then, even damn annoying to some of his friends, while some of his other friends were genuinely amused by, and saw value in, his musings—and his however far-fetched extrapolations. In Bedloe's own opinion he *was* opinionated. *Very.* He was quite aware of it and quite aware that it rubbed some people the wrong way. Especially since many of his opinions were contrary to popular belief. His friend Barry once gave him a couch pillow on which was printed: "You can agree with me or you can be wrong." It occupied a prominent spot on their couch and always made him smile whenever he looked at it. For his part he wondered how it was that everyone else didn't admit they *too* were opinionated. How could one *not* be opinionated? To have opinions meant that one thought about things — or having experienced them then formulated ideas regarding them—which was something *everyone* did. Also granted, far too many never gave any thought at all to whatever it was the were opining about. Bedloe's concern was with people who could, and did, still think. And, of course, they were becoming scarce. Anyway, to him, the difference between opinionated people and those who *thought* they *weren't* opinionated when in fact they *were—everybody* was—was simply how strongly held the opinions were, and how willing one was to defend them openly. Even when they flew in the face of the popular viewpoint. *Especially* when they flew in the face of the popular viewpoint. And when people pointed to someone being opinionated as a criticism he couldn't help but wonder at them not seeing the absurdity inherent in their having the *opinion* that someone was *opinionated.* At any rate, the frustrating fact was that while some of this got through to James, he could not get through *any* of his opinions which contradicted what the boy saw on FAIR. Even when he couched them on a street level he could not make the boy see the evil criminality of this government.

Before the New Populists scrubbed the history books and the documentary footage, he'd read about what happened in what was then Germany one hundred seven years ago, and it seemed to him sometimes as if he was raising a Nazi youth. He couldn't help entertaining these kinds of dark thoughts even though he loved his son and he knew his son loved him with the same depth of feeling. But try as he might to fight it, he was beginning to lose patience with his son's belief system. When he tried to shut the TV off his son would have none of it, and it further infuriated him that the damn thing sometimes turned itself on! So all day and night he was subjected to the dumbest shows and the most insidious and ultimately dangerous propaganda imaginable courtesy of FAIR News and any one of the now 300 of the 460 FAIR channels. If they said black you knew what you'd be getting instead would be white. And then, after you *got* the white, they would explain in great detail how this white was *really* black and not to worry because it was really *much* better—take our word. And, *anyway,* we *never* said black in the first place.

In his darkest hours he could imagine a day when his son, acting as any good Nazi youth, would turn him in to the authorities. Admittedly, he realized that this scenario was pretty much a stretch. Yet, he sometimes thought that the part of him that allowed himself to be subjected to night after night of dimwitted cartoons and sitcoms was that part that harbored this very fear, and so perhaps he was being prudent in just going along with it all while still trying his best to talk some sense into the boy.

What libraries that still existed were devoid of anything that contradicted the regime as well as anything provocative or remotely interesting. What books that were available were not books to get lost in, but rather state propaganda written by state sponsored hacks. *My son thinks it's a good thing when he hears the new Chairman say: "we are also granting each and every one of you, and all our citizens, more personal responsibility." What I hear is: "you're on your own suckers."*

Bedloe sympathized with families like his own which were torn apart, scarred by the unfortunate happenstance that one side of the family was very well-off and the other side were Associates. One uncle liked Conover and another opposed him vehemently. It was like what happened in our Civil War—brother against brother. *How did these families handle that? Would they ever again sit down together to Thanksgiving dinner? What was Christmas now like for a family now torn apart like this? What about the immigrant mothers and fathers deported —without their newly orphaned children?*

Even the movies starting sometime in the fall of 2021 were under strict governmental scrutiny allowing nothing with even the faintest sniff of an anti-government slant. Cinema was fine just as long as it adhered to the New Populist message. It hardly mattered to the Socees though, since what little money they had was not being spent going to the movies. As a result the film business, whose audience was now reduced by millions, began being subsidized by the government, and what came out of it was either heroic action, fantasy, cartoons, fluff—and always propaganda. All B-Grade and *all* with *lots* of explosions. He envisioned a future Oscar telecast: "I want to thank the academy for this Best Explosion Oscar." All the cartoons had huge explosions. Actors and directors were put out of work, and any artist of any sort who protested the administration was brought before a select Congressional committee, summarily found to be an enemy of the state—and "disappeared." And, whatever films *did* get made bore a message that read "If You See Something, or Hear Something, You'd BETTER Say Something." This message appeared before and after each film against a background of the flag flying gloriously in the breeze. *I can't remember when they added the words "hear something" or "you'd better" to that.*

He thought of the famous chef who characteristically referred to himself as a "cook"—sort of like a concert violinist referring to himself as a "fiddler." A man who was, in actuality, far more than just a chef. He was a critically acclaimed author who possessed a caustic wit and the heart of a radical. He was an activist and an unapologetic clear-eyed narrator of America's moral failures who used his award winning TV show, which was ostensibly about the world's cuisines—especially La Cucina Povera or, as he called them, the "nasty bits"—as a vehicle for political and social justice. A *New York Times* editorial writer wrote: "a man who brilliantly and bravely wove political education into food culture that provided the kind of historical context and compassion for the oppressed that Americans need now more than ever." She added; "may his compassion and indignation live on." This remarkable man committed suicide in 2018 at age 61. Why, he wondered at the time, didn't the vast multitudes across the globe who mourned his loss with the shock and sadness befitting the loss of a Gandhi honor him by then taking up his righteous indignation?

So, getting destroyed on M-POW!-r, and tripping on the kaleidoscopic cartoon colors on the TV, was unfortunately useful in taking his tortured mind somewhere far, far away.

Still

in a zombie-like trance and hardly aware of walking through the icy sleet instead of taking the Straddling Bus to the subway, James trudged the seven long blocks out of the Financial District to the train that would take him home. How he finished the day's work was a small miracle being that his mind was preoccupied with concern for his father. He didn't see Lacey after the phone call and was glad that she was out on a run when he left for home. He didn't want her to see him so down. Nor did he want to, in effect, cry on her shoulder. Everyone had problems and he knew she had her own. His boss, asking what happened, perhaps already knowing what the upshot of the call would be—would only shake his head in sympathy when he told him. *Maybe he does have a heart...I dunno....*He sat there as the stops came and went through the tunnel and then out and onto the elevated track under which they lived. *Why'd I never noticed the state of these people on the train before? They all look sick...Did I see it and just ignore it? Only a few of 'em aren't sneezing and coughing. I'd be shocked if they've ever seen a doctor. Not since they were born anyway. They're probably not as old as they look too.* The train slowed—*Aw heck, not again*—and stopped. *Crap!* He sat there looking around him. *Is he right? Do we put defense ahead of our health and well-being? What good is it if we're dead anyway? Wouldn't it be righteous to make it easier for people to get medical care? Not all free, but at least it should* *be possible to see a doctor without it costing almost a whole month's salary. For just a consultation? For just a prescription? Two hundred and fifty dollars? It's a clinic! We need a strong military but... There's gotta be money... All these wars, cyberwars... Threats from other countries...I...I dunno... What do I know?*

He needed to stop his mind - for a little while at least. *I gotta see my guy. Do I have enough? Don't check your cash in the train.* The train started back up. *I'll get off at my connection's stop 'n do it quick 'n jump back in if I don't have enough. If I do I'll get a four-pak. Pop'll appreciate it. I can already hear him when I tell him about the phone call to the clinic. It'll be the fascists this 'n the system that. It'll be more blasphemy about the "shitstem." Holy... Too many of these people don't even have front teeth!*

He got off the train and looked around before taking out his money and saw, as he had hoped, that he did have enough for a four-pak. He walked to the litter filled metal stairs and down to the snowy street. When he came close to falling down half the flight as he slipped on one of the icy steps he was glad he knew enough to be holding on to the railing. Even though it was ice-cold. *I could've broken my neck... then what?* It was already dark and he hurriedly walked the two blocks through the slush to his connection - looking around over his shoulders as he went. He reached his man's building and rang the downstairs bell. After a short while a static-y unintelligible voice came out of the intercom:

"Wh** I* *t?"

"Straddling Bus."

The buzzer sounded and he pushed open the heavy door and stepped inside the dimly—lit hallway. A waterbug skittered across the stained torn linoleum floor. He began the climb up four flights to his connection's apartment. *More trash.* A baby was howling somewhere above and a dog was howling in response until his owner shouted something unintelligible and the dog whimpered loudly and ceased its commotion. It was not a pleasant building to live in. *Why even have a dog? The stink can keep anyone away.* On the dimly lit third floor he counted out the bills he would need.

On the fourth floor he knocked on his man's door. The peephole slid open and then closed. He heard the door-jammer police lock removed followed by a succession of chains being slid open. The door opened just wide enough to allow him to step step inside the dark apartment. The door was immediately closed—and locked—behind him. He quickly handed his money to the man who carefully counted it. Then:

"It's ten more."

"I don't want a six, I only want a four."

"Price wen' up. You wan' it?"

He stood there slowly shaking his head at this news. "Well...?"

You're kidding me. "Yeah."

He went into his pocket and handed the man his last ten. The man turned and disappeared into the apartment. *Even the damn M.* He waited until the man returned with a crumpled grease-stained paper bag containing the M-POW!-r four-pak. He turned to leave.

"See you nex' time kid."

Accompanied by the attendant clatter the police lock and all the chains were returned to their usual positions as he descended the fourth floor stair. *Ten lousy bucks more...*Now to get his precious package, and himself, home safely. The baby was still howling as he quickly exited the building and moved down to the street.

Once out of the building James began to double-time it back to the train. He usually tried to score while it was still light out. It wasn't often that he was in this particular neighborhood when it was completely dark. Only one street light was working and it was at the end of the block and was going dim every five seconds or so. He was now quite aware that he was doing something risky. *This is too stupid.* The memory of being mugged once before came back. He'd gone the one block when he saw two men turn the corner up ahead and approach from the opposite direction. *No, not again! Do I cross the street? No! Don't! It'll signal I have money. They probably already saw the bag. Cripes! Can't hide the bag now, it'll be too obvious.* He felt his heart pounding out of his chest as the men drew nearer. One of them was looking straight at him…then downward at the bag. He quickly averted his own gaze away. *Holy… Do I cross? Run? Why aren't there any soldiers in the street in this neighborhood?* Now the men were ten feet from him. He had to keep walking straight ahead and he had to look confident… unafraid. *Smile.* He steeled himself; *Smile idiot!* Heart pounding, he smiled at them as he was about to pass; *Speak! Say hello…something…anything…*

"Nice evening."

"Little cold but…"

And they were past. *Oh, my Lord!* James crossed himself as he looked back—relieved to see they were still moving up the street away from him. He got to the el and quickly clambered up the stairs. The platform was empty. *Good!* He peered anxiously up the track for the train. Two well-fed rats scurried across the tracks. The train was nowhere in sight. He stood shivering. *My feet are freezing.* Five minutes, ten, fifteen. *C'mon for…* Without a watch he'd honed his sense of time. He was usually pretty close, give or take a minute. Finally, in the distance a train was coming. *Lemmee get home, out of these wet things and into a warm can of whatever. And a can of this M.* The train was approaching the station. *Thank heaven for litt---what? C'mon! You're not sto…You mother! You…crap…CRAP!* He could make out the dim sign on the front of the first car as it sped past him and continued on. "Ou of Se vice." *DAMN! Now how long? I gotta get home, he'll be worried. I should open one of these cans. No! I'm gonna get stoned in my own home.* Twenty very long, very cold minutes later a train finally squealed into the station.

He was safely on the train and going the rest of the way home. *If I can help it this'll be the last time I score after dark. It isn't worth that huge dose of paranoia…not even for M. Only when it's light.* He sat there decompressing. *Cripes, I have to tell pop that a visit to the clinic is out. It's gonna be another what-did-you-expect night. After what I just went through in this whole fouled-up-lousy day I'm gonna get good an' blitzed tonight for sure. Maybe I'll wait a day…or two…or three even to tell him this lousy news. Tonight I'm just gonna bliss out in front of the TV. I know one thing; I'm gonna have to get him some medicine somehow.*

James

could see it was dark inside as approached their front door . *He's not home yet?* He opened the door and switched on the light. *He'll be hungry - I hope. We have…a Natasha's® Norwegian Stew…I hope he'll eat this. It says it's "Fjord Pjure," 'n it's good rat. He says it's been dead longer than the fjords. I dunno…nothing's good enough.* He sat down, and took off his boots and wet socks. He went into the small bathroom washed his socks and hung them on the towel bar. Back in the kitchen area he set the small fold-down table with a bowl and a spoon for each of them. *I need to tell him about the clinic… and I have to ask him about meeting Lacey. I should probably ask him about Lacey first though. I'm glad I didn't see her after that phone call.* He turned on the TV. FAIR News was showing the latest holo-films from one of the desert wars with the twenty-eight United Arab Federated Countries. *I still can't believe I missed when twenty- two became twenty-eight. Damn… we're taking heavier than usual casualties.* He stood there watching the war footage. *I have a girlfriend. I can't sign up for the war with Canada.*

They'll both be happy about that.

At the same time James was getting ready to eat rat, the girl he knew as Lacey was wondering how James' phone call went and wishing she hadn't missed him so she could ask. She stepped out of the backseat of her Andro-car and went through the massive entrance to her building, held open for her—as usual—by her android doorman. As she did every day, she entered one of the maglevators, felt for her key card in the pocket of her cargo pants, fished it out, slipped it into the slot, looked into the iris scanner and unlocked the maglevator allowing it to take her up. *I have to ask him. I have to know.* She entered the large foyer of their penthouse, took off her boots and placed them in the basket on the mat beside the elevator door. She hung her coat and scarf in the huge double walk-in hall closet. She knew her parents would be in their respective offices. She padded down the hallway pausing to sniff the fresh flowers on the large consoles and then continued to her father's first floor office. She was through debating herself whether or not to ask her father if she had been placed in the messenger office because of a specific target. She reached his office where he was at his desk—sitting back in his chair. She could tell he was reading his eyeglasses computer. She softly tapped on the open door. He rose, took off his glasses, walked towards her and kissed her on her cheek.

"Let's go upstairs."

She took this to mean there was something important he wanted to show her. *Alex, don't chicken out.* They walked down to the end of the long hall and got into a small private elevator. He looked into the iris scanner and pressed four. The elevator started upward.

"Good day today?"

"Okay."

They stood side by side as the elevator neared the fourth floor of their penthouse.

"Oh?" Was his response.

One would need to put him under an electron microscope to make out a barely imperceptible look of concern; a nanometer's narrowing of the left side of his left eye. As quickly as it came it went. The elevator door opened onto what he called his situation room. He sat behind his desk and bade her to sit in one of the leather chairs.

"Dim lights please."

The room went dark.

"Skylight, show us the latest beheading piece."

Immediately, a hologram in the center of the room showed four people. Three of them were dressed in white thawbs and keffiyehs and the fourth was a young American soldier whose hands were tied behind his back. One of the Arabs prodded the soldier with his assault weapon. The soldier lurched forward. As he did, she felt something she never before had felt when she watched this kind of thing. It was…guilt.

"Taduth!"

"Speak!"

One of the Arabs then smashed him in his head with the butt of his rifle. The boy fell to his knees. Blood began to flow copiously down his face. Her father watched her. She remained impassive while feeling a revulsion.

"Speak dog!"

"TADUTH! INFIDEL!"

"TADUTH!"

He was hit again, this time in his back. He was in obvious pain. She watched in horror. *I know we need to keep people aware of all the threats we face but why this?*

"SPEAK!"

"TELL YOUR STUPID AMERICANS HOW IT WILL BE!"

Finally, through the blood and wincing in agony;

"We...can't...win. We will...be...destroyed. We...have to...give up the fight."

Again, he was smashed in the head with the butt of a rifle. He fell face forward onto the sand. One of the Arabs pulled him back up by his hair. Then another kicked him in his side. The boy was now crying. She forced herself not to react with revulsion. *What is happening to me?*

"Please...no more...please."

"Dog!"

One of the men now pulled up his thawb and began to urinate on the boy. On his face. The others laughed. *I have to see this?*

"Alex, are you alright? Skylight, stop!"

The hologram froze.

"Alex?"

"I'm fine."

Her father looked at her.

"Skylight, continue!"

The man finished urinating and shook his penis on the boys head. She watched, disgusted at what she was seeing. The boy was sobbing uncontrollably. One of the men looked straight into the camera;

"This is your brave American dog of a soldier. Now watch closely." Another of the men produced a scimitar from behind his back.

"We are going to cut your head off dog—and then shit on the stump of your neck." *Oh God...No daddy, it's enough. The point is made.*

He noticed her discomfort.

"Skylight, stop!"

The image froze again.

"Thoughts?"

He expects an honest opinion. "I think it's too much. The point has been made."

"Hmm…I agree. Skylight, back up to word 'dog.'"

The image rolled back.

"Skylight, full stop after word dog." *Omit action and sentence following word dog.*

"Continue."

All she could think was: just after dog? The hologram continued: the boy was blubbering.

"Don't! Please…I'm begging you…please!"

"See how your cowardly dog of a soldier grovels. He can't even die as a man! All you Americans are cowardly dogs. And you will all die. Quake in your beds because we are already among you."

"Skylight, stop. What do you think of it this way?"

"It's…It's frightening."

He wasn't sure how to take her comment.

"Skylight, continue."

The hologram came to life again.

"Let this be a lesson to all American infidel dogs."

The boy's scream ceased immediately as the scimitar sliced through his neck as if it was a tomato. The head fell to the sand and rolled a few feet. The blood spurted from the headless torso's neck as the body spasmed and lurched forward onto the sand. One of the men picked up the head by its hair and, grinning, waved it about. They all started chanting. Alex was horrified. *This never bothered me before*—

"Allah o Akbar, Allah o Akbar, Allah o Akbar…"

"Skylight, end program!"

Why did I ever have to meet James?

The hologram disappeared.

"The rest of it is just dancing around yelling fanatically. Death to infidels, death to infidels…blah blah…The usual."

Afraid of the answer, she managed: "Are they real?"

"All droids. Except the soldier. Terminally ill…AIDS. We made him a very fair deal—this in return for a generous anonymous payment to his family. *Aids. Oh God, this is not right.*

He stood. "Alex, what is it?

She knew she had to take this moment to ask him about the messenger job. And it had to be blurted out quickly before she could stop herself. She wanted to know—and, at the same time, she didn't want to know.

"Daddy, I need to know something. The messenger posting. Is there a specific target?" She held her breath.

"Why are you asking?"

"I need to know…Please."

He sat back in thought. For thirty seconds which, to her, felt like thirty years.

"And knowing this will make a difference to you?"

"Yes."

"Alexandra…What is it?"

"Please, Daddy…if you love me please tell me. I am trying not to implicate someone who may be completely innocent." *I'm lying…I can't lie to my own father. I can't do this. I have to tell him.* He waited.

"There's a boy. I suspect his father is dangerous."

Her father took off his glasses and rubbed his temples.

"What's his name?"

Oh Jesus.

"Alex, this is important. What's his name?" Her mind was working furiously.

"Father, let me make certain before I make any accusations."

He studied her closely.

"Alex, I know you…You can't be feeling sorry for these people. They're dangerous. You can't let yourself get too close."

"I'll do my job."

"You're certain?"

"Yes. Yes, I am." But she wasn't certain.

"Well, you can think it over while we're in The Maldives.

Why did I do this? She knew that because of what she just told her father he would now go through the TV holo-vids of all the employees in the messenger office. She also knew that surveillance cameras would have a record of her and James being together. If she begged off now it would make her complicit and disgrace her father. She was trapped. Feeling a bit sick to her stomach she went up to her room to get ready for a dinner she was in no mood to eat.

How

long is it gonna take me to get two hundred and fifty dollars? He's gotta get to that clinic. I have to get him there. James was so preoccupied with this turn of events that he hadn't switched on the TV—which now switched itself on. FAIR was showing the latest news and battle footage from the United Arab Federated Countries war. It looked as if our troops were surrounded but were still waging a heroic battle against great odds. Suddenly, the broadcast was interrupted by another sickening beheading video. One of our soldiers was kneeling on the sand surrounded by Arabs. One of the men was waving a scimitar around wildly while screaming threats and obscene insults into the camera. He knew this because there were sub-titles. FAIR always said, it was in the interest of factual reporting to show these translations. The soldier looked about eighteen years old and was crying and trembling with fright at what was about to happen. *These criminals… They don't even cover his eyes or put a hood over his head!* Suddenly the man swung the scimitar and severed the boys head from his torso. Blood spurted everywhere. The head fell onto the sand and rolled a few feet. It was sickening. Heartbreaking. *Holy… I would gladly kill these people!* Already in an uncharacteristically foul mood James wanted to put his fist through the TV. Then, the message; "Dissent Equals Descent" appeared on the screen. *Man, am I glad for FAIR News keeping us informed about what animals these Arabs are. We're gonna win this thing…no doubt about it. We got a great military, an' they're obviously important, but… I still think we need some of the money we spend on them to be spent on us.*

The siren sounded and a stentorian voice said: "This is a FAIR Science report. Scientists are now in complete agreement that the weather we have been experiencing has nothing to do with the work of our important mining industry and that fly ash, a coal by-product, may, in fact, soon be employed to make the weather better. We at FAIR say have patience, we will soon be experiencing far better weather. This has been another FAIR Science report. Be well." Then, the on screen ever-present reminder: "If You See Something You BETTER Say Something.

There was a BashBall game on tonight which he was really looking forward to seeing. *Barbaric or not, Pop'll watch it after a few M's… I'm glad I scored a four-pak. She said something about watching a BashBall game with us. I'll ask him if she can come over and watch a game.*

Even as James now watched the war's horrors on TV he couldn't keep his mind from going to Lacey. *I'm sure if he agrees to meet her he'll really like her. 'Specially since she shares some of his views—and her father's most definitely aligned with him too. I dunno, am I wrong? No, I'm not! Lacey…Man…She seems to know some things that I have no idea about. Sneaking into a movie? I'd never think of that in a million years. Am I glad we didn't get caught.* The siren sounded again: "This is another FAIR News Science report. New Evangelical Science Council findings prove that Evangelical School textbooks are indeed correct regarding the age of the earth. Dinosaur bones found in Wales have been carbon-dated and shown to be six thousand, seven hundred and thirty-two years old. Fossilized bones of humans were found buried with the bones. Once again, the inescapable conclusion is; man and dinosaurs co-existed. This has been a FAIR News Science report."

I dunno, that man we all saw that day in the Financial District…he hadda be high on something to storm into that auto-café and open fire on all those people having lunch. Why didn't they show that stuff on FAIR? That NRA guy who showed up immediately said it had nothing to do with guns? I'm not sure how he could say that. And I'm not so sure about that new law mandating kids in the Evangelical schools being issued assault weapons. But, I guess it's better protection than just having a sidearm. Come on pop, I'm hungry. Two hundred fifty dollars? I don't even have the money to take her out on a date. Come on with that raise. I wish I was qualified to do something like...a mechanic or...I wonder if I could've learned a trade in what they called High School. His father had told him that way back in the eighties the people who became the New Populists began a "war on education." *How he could say there was a war on education? The Evangelical school I graduated from was...It was excellent. This "war" stuff is...I mean, it's pretty far-fetched. I love him but he sees conspiracies everywhere. School gave me a solid grounding in everything. Faith in God, a healthy skepticism in all these "facts." I mean, I know my country's history. I know the benefits of abstin—Oh, what if that's an issue with her?* He crossed himself as he looked out of the window skyward. *You'll understand. Please. Amen.*

I wish I could do something that would earn more money, more than ten bucks an hour anyway. I sure hope Jeffers Jr. will keep his promise to break us out of the Socee class pretty soon, but...I need more money now. I have a girlfriend! He sat back and closed his eyes. *Man, we'll get a nice apartment somewhere in the good section of town. 'N when I come home from the office I'll bring flowers for her, or some kind of surprise—maybe a nice bottle of wine. We'll sit down to dinner together to eat and talk about our day...and, after dinner we'll do the dishes together... We'll have two children—a boy and a girl so we'll get the eight hundred bucks. I'll take our boy to the park and teach him how to catch a baseball and she'll take our daughter to dancing lessons...Man, would we be happy...Like on that sitcom; "Honey, who needs money?" If I'm ever gonna make more money it isn't gonna be from my messenger gig. It's gonna have to be with a better job.* All of a sudden James was feeling things he had never felt before regarding his self- worth, and he didn't like it. *Everyone I know, except for my clients, and some of the people I deliver packages to, is a Socee...I never come into any kind of meaningful contact with anyone else. She doesn't have any kind of money either. Why else would she be working as a messenger...*

and have to sneak into a movie theater? It was fun but…I'm glad that the Servers are big on law and order. Still, I hate to think what would happen to us if we got caught. Although, how come there's still a lot of bad people roaming the streets and you gotta be careful not to be out too late at night? A lotta people think that working for a living is for suckers. They'd rather just take other people's hard-earned money. Maybe that's how some of those people at the clinic can afford it. That time I was mugged…It was fouled up that the soldiers who used to patrol that area pretty much looked away. I dunno, maybe they're just there for the big stuff…Violent protests and such.

A FAIR News report on the country's cyberwar with PanAsia caught his eye. *Man, I'd love to be able to take part in this kind of a war. I'd love to know how to do cyberwarfare. Our enemies do way more damage in cyberwars than any boots-on- the-ground war. Our soldiers are still being wounded in those, even worse killed. And, even worse than that—beheaded.* He watched the war news. *How do the parents of a soldier who was beheaded on TV for everyone to see…how do they deal with it? The family has to be left destroyed by it. Do they get the body—and the severed head? Do they get that back for a decent burial? These wars are terrible. Every day in this war with the twenty-eight Arab Countries we lose our bravest and brightest. Our power grid, the reservoirs, our mass transit, our very ability to exist…it's all threatened by these people they call "state sponsored" hackers. I wish we had a computer, and I could use the thing they call the internet. My clients use it. I'm not a security risk. I bet I'd be a great cyber-hacker an' probably really help our country's security.*

How the heck can I invite Lacey to dinner at my place? She said that the food at Greasy Lee's was less than mediocre. The more he thought about it, having a girlfriend presented some vexing problems. *Hey—stop worrying! Okay? Her family probably eats hash just like we do and she looks like she can get with whatever the program is. Well…they don't pay rent so they may eat a little better than we do. Or a lot better. She's a sweet down-to-earth girl, and she likes me 'n she's fully aware of my deal. Our deal. She's a Socee too. She's not expecting to be wined and dined and brought flowers and all that. It'd be nice but… Yeah, we could watch the game at our place which wouldn't cost anything and she could meet pop at the same time.*

In the last year he'd been propositioned by two of his clients who said they would pay more for additional services. He never asked what they meant exactly by "additional services," or how much more money they were talking about. And, now he couldn't believe that he was considering reminding them of what they'd said. *Judging by how often I see them I'll probably be seeing most of them in a few days —maybe even before then. I'm gonna ask. I need this two fifty. Quick.* He heard the coughing before he heard the creaking. *Good, he's home.* His father opened the front door.

"Pop, you okay?"

John took off his coat, hung it on the nail and went to the rear to change. "Pop, are you *okay?*"

"I'm okay, I'm okay…don't worry. Sorry, I'm late. The train. You hungry?"

"You know you don't sound so okay."

"James, I'm fine. There's a game tonight."

"Don't change the subject. We gotta get you to that clinic."

"It's a hundred dollars. I don't 'gotta' go to any clinic. Forget it."

I wish it was only a hundred. I have to tell him. But for the moment he thought it best to drop the subject. *I almost have enough get him some cough medicine.* John came back up front.

"We had a can of mixed meat hash and I'm boiling an Idaho. How was work today?"

"Fabulous. James, you mind if we shut the TV off while we eat?"

James turned the TV off.

"Walking one block let alone three in this crap is brutal. You know, I remember when we used to at least have snowplows cleaning the streets. But those days are gone my friend. Gone and forgotten." He coughed.

I gotta get him that medicine.

"I dunno…the streets in the financial district are still plowed. And heated.

"What does all that tell you?"

Bedloe's head would have further exploded if he also knew that StreetHeet LLC, the company that engineered and installed the sidewalk heating systems in all the neighborhoods of the elite, was a wholly owned subsidiary of RanConCorp.

"Pop, that area has to have special attention. It is the business center of the city and people need to be able to get around easily…no?"

"Why so more than us?"

Oh, Poppa…I don't feel like getting into one of these dialogues. The game…

"It's a good game tonight?"

"I don't know. Hey, did you see our guy?"

"I got a four-pak."

"Good man."

"Let me have your plate."

James dished out two plates of hash and potatoes and they sat down to eat. They ate in silence for a few moments.

"James, are you okay? You seem a little…low energy."

"I'm fine, Pop. Just a tough day. How do you like the potato?"

"It's good. Thanks, kid."

John took another spoonful of hash.

"Boy, what I would give for a cold beer to drown this stuff though."

"We don't have any ice. We need to get a mini-fridge."

"With what?"

"I'm saving up for it...and the heater." *I can't tell him about the two hundred and fifty dollars.*

"I can kick in a few bu—" John smacked himself in the head.

"Fuck m—oops, sorry kid, sorry. What am I an idiot? It just now dawned on me—we can always keep beer outside buried in the snow—or anything else we want to keep cold."

His father got up, took the M-POW!-r outside, buried it in the snow, and came back in.

"Why didn't we think of this sooner? This whole freaking city's a fridge most days. I'm springing for beer tomorrow night. At least global warming'll be good for something."

The TV turned itself on and FAIR News interrupted them: "Live from the Front!" the voice intoned. "Watch our valiant soldiers as they battle the forces of evil. Tonight after the big game. Then, an all-new "Making of Dillyman and Gloober. The boys as you've never seen them before."

"Please turn it off, James."

"Wow, unbelievable huh?"

"Yeah. Incredible too."

James smiled and turned the TV off again. They both took some spoonsful of hash. Then:

"Between you and mom...when you first saw her...it was - what's that old expression—love at first sight, right?"

"That's what it was."

"Pop, I think it's like that with the girl I told you about...Lacey."

"I think that's great, James. I'm really happy for you. It would be good for you to have someone special in your life."

"She's *so*…She's wonderful, Pop."

"Then I hope with all my heart she likes you back."

They continued eating.

"I think she does. And I'm wondering; you think if she wanted to watch a game with us you'd be okay with it?"

"Uh-huh…Yeah. I'd very much like to meet her. Where does she live?"

"Down near Chinatown. And get this, they live rent free because her father is a doorman in another building their landlord owns. That's his salary."

"That's a heck of a break. Yeah, if you like her I'd love to meet her."

"Great. That's…I'll set it up. Hey, let's get the M-POW!-r."

"Let's let it get a little colder. She wants to watch a game with us? A BashBall game?

"That's what she said. She just wants to meet you. So…sometime next week might be okay?"

"I guess. Sure."

"Okay…I'm gonna tell her that we're on for a night next week."

"She's smart huh?"

"Oh yes. She's a little shy but very sweet. And kind."

"Let's make it next Thursday, it's my early day."

"Great! And her father thinks a lot like you too."

What? James…What? There was a long…long…long silence. Then:

"Excuse me? James? Her father? What do you mean?"

Oh...you idiot! Why did I say that?

"How does she know what I think?"

He sat there silently regretting what he'd said.

"You told her what I think? Things I've said to you?"

"Dad, she's a Socee just like us, and she's also a little down on a lotta stuff."

"A little down on a "lotta" stuff? I've asked you a hundred times..."

"I'm sorry...I shouldn't have said---But she's one of us. I know it."

"I really wish you hadn't."

"Pop, please don't worry. She's on our side...and you are gonna love her. I'm telling you. I know it. So, next Thursday?"

"I'm *gonna?*" He was dismayed by what James just told him.

"Sure, Thursday. But still James..."

He sat there slowly shaking his head. And, an uncomfortable silence hung over the rest of dinner.

The

main opposition of The PEEPS in Congress was the aptly named Lemon Party. Aptly named he thought because they were all curdled. A gaggle of self-righteous mouth-breathing knuckle-draggers with little or no knowledge of history, economics and The Constitution, which they were ready to proudly defend with the flag of all their inglorious ignorance flying. An ignorance, Bedloe was certain of, that was the result of a gene pool into which too many people had pissed.

These useful idiots of The Money opposed increasing the size, scope and power of government at any level, for *any* purpose save religious. They were against funding any program which sought to help ordinary less well-off citizens—*their own constituents!* And their own constituents were *all for it!* Again, yippee! Woo woo! Fuck us! The Lemons were uncaring sock-puppets. Ultra-Right, self-serving, "Christian" hypocrites. Polls clearly showed that most of the electorate did not like this destructive intransigent bunch. And, right backatchya, the Lemon Party members of congress who were elected to govern *didn't like government.* So there!

The voters who elected these folks were plainly, and understandably angry. But they weren't exactly clear as to who it was that they should have been angry *with.* That, coupled with how relatively ill-informed they

were by their major sources of "facts." Right wing radio, fake internet news
and what became FAIR News, and how easily they could be whipped up
and manipulated to act against their own interest, made for the perfect
Loyalist/Money storm. Bedloe could not fathom how these people ever
got *re*-elected. Their entire agenda consisted of no new taxes on the
wealthy one per cent, raising the middle-class tax bite, tearing gaping holes
in the social safety net and, *most of all,* destroying the "nigger" who had
the downright temerity, the unmitigated gall, the fucking nerve, to get his
skinny black ass elected to the highest office in the land in the first place.
One of the all too rare times The Money lost a *tiny* bit of ground. However,
their boy Conover took great pleasure in erasing all of this honorable man's
achievements. A man who once had the uppity-nigga-nerve to publicly
make fun of the once and future Wolf King. The Family's man. The perfect
fool. The monster who, because of the advent of world-wide connectivity,
became history's most effective despot."

For someone to vote for these Lemon Partyers meant to him that
they were either very rich, very ignorant, very against the working class,
which ironically, most of these misguided Loyalist voters belonged to, very
jealous, or just plain out and out racist. But Christians. Oh yes, they *were*
Christians. He opted for a noxious stew of all of it. And, "Christians" was
the mirepoix.

What too many of the voters conveniently forgot, or conveniently
forgot to remember, was that "this black bastard" inherited two wars—not
easy to disengage from—which cost us six trillion tax dollars and was a
major reason for the economic slump and loss of their jobs. At the same
time The Money's front men, the Lemonade-led Loyalists, were busy
saying "no" to most of the PEEP president's proposed jobs programs to get
us out of this ditch the Lemons had been busy digging. The voters, many
of them in the rust-belt, were assaulted by blatant lies "explaining" why we
were in the predicament we were in. FAIR News was their megaphone.
And, the Loyalists had been smearing Conover's opponent for thirty
years even though she had performed admirably in many high offices
in government. Because Conover's predecessor also had the misfortune

of being an intellectual, and would rather think something through in possession of all the facts before he made a decision, the Loyalists and FAIR News continually portrayed him as indecisive, and PEEPs in general as "elitists." Meanwhile, the Loyalist/Lemonaders, who themselves were among the wealthiest among us - and who fronted for the *real* Elite - masqueraded as the party of the people. This, combined with *real* phony news, lies about his opponent, a hostile Nation's interference, The Electoral College, screwing with the mail and voters who had lost the ability to see through the smoky miasma and think critically, led us to one Ransom B. Conover Sr. A serial liar and gifted grifter running a *very* long con.

The result of all this propaganda was that the PEEP's popularity with the American electorate was declining even though they continued to be the reasonable, conciliatory adults in the face of self-interested, uninformed, unreasonable, uncaring and intractable children. Perception was, and still is, *everything* - whether facts backed it up or not. It was what mattered in our new virtual, instant society. And what mind-fucked John and Jane Bedloe at the time, and the paradoxical part of all of it, is that those Loyalists were behaving in a way that they both begrudgingly had to admire; they were taking a hard, albeit unprincipled stand for what they believed in. Unfortunately, he now knew what the Loyalists believed in led to something far worse than anything they both could have ever imagined; Jane's untimely death, a totalitarian state and the harsh conditions and attendant isolation that Bedloe, and every other person considered to be an "Associate," now found themselves trapped by.

Because the mail, the internet, landlines and cellphones had been taken from them—for "security" reasons—Associates all over the country, and the world, eventually lost all contact with their families and friends. There was no way to call someone to make a date to meet, no way to know if they were even still living or where they were since the last time you'd seen them. No way to keep in contact with grown children who had moved away, parents who lived in another state or friends who were scattered all over. This lack of ability to be in touch even affected those of the above who might just live in another part of the same city. This made things difficult for the underground resistance and made for a terrible situation for Socees to be in—besides all their other attendant hardships. Just to get together for a drink or a bite was a hit and miss proposition. The State had disconnected all landlines and cellphones and caused the internet to go dark on a Monday at three-thirty in the morning across all time zones absent any prior warning. People woke up to find they were now cut off from their families and all their friends. FAIR-TV gave them the news the day after the event explaining that there was a "coordinated series of terrorist bombings in seven states all across the country that killed two thousand and seventy-three people and had injured many, many more." There was also "a terrorist threat of more bombings which makes it necessary for all unnecessary and un-secured communications to be discontinued." FAIR explained that this action was taken by Homeland Security for the protection and safety of everyone in the country. But, not to worry…"all these measures will be lifted as soon as the danger has passed."

Then there was "Homeland" Security. The word homeland disturbed him as far back as he could remember—as far back as when he was fourteen and still able to study history via the internet. He knew that the history we read in schoolbooks was, to be generous, a bit less than factually correct and rife with erroneous information. Sure, our first President chopped down a cherry tree at age six and, of course, he threw a silver dollar across The Potomac—which is over a mile wide etc. By fair means or foul, the history books Bedloe read while in school conveniently missed the inconvenient fact that old George became a slave owner at the ripe young age of eleven! Washington owned over 120 slaves who he deemed "proper" to whip, and when they tried to escape he pursued them relentlessly. Okay, understandable---Washington was a product of his time. But, Bedloe's high-school history textbooks should have included things like this, and not be sanitized to create a false narrative. Bedloe had to learn much of our real history from Google. Now, there was no Google. Or Snopes. Or even an internet Well, not for Associates anyway. Sure, when Bedloe was in school there was some disinformation. Still, too much of it showcased our mythic nationalistic wonderfulness. But now, it was all wonderful. All disinformation. A made-up fairy-tale of America's goodness and light littered the pages of every teen-ager's "history" text. Among the many other falsehoods he'd read in James' Evangelical school's history book was that the Department of Homeland Security was created "purely to protect our civil liberties." Well, the department's title was true anyway. Also, back when this excuse for more Big Brotherism was created, Bedloe thought that the word "homeland" had a little too much of the stink of the Nazi's nationalistic "fatherland." You know, that old "über alles, in der welt" thing?

After reading much of the history about the aftermath of 9/11 he knew that the administration, which had ignored the warnings of such a threat, immediately created the Total Information Awareness Office. A lovely way to keep closer tabs on the country's citizens then they should have been able to. Building on this, Conover and his pals then created TATAS, The Total American Truth in Alert Security office. Bedloe blogged a bunch of satirical pieces about that one. TATAS was a "security" program which empowered the government to keep a computerized dossier on every American citizen. Massive amounts of information was collected about the tens of millions of Americans who fly each year. Then there were the Social Media "influencers" who influenced us to embrace the inane - and whose 2.3 billion users world-wide had their personal data shit out world-wide as well. Information "dump" indeed. It was saying to privacy, as the Lone Ranger said to Tonto when they were surrounded: "adios motherfucker.

By 2017 the seeds that were sown in 2001 with Homeland Security and The Patriot's Flag Act and in 2003 with the Total Information Awareness Office had developed deep roots and poisonous fruit. It was certainly "patriotic" of The Loyalists to clamp down on The Bill of Rights while waving the flag. A fundamentalist Right-wing Congress's fantasy made manifest. He wondered whatever took The Money so long.

Bedloe now longed just to speak with his parents. His sister and brother. His old friends. Prior to the internet going dark for them he and Jane had stayed in touch that way with their families and with friends who were scattered all over the globe. They once spent a summer in Los

Angeles and had formed friendships with people who they stayed in touch with and subsequently traded visits with for two weeks at a time—until that was no longer possible. While in Los Angeles they also met people from Australia who they became close with and who, when they came to live in New York, they saw constantly. And when the Aussies moved back to Sydney they were able to visit them and also stay in touch with them via the internet. He had also stayed in touch with all his childhood friends. They had dinners with all their New York friends new and old. Some of these people who he knew since kindergarten —forty three years. Others for less—but who were still dear to both of them. His old childhood gang met at least once a month at a diner in the East Bronx. They had been doing this for many years. Sometimes Jane would come with him. They would travel up from Manhattan on the two train and were picked up at the Gun Hill train station by their old friend Sacky who drove in from Hartsdale. Others would drive in from the other suburbs and from the other boroughs. This was a wonderful event, now for years impossible to organize. For the last twenty years, he and every other Associate around the world, had lost all contact with all the people dear to them who didn't live with them. This situation of separation and loss of communication was all in the service of "national security."

He had always considered all the trappings and catchwords used by every Government to foster patriotism—an anthem, flags, nationalism, national security—to be things that kept people apart. Like religion they all had the effect of creating an "us and them" mentality. He believed they were constructs whose aims were to instill unquestioning obedience in the citizens of every country. Things that would make them feel superior. No less great a thinker as Albert Einstein said he hated "all the loathsome nonsense that goes by the name of patriotism." Leo Tolstoy wrote: "One would expect the harmfulness and irrationality of patriotism to be evident to everybody." In Bedloe's own opinion these unquestioning unequivocal flag-pin sporting "patriots" who quoted the Bible, chapter and verse, and loved them some Constitution—the *one* amendment they gave a damn about anyway—possessed one rock-ribbed attribute. Theirs was an unswerving allegiance to the flag. "My country right or wrong," went the old saying. He was certain that this unquestioning nationalism made people more disposed to want to go to war. In any event, the authoritarianism he now lived under had made successful use of all these constructs to subjugate the populace.

He wondered about his old friends. He would love to be able to pick up a phone and speak with them...or see them over dinner. Catch up, as it were. However, as it was, each person considered to be a Socee was now isolated, marooned as it were, on a tiny island of one.

Three

days? Four? John Bedloe was trying to remember how many days it had been since he had allowed himself a warm shower. To keep the water bill manageable they had limited themselves to a maximum of two warm showers a week. The rest were cold...and *all* were quick. Very. *A man shouldn't have to wear the same underwear this many days. The ones I washed in the sink just won't dry inside. We have to bring a laundry in today and the cost is going to break us. Both sheet sets are dirty, and doing them alone will be expensive. Those dumb D&G t-shirts? How fucked-up must we have been to do something so stupid? And, if they'd arrived already at least we'd have a clean tee to put on. Cough medicine; another unexpected expense.* His cough was now worse which he tried to shrug off. *We can't walk around like this. We have to do the laundry. He's got a girlfriend. His clothes have to be clean. He needs boots...We need a heater. We're eating shit.* He tied his sneakers—with some effort. *What was that old movie? It's a Wonderful Life?* Today was one of his late days and before his son went in to his job he would have to help him finally bite the bullet and bring this pile in. His son was in the front making the oil-slick they named Kaw-Fee...*Another slap in the face.* He walked up to the front.

"James, we *must* do a laundry today - I have twenty bucks...How much cash do you have?"

"Aw nooo…I wanted to put some money down on a pair of new boots but…" *And your medicine.*

"You know if you have a girlfriend now you should at least think about wearing clean underwear. Cash. Get it up."

"Lemmee look."

James fished in his pocket, brought out a few crumpled bills and counted out a total of thirty-four dollars. *Well, there goes that.*

"Good. We'll still have a few bucks left over. Help me gather it all up into the pillow cases."

Together they stripped the two cots and went back to front picking up all the soiled laundry and packing it all into the four pillow cases.

"Pop, you wanna have your Kaw-Fee before we go?"

"No. Let's go. You have to get to work. The sooner we get it in the sooner we get it back. I'm sure we're going to be without sheets for at least a couple of nights because the soonest we can get all this back will be a few days.

"Lemmee just knock this cup back."

"Did you eat breakfast?"

"Two Twin-Keez. I'm good."

#

The two men plodded through the slush and snow to the only laundry within ten blocks of their place. As they neared it they could see a hand-written sign on the door. "Opining late today. 11 o'clock. Sorry for incanvenience."

"Do you f—do you believe this? The one lousy day!"

"Unbelievable."

"No…again, believable. Look, you go to work. I'll wait here for this place to open - okay?"

"Pop, I'm really sorry I can't wait with you…but I really gotta go in."

"Go…Go ahead, I'll be alright. Go."

Reluctantly, James backed away and headed back to the train. *He's standing out there in this weather with that cough.* And I still haven't told him about the two hundred and fifty dollars either. Again, he had that same uncomfortable feeling; *now besides letting him down, I'm not being completely truthful with him.* Yet, with all this, his thoughts all the way downtown were on Lacey. He couldn't wait to see her. He could not shut her out of his mind. So much so that transferring, he got on the wrong Centipede and jumped off just in time. Walking the two blocks to the office: *You're thinking about her? Not your own father waiting in the cold?*

# # #

It was cold…at last the door to the laundry opened and Bedloe was waved in. He laid all his laundry on the scales and waited for the man to tell him the cost. It was fifty dollars and thirty eight cents. *Holy shit!* He counted out fifty-one dollars and waited for his change.

"Two of our machines are down so this may not be ready 'til…the day after tomorrow?"

"Are you pretty sure I can get this day after tomorrow?"

"Umm…I guess."

"Because it's a long walk from my place and if it isn't ready…I mean…"

"I can't promise…I'll try my best."

"Okay…I'm going to trust you'll get it done. Thank you."

"No problem."

Don't! Don't say anything. He's just trying to keep a business going and he's dealing with machine break-downs, no service and angry customers. Two of which had now entered the laundry laden with bundles. Nodding "thanks" he turned and was back out on the slushy street walking the ten long blocks back to their home. Nothing was *ever* a fucking problem. Even if *every* fucking thing was.

We kids did the laundry for mom in our building's basement laundry room. Sixty apartments, three machines and three dryers. But at least the machines all worked. My brother and sister...I haven't heard their voices in forever. I taught Roberta to walk. The three of us slept in one room. Marv and me on the roll-out. We grew up in the Bronx, and now I'm right back where I started. My life in full circle. I wonder how they are. I hope as well as possible...considering. He knew from their last conversations maybe seventeen or eighteen years ago that his sister had two children, a girl and a boy, and was working in the Post Office while her husband worked in a hospital. His brother was a waiter in a restaurant in Boston. He worked lunches. He remembered that day, early in the morning, when he left James with that wonderful neighbor. *I went to where Marv lived and he wasn't home. I spent an hour and a half on the stoop of that brownstone for him to return. I took a shot. But without a phone it just didn't happen.* He finally gave up and traveled another four plus hours back home. *Eleven hours spent trying to see my kid brother.* His neighbor, fearing the worst, was relieved to see him. That was fifteen years ago. He never again tried to do such an impossible thing.

What did people do? Who can afford any medical care - even the clinic? He saw all this happening years ago as the New Populists finished what the Loyalists began; snipping away at the social safety net until the hole in it was so large that everyone had finally fallen through and had landed in this terrible place. *I'd gladly welcome putting up with the things that bugged me twenty-five years ago that my friends thought I was nuts to be bothered with. People walking into me because they were continually staring down into their cell phones. The one hour wait at the doctor's office before they could see you. The increasingly long lines at the under-staffed government offices like the post office. I'd gladly give anything to have these trivialities back again. That's what they were Johnny boy—trivial bullshit annoyances. Man, was I angry. Still am. I'll tell you, if anything proves the theory of relativity…My friends were right.*

Bedloe checked the time on TV and realized he still had some time before he had to get to work. In that brief moment that the TV was on he saw the new Chairman Jerk-off Jr.'s stupid face. He was saying something to do with the Server Defense Department. *Of course Canada's about to invade us.* He spit on Jeffers' image and shut the TV off. *It would be more fitting if this country's name was Gullibullshit - or even better, Gullibelieveme. It's too bad gangs of the terminally ill didn't pick up assault rifles back then, go to D.C., and rid us of all those amoral criminals who de-funded health care and made our lives miserable.*

He took the Kaw-Fee off the shelf. *I need something hot.* He looked at the Kaw-Fee can. "Virtually Real." His laugh was a sardonic burst. *Virtually; the preferred word of swindlers everywhere.* He spooned the ground Kaw-Fee into the pot. *Imagine "virtually" when we grew up. Come on man - that's virtually a home run! Yeah, you know what - you're a virtual asshole!* He took a cup from the shelf. *Not that I can, but go ahead—buy a car that gets virtually thirty miles to the gallon. Just don't complain when it gets twenty seven. Hey —twenty-seven is "virtually" thirty… isn't it? We've become so dumbed down that we can no longer recognize when we're being lied to. Another nail in the coffin of intelligence. This is a country where twenty plus years ago guys spent money on special shirts that you could wear "un-tucked."*

The Kaw-Fee was made. He poured a cup. *God…this liquid piss really —not virtually —really never gets any better.* He made a sour face. *That's another reason why Loyalists got in; Millennials. Lost in all their "incredible" virtual worlds and far too busy to vote while their brains rotted. I'm a damn Millennial. Elections we stayed home playing virtual reality games or some game on our cells. We polluted our language with all the "awesomes," "incredibles," and "unbelievables." No problem, right? We didn't look ahead, we looked down. At our phones. Too many times I was the only person on a train or a bus who wasn't looking down at a cell phone. Even when we crossed the street we were looking down at a phone.*

This was another of the many things that drove him to distraction back then - and one, of the many, he fervently wished he had the opportunity to put up with again. At the time people would walk smack into other people while looking straight down as they were texting, or chirping, or tweeting, or twerking, or whatever, on their latest $1,250 iPhone, or whatever else it was that had just became obsolete twelve minutes after it was put out. This zombie-like behavior had really spiraled too far out of control for him. If it wasn't some ordinarily private person yelling into their cell phone in the bank, telling the world, and more importantly him, that their anal fistula was going to be being drained, which image he now had to take with him to dinner, then it was some pubescent tween, thumbs moving at the speed of a panicked hummingbird who was "virtually" everywhere except where he or she actually *was*. They had no clue that they were well on their way to being Cyborg 1.0's. Well...

He once saw a guy, looking down while working his thumbs furiously, walk right in front of a moving car. It's a good thing the car was in New York traffic and doing only ten miles an hour. But, the thing was, he never even *looked up* as the car stopped short, just kept right on blissfully texting and walking. He imagined someone on their cell phone—maybe at their friend's grandfather's funeral service, "...I mean, I'm on the treadmill, and like this creep just comes right next to me and—excuse *me* mourners, but like I'm *trying* to have a *conversation* here..." And then deigning to note the mourners' dagger stares, they'd begrudgingly change to texting, and, eyes down, walk into the priest delivering the eulogy at the gravesite and knock him head first into the freshly dug grave. *Is this why Mother Nature in Her infinite wisdom gave us opposable thumbs? Was this Her Grand Design? Did She plan for that cell company I called Yor-eyes-on? I knew women are good contingency planners, but this was really a step too far. Sure there was a need to be in constant contact if one was in the middle of a business negotiation, or if one had any kind of situation which required ongoing attention. A doctor.* Bedloe's beef was with the guy who texted "had 3 tinis heading to car dond wory not durnk" and, as he's texting, he reels into his car and backs up seventeen feet - leveling some poor guy's fruit stand. That guy. *It used to be that when you had a telephone conversation it was usually private, even if it was about nothing more than passing the time of day. Public telephone booths had doors on them for a reason. Did we all need to hear about someone's oozing herpes sore while on the checkout line at the supermarket?* At the time he envisioned a new procedure, a Radical Cellectomy, wherein a tiny cell phone is surgically implanted into everyone's skull at birth. *We had a dysfunctional need to be in constant contact about anything and everything under the sun. With someone or anyone anywhere. That nice customer service person in Mumbai for example. It was a symptom of some great world-wide existential crisis of the fear of being alone with one's self - even for a moment. How depressingly ironic that this condition of alone-ness is now the norm for We, the Associates.* He sipped his Kaw-Fee. *God, I yearn for all this dumb shit to still exist in my world. I wouldn't complain about any of it. Not now. Not never. Not even this sludge.* He sat there suddenly struck by what he was now thinking; *why the fuck did I care anyway when so many others seemed not to? Why was I so angry at all this shit? Why am I so angry at it still? Hey...wait a minute Johnny boy...look what you are. Look how you live. Why wasn't everyone as angry as you were when our country was stolen from us?* He slowly rose from the table and rinsed his cup in the sink. *FAIR News. FAIR fucking news! Fuggedaboudit...It was a fixed fight. Go to work Johnny. The exciting world of Melamine maintenance beckons.*

In

the auto-cafe James and Lacey were eating the last of their Scarab fries or, to be more precise, she was moving them back and forth on her plate. He was eating.

She tapped the table for the check. *Alex, you have to…You can't let it go…You need to show your father the facts. And it is possible his father is harmless anyway.*

"Just so you know, I'm serious about wanting to meet your father."

"I know. I asked him and he said it was okay, he'd love to meet you. He wants to make it next Thursday because it's his early day."

She immediately knew that she had to agree to this date although, until he said Thursday, she remembered something she had completely forgotten about. Next Thursday she would be leaving for the Maldives on her family's annual five day retreat to the sun. After saying so many times that she wanted to meet James' father it would be strange to say she couldn't make it. And, even if she said that, what about saying she couldn't make it when he said Friday? Or Saturday? Or…

"Thursday sounds great." *When I get back I guess I'll say I was sick. Oh,*

Alex…O what a tangled web…

He smiled. "Well go together after work."

The check slid out of the table. They got up, he took her coat off of the coatrack and held it for her to slip into. As she did their bodies came together. He put his coat on as he followed her to the cashier. They each paid their five dollars and left the restaurant. As soon as they were outside and on the sidewalk she took his arm.

"I wish we took the same train. Or at least we went in the same direction."

They walked up the street past the soldiers towards the Centipede station. He had kept his dry socks on and was glad for the heated sidewalks and plowed streets. She thinking: *He feels strong.* What he felt was akin to hitting the big prize. *Pop's gonna love her. God, the city looks great! The snowflakes twinkling in the bright lights, people bustling to and fro, the beautiful store windows.* He was walking on a cloud with this wonderful creature on his arm. They stopped every now and then and looked in the store windows and when they did they moved in close to each other. *Her hair smells so good.* If he knew what one hundred and seventy-five dollar mango lime shampoo and one hundred and fifty dollar aloe coco-peach conditioner smelled like he would know why.

They reached the Centipede station, descended the stairs, flashed their TransiPasses at the eye, and before they each went down to their respective platforms on the opposite side of the tracks she stopped, moved close, and looked up at him. *Please kiss me…*It was clear to him she expected him to kiss her. After some five seconds he did. She melted into his arms. *This is… insane. Why can't I help myself?* This kiss was a bit more serious. For both of them. They stood there kissing that way for at least thirty seconds. Finally, she moved back slightly.

"I should get home."

"Yeah…me…t-too."

Jesus man...be cool.

They were both trying not to breathe so hard—and failing miserably. She broke away and headed for the stairs going to the downtown train.

"See...you...tomorrow."

"Safe home."

He stood and watched her as she got to the stairs and disappeared down them. *I love this girl.* He turned and hurried down to the uptown platform. As he reached the platform her Centipede pulled into the downtown side. She got on and blew him a kiss from its window as the Centipede pulled out of the station. He watched it until it was gone. He looked up the track. *Cripes, I have to tell pop about the clinic. I have to.*

He had a forty-five minute train ride to ponder how he would do it. She, on the other hand, would go two stops, get off, go up to the street and meet her already summoned Andro-car to take her uptown. All the way to the Upper East Side all she could think about was how she felt when she was with him. And then; *how have I let this happen? I'm in love with a boy whose father might well be an enemy of the state. And I am a liar. Good one Alex.*

#

After work on the same day that his son and the girl he was crazy about were eating Scarab fries, John Bedloe got on an elevated train. He was going to another upscale neighborhood where he was sure he would find a pharmacy. Eight stops later the train burrowed into the tunnel and seven stops after that he changed to a straddling bus. Two stops later he ascended to the heated sidewalk by way of the spiralator. He walked one block past the soldiers and found a pharmacy. He walked up to the pharmacist and asked him what aisle the cough medicine was in.

"Aisle ten, sir."

Sir? I haven't heard that in a while. I guess being in this neighborhood makes me a "sir." He searched the overhead signs for aisle ten and made his way to it. There were a number of cough remedies on the shelf. He walked back to the pharmacist:

"So, uh…can you tell me which of the cough medicines is the most effective?"

"The strongest is the C-Coff."

"How much is it? "

"Nineteen dollars."

Nineteen dollars? Are you fucking kiddin—

"And the Coff-Eeze is seventeen."

"Ah…Is it any good?"

"It's got some codeine."

"Why is the C-Coff two dollars more? Is it better?"

"It's a little stronger formula…a little more codeine."

"I'll get that one then. Thanks"

"Awesome, no problem."

He checked the box of C-Coff. The first active ingredient was codeine 6.25 mg. The label on the Coff-Eeze—5.5 mg. Did .75 mg difference matter that much? Either one was most of what remained in his pocket after the laundry money. He decided that he'd buy the C-Coff. He paid and walked out into the falling snow melting on the heated sidewalk.

He was on the straddling bus on the way to his train: *Awesome, no problem. The exacta of robo-speak. My lucky day.* He detested the expression no problem as much as he detested awesome. It seemed like he heard it ten times a day for the last twenty-five years. *Nothing's a problem. We're "Associates" for shit's sake. Nothing's not a problem. You can try to put a brave face on things, but it's such a transparent unwillingness to come to grips with the reality of the situation. No problem...I dunno why I can't help picturing a safe plummeting straight at my head from thirty stories above. Or the ground's going to open up and swallow me whole. When did "no problem become the answer to "thank you"? What ever happened to "you're welcome?" Or, "you're quite welcome?" This assumption that it's all good without any knowledge of what someone may be dealing with...My left kidney is killing me, my cat is sick, my wife is mad at me because I insulted her mother, oh - yeah, our water is diarrhea brown. And...we are fucking something called Socees!*

He felt this way as far back as when he was about twenty one, had returned from fighting in a phony war and all of a sudden everyone was saying "no problem" all over the place. His friends laughed at him for taking what they called "shit like this so seriously," but he took it as yet another sign of the erosion of the language which was further dumbing down and lobotomizing the culture. *If that poor pharmacist only knew how much of a problem it was for me to buy this medicine. I have to make a choice between my health and doing the laundry.* Then, perhaps guided by thoughts of his lousy health coupled with searching for some comfort he was led back to when he was fifteen, the summer before he met Jane. *I was healthy as a horse. Off from school and stoned...but healthy. Funny. Whenever someone looked around, and asked what day it was we had to check a newspaper or a cellphone to find out. It's crazy, but we didn't know what day it was...and when we finally checked - it was invariably Friday. And Berrs coined the expression that was our lifestyle; "Every day is Friday."*

It was now snaining as he gingerly walked the four blocks through the slush to change to the train. He smiled recalling that expression. It represented to him a youthful kind of unappreciated unburdened freedom that he now wished he could re-live. *Friday... the ledge overlooking the week-end. A jump away from fun...expectations. A movie, a softball game, pizza with Jane and the crew. We hung out...maybe had an adventure... usually after getting a nice buzz on. My teen years. No cares and anything that was a bummer always in the rear view mirror.* The thing was; they felt that way no matter what day it might have been. It just always *felt* like Friday.

And it wasn't a slacker kind of existence. *It was the exact opposite...We were filled with hopes, big dreams... Like Jeff said that time; "a shitload of joy."* His laugh was out loud - but short. *Every day is Friday.* When he and Jane were dating he told her this expression and she loved it so much that when they had their first apartment she had it printed on heavy ecru linen paper, framed it, and hung it in their living room.

Now, the thought occurred to him that lately he seemed *only* to be alive in the past. And that he was otherwise—well...dead. It was certainly no great revelation to him that the joy of his youth, his past, was gone — never to be again. That was the natural way of things. The surprise was the present. What his adult life had become. It wasn't only that his youth was spent in another lifetime, it was more like it was spent in another galaxy. Every day now felt like Monday. With snain.

After what had to be at least a half-hour the old train rumbled into the creaking station. Only a few people were in his car. *It's easy to tell where the good neighborhood ends and our lousy neighborhoods begin. The smell turns to rotting garbage and the soldiers get off.* He coughed. *Motherf...to have to choose between taking care of this cough and being clean. Fucking crazy.* The train lurched to a halt. *Now what?* And stayed stalled.

James wants to go to Mars but I can't get home on the train. Billions of dollars so we can poke our noses into space while the trains don't run. Minutes crept by. *When will this fucking pile of junk move? Let's go to Mars. Yeah, for that good old Nationalistic pride... that "boy, are we great, or what?" feeling. Who says we have to colonize other planets to ensure mankind's survival? Why? We should just fucking die out. We are not so wonderful.* He thought of a line from an old sarcastic song he liked called "*Going into Space:* "We're all done down here, let's go fuck up some other place..."*And anyway, a spaceship travelling at a million miles per hour would take four thousand years to reach the nearest star system that might - might - be hospitable. Should I tell him about the President we once had who was a real General who said; "every rocket fired signifies, in the final sense, a theft from those who hunger and are not fed, those who are cold and are not clothed"? How the fuck can people fall for this waste of their tax money... Their "contributions." Man, it is just too easy to swindle us out of what little common sense we have left. I love the argument about all the medical advancements as a result. How 'bout we just invest in medical science and skip the damn rockets?*

With a sudden bone-jarring lurch the train started up. He shrugged his shoulders because he also knew, in light of what his world had become, that it was silly of him to think of many of these things now. *I'm on the right side of a history that no longer exists.* Still, it afforded him some measure of solace. His fertile mind had escaped the gravitational pull of his existence once again.

He took a couple of healthy swigs from the small bottle of cough suppressant. *This shit better help.* The train squealed into a station. *Now what?* He was just a few stops from his own station. A group of thuggish looking young Socee men boarded. He saw them get on and instantly his alarm bell went off. They were very loud and very high. *Don't look at them.* It was too late.

"Whut you lookin' at grandpa?"

Ignore them.

Djyou you hear me old man?"

Just ignore them. They walked towards him. A different voice bellowed:

"Whassa matter...you fuckin' deaf?"

They were now standing over him. Grins plastered across their leering faces. *Okay, pretend you're deaf. They'll leave you alone.* He made some semblance of deaf signing at them. They were now standing over him. Grinning stupidly.

"Muthafucka *is* deaf!"

They were now jumping around and laughing at their good fortune at finding someone so apparently helpless. One of them leaned in close to his face while pointing at the paper bag.

"WHUT - YOU - GOT - IN - THE - BAG - THERE - DUMMY?"

The creep grabbed the bag from his hands. He tore the box out of the bag and looked at it:

"What is it?"

"It's fuckin'…cough shit?"

"Cough shit? You givin' us cough shit? What the fuck man."

Keep signing.

"Shut the fuck up dummy!"

This made them laugh even harder.

"Shut the fuck up? Streetboy tol' him to shut the fuck up! Hey man… YOU - ARE - WAY - TOO - FUCKING - LOUD!"

They were jumping around doubled over laughing. Again, that feeling of impotence. *Fuck this shit.* He rose quickly from his seat:

"GIVE ME THAT FUCKING BOX YOU FUCKING ASSHOLE!"

"He ain't deaf. He ain't a deaf mute. What are you—a fuckin' joka?

"He's a fuckin' joka muthafucka!"

Another man grabbed the box, took the cough medicine out and smashed it onto the train floor. Bedloe lunged for him. As he did, someone grabbed him from behind pinning his arms.

"YOU IGNORANT COCKSUCKING BASTARDS!"

"Yo, Street—grandpa called you innorant! Does he know somethin'?"

They howled with laughter. Suddenly, one of the boys punched him in his face—hard.

"Hey, it's Jackson!"

"It's Jackson!"

Laughing crazily as they careened to the door:

"We dint get his money!"

"Money? He's a fuckin' Socee. He ain't got shit. We got plenny offa that rich guy."

"Let's get a beer at The Clown."

And they were gone as quickly as they had appeared. As the train pulled away he slumped back down in his seat and wiped his nose on his cuff. *Fucking scummy world!* He looked at the cough medicine spread all over the floor of the car. *Ignorant bastards!* He looked at his sleeve. There was a fair amount of blood on it. He gingerly felt his nose and winced. *It's not broken but...Lousy punk-asses! I ever see any of them again...Gee, I wonder why none of the puppet soldiers that could've stopped them were around.* Now, besides no money because of the laundry there was no medicine. The blood was subsiding and he blotted what was still there on his sleeve. *He can't see this. I'll take this off before I get home.* He had another coughing fit - and this one hurt. And he still had to get their laundry out. *Fuck this fucking shit!*

# # #

The can of Natasha's® Norwegian Stew had been simmering on the hot plate for a half-hour. Now, he was beginning to be worried. *Where is he? National Security my...Why can't I call him?*

# # #

As he began his walk home from the train, which yet again had been stalled adding to his rage, the anger that had been building in John Bedloe over the punks who emasculated him on the train breaking his medicine and mocking him had turned white-hot. The dark thought which had been stewing since then was now something he *knew* he was going to act on.

I'm not a motherfucking punching bag! I exist! I am fucking getting even! As
he approached their home he took off his coat and tried washing the blood
off of the sleeve with the snow. *I have to hide this blood.* He opened the
front door, entered quickly, and draped his coat wet and bloody side down
over his arm. As he did he heard: "*…and,* he was ready to go again in
three minutes!" More hilarious canned laughs. He immediately knew that
his son was watching the witless FAIR TV sitcom "Three Ladies and a
Droid." Except James' mind wasn't on the TV, it was on the fact that he was
making less money on his side job because of all the time he was spending
with Lacey after work. *It's gonna take me a while to get this money.*

"Pop, where were you man? I was really worried."

He pretended to cough so he could cover his nose with his other hand
he brushed past his son: "I'm sorry kiddo, I was having a cup of coffee with
one of the waitresses at the diner. I gotta go to the bathroom real bad."

He went into the bathroom to try the hand soap on his coat. After
scrubbing the sleeve hard for a while the bloodstain seemed to be washing
out. *Now where am I going to hang it where it will dry? Forget outside. I'll
hang it on the front door hook as usual, with the sleeve facing away from the
room. If he asks I'll say it got dirty, and I had to wash it in the bathroom.* He
then washed his face and the bit of caked blood beneath his nostrils. *I am
gonna come for you, you fucking punk shitstains. Enjoy yourselves while you can.*
He gingerly dried his face, walked up front to where his son was stirring
the pot of Natasha's, and hung his coat on the door hook as he planned.

"You hungry?"

"Not really. You go ahead."

"A waitress huh?"

John tried unsuccessfully to stifle a cough.

"The heck with all the other stuff we need, I'm getting you some cough
medicine."

John wanted to tell his son about what had just happened to him on the train. He wanted to but he was ashamed and couldn't.

"I'm really beat, James." *What a comedian.* "You mind if I sack out early?"

"There's a game tonight."

"You'll tell me about it tomorrow. Okay? Get a good night's sleep. I'll see you tomorrow."

And he shuffled off to the back, undressed and got into bed. *You motherfuckers are going down.* And, with that thought repeating in his head, he finally fought his mind to a hard won draw and fell asleep.

Five

figurative minutes after she'd become the thoughtful young woman of
sixteen years that she now was, Alex discovered that most boys her age - and
in her strata - were gulping leering teen-age idiots on their mindless way
to becoming gulping leering idiot adult men. Now, some nine thousand
miles away from where James' father fought for sleep, she also lay awake
- thinking about James. He possessed an innocent shy earnestness which
she welcomed. He was considerate and kind. She knew that, unlike the
others, he also found her attractive. And it didn't hurt that he was quite
a handsome example of the male species. He was the first boy she'd ever
shared a meaningful kiss with. She even fantasized having sex with him
- a thought she'd never had about another boy. And, in the last few days
on Soneva Jani, it drove her to pleasuring herself, something she wasn't
in the habit of doing. *This thing is impossible. How has this happened? His
father is...maybe is an enemy of the state! He's a Socee. My parents, especially
father, would dismiss any notion of any kind of a relationship, let alone a life
shared by us, as an unequivocal impossibility. I need the strength to stop this.
It's out of the question.* She also could not believe how little time it took
between their first meeting and the way she now felt about him. Never in
her craziest dreams could she have conceived of this kind of a complication
in her normally uncomplicated life. She had finally met someone who was

attracted to her. Someone who thought she was beautiful. Someone who made her *feel* beautiful and who she was attracted to. And, there was the possibility she would have to take down his father. More painful, she also knew that it would be impossible if James' father was arrested or not, to ever continue seeing him. There could be no secret affair short of running away with him and thereby running away from what she was increasingly sad about; her chosen life's work. Her calling. Or rather, what she had *thought* was her calling. And, her family. If she still wanted to advance her career, still wanted to be a part of her family, she knew she would have to cut this unwieldy thing off at its knees. But she wasn't at all sure she had the strength to do this. And, if she ignored what she suspected about James' father, it would come back to her and, even worse, land on her father. She saw no way out of this lousy predicament.

Now, under the blazing Soneva Jani sun, she was trying not to get too tan. It was the last day of a five day mini-vacation that her father took them on every year since she could remember. She had always enjoyed this trip far more than she now could. They took a hypersonic jet for the eight thousand nine hundred mile nine hour flight at Mach 5 from New York to Malé International Airport, and then a scenic 45 minute seaplane flight to Soneva Jani. At $10,000 each for five round trips and $38,500 a night for each of them in a fabulous plantation-style villa on a private beach. Her parents needed this. It was paradise, but she would have chosen to stay behind and be in true paradise with James. This was one of the forty places in the world where the effects of global warming were somehow not yet manifest—however the signs were there. These were the provinces of the super-rich. God, she observed unamused, seemed to make miracles for people with money. In any event and miracles aside, as a hedge, plans were underway to soon Virtu-Dome all forty of these places —along with some of the wealthier residential enclaves in the world.

She had always loved the warm ocean water and stunning white coral reef that materialized for just a few hours a day, and the open-air theater on the beach. She still had no idea that the "stunning" whiteness of the reef was because the globally warmed ocean water had bleached it, and thus, it was dead. And, of course, who wouldn't love the five bedroom guest house with the unbelievably comfy king-sized beds and the sheets she was amazed by, and which she later found out were bespoke and cost $4,500 a sheet? Now, she found this...obscene. The first time her father slept on them he immediately ordered two sets for each of the six bedrooms in their New York penthouse, and two sets for each of the six bedrooms in their villa in Mykonos at $12,000 a set. As he said to his wife; "when you see a bargain, grab it."

Her pressing worry at the moment was, that since she was supposed to be an Associate, she definitely couldn't get *too* much color and trusted her wide-brimmed floppy straw would at least keep the sun off of her face. Though she had managed to keep her face protected enough from the Maldives' sun, her forearms and hands were still a little too tanned. This would not present a problem while she would be outdoors doing the messenger job and wearing gloves...but indoors, even with long sleeves, it was another thing. She *might* get away with keeping her gloves on in the office since they were in and out with deliveries quite quickly. *But... No! I can't. It would look funny. And meeting James for lunch would definitely present a problem.* Still, she would have to take a few extra days away from the messenger company to lose whatever color she *was* getting - especially on her hands. That would be something easily arranged by her father. As much as she wanted to be with James, she knew she couldn't go there looking darker anywhere on her body.

She spied her mother walking up the beach towards her doing Arabesques and Pirouettes in the surf's edge. *She is so beautiful...still so graceful. I would have loved to see her Odile in The Dying Swan. They said it was one of the best ever. It made daddy fall madly in love with her - and I don't think she was at all easy to win.* She knew he was a bit of a "Homme à femmes," back then. From pictures, she knew he was handsome and, even at a younger age, distinguished looking and had an easy way that hid a very shrewd mind. He was still her idol. Her mother walked up to her and purposely positioned herself so her shadow was cast over Alex.

"Cheri, n'obtenez pas brûlées."

"I won't."

"Well, I *do* think you've had enough sun for today. Rappelez-vous, vous a brûlé la dernière fois, Oui ? You had chills and fever that night and you missed dinner." She knew her mother was right and arose from her beach chair.

"You don't want to miss dinner tonight. He's preparing one of your father's favorites; a seafood tower. And dozens of oysters."

They began walking towards their guest house.

"And, chère fille, a couple of bottles of an *amazing* riesling no doubt."

No doubt.

The

past couple of days had been really lousy. His father's mood had darkened a lot and his cough was getting worse. *I gotta get to a drug store and get him some medicine. Why hasn't he already bought it? Was it the laundry money? I'm not a good son. I should've done it already. But the darn laundry tapped me out too and... Man, I hope what I have is enough. Those two clients wanted oral? No way. I could've used their money but...Two of my regulars too. And where's Lacey? She hasn't come in for two days. Is she sick? I hope nothin's happened.*

The day wore on. James almost made a mistake with a delivery because he was so preoccupied with his dad, with Lacey, and hoping the drug store, wherever it was, would be open when he got there—it was a business area after all and most stores tended to close on the early side. Making a mistake with a hand-off was a cardinal sin in his line of work and could cost a messenger their job. *Damn, they're usin' more droids and drones for package delivery —even for some of the personal hand-off jobs. A drone can't really get into an office but a droid...I better not be replaced by a lousy droid. It's a good thing they don't wanna go for the thirty thousand or they'd probably already have one and goodbye job.*

#

The temperature had fallen quite a bit in the last two hours as he walked through the falling snow to the drug store. *At least the sidewalks are dry in this neighborhood. If pop was here he'd go on a rant about it for sure. The warmth feels good. The lady said it was two blocks down and two blocks to the right.* He walked on. One more block. He finally got there—and couldn't believe that the drug store was just closing. *What the heck!* There were people still shopping inside, but the guard made sure that no one could get in, just out. *There's gotta be another one nearby, especially in this neighborhood.* And, if there wasn't, he was going to get on a straddling bus, take it a short way to an upscale neighborhood, and find one. He waited until a woman came out of the store and asked her if there was another drug store nearby. Of course, like him, she only worked in the area and had no idea. He waited for someone else to exit the store. There was a man carrying a briefcase coming up the street. *Maybe he knows.*

"Excuse me sir, but can you—

"DigiCurr, sorry."

"A drugstore…I only wanna know where there's another drug store around here?"

"Go away."

He passed quickly. Another woman, holding the hand of a young child, came out of the store.

"Excuse me Ma'am…do you know where there's another drug store near here?"

Even though there were soldiers patrolling this area, her reaction was to immediately grab the child and place him behind her back—as if he was some sort of a criminal or something. *Lady - you kidding? Okay, okay…No threat…unthreatening.* In a very calm way he asked again.

"My father's ill. Do you know where there's another drug store anywhere in this neighborhood, or in a neighborhood fairly close by? Please. If you do, just let me know. I *have* to get him some medicine. It's *all* I want. This one is now closed."

After a few seconds, while she debated what she should do, and he stood there with a benign look on his face, she turned away from him—and took what looked to him like a really small flexible card out of her pocket.

"Okay Flexi where is there an open drugstore besides this one near here?"

Wow! I've seen one of those on TV. After maybe five seconds:

"There's an open pharmacy at number Fifty-one Edgar Street Sheila. Blake's. It's open until ten o'clock tonight, Sheila."

Awesome! But, where's that? I've never delivered anything to Edgar Street. Never heard of it.

"Thank you ma'am…so much. One more thing—do you know how to get there from here?"

"I…believe…it's four, no five, blocks down and—Wait, you have plenty of time. I'll ask."

Again, she spoke into the card, and the card told them that, from where they were, Fifty- one Edgar Street was four blocks south and three blocks east. She smiled.

"There you go."

He thanked her and began his walk downtown. *Wow, that thing was thin as a playing card and what…two by three? And it was loud and had her voice. I can't…Why don't we have that?*

He finally reached the drug store and found a cough medicine he thought would help. It had 6.25 codeine, more codeine than the next one had, and though it cost twenty-one dollars—two dollars *more* than the next expensive one was—he purchased it. When he reached the check-out bot and scanned it the bot said "this medicine contains codeine" and asked him to prove he was over twenty-one.

"What? Are you kidding me?"

The bot answered "No. I do not kid." He grabbed the cough medicine off of the scanner, stormed through the huge store to the back where there was a live person in the pharmacy - a woman. He showed her the box.

"Excuse me ma'am, I need this for my father and the check-out bot says I need to be twenty-one to buy it?"

"Yes, it has codeine in it."

"You mean people can't buy cough medicine anymore?"

"Under twenty-one? Not with codeine. I'm sorry, but it's been the law for five years."

"But... My father *needs* this!"

"Then he can simply buy it in any pharmacy in the city. It's quite easy."

He stood there with a stunned look on his face. *Simply? Easy? Are you...*

"I'm sorry. Is there anything else I can do for you?"

Shaking his head "no" he turned to leave. *Screw this, I'm taking it.* He walked back to where he had picked the box off of the shelf, faked putting it back, And, as he started down the aisle to the front of the store, he slipped the box into his coat pocket. *Walk slow.* He knew he was taking a big chance but he was determined to get his father some kind of medicine that would maybe give him relief from his nagging cough. As he approached the door a man stepped to his side, grabbed his arm and shoved him hard into the wall.

"You know that's not very smart."

The man reached into James' coat pocket and took out the box of cough medicine.

"Not a good idea, kid."

He took out a small cell and spoke into it.

"Shoplifter at Blake's Pharmacy Fifty-one Edgar Street. I'll hold him."

"Please, lemmee pay for it. My father needs it bad. Lemmee pay for it and go home. I'm not a criminal! I'm just trying to get my father some medicine! Please!"

"It's my job, kid an' I don't wanna lose it. It's in the camera. Sorry."

You're sorry? You're...I'm in big trouble. His thoughts grew darker by the second. *What the heck's gonna happen? What are they gonna do? I am so screwed...This is bad.* He stood there, the man close to him with his hand on his arm. About three minutes later a car braked to a stop outside the store and two men, rather one man and an android, rushed inside.

"This him?"

"Stealing this box of cough medicine."

"Please...Come on...Lemmee pay for it! I have the money!"

"If you have the money why were you stealing it?"

If I say because it had codeine it could get even worse. He didn't answer.

"We'll take it from here."

They hustled him out of the store and into the back seat of the car. *Oh Lord...how did this happen? What have I done? What's gonna happen? Why did I think I could get away with it? Pop...I can't even let him know. Those men who were caught stealing from the Citizen's Ultra-Superior Food Market were put to death.* He was trembling with fright as he crossed himself.

"W-Where are we going?"

"Relax, you'll see when we get there."

Relax? You want me to relax?

"Am I g-gonna be able to go home?"

"You'll find everything out when you're booked and arraigned."

Booked? Arraigned? He sat back in shock and scared to death at what was happening. *What have you done you dumb idiot?" What the f have you done?* The car finally came to a halt in front of an imposing building in mid-town and he was hustled inside where uniformed androids sat before computers doing routine police work. He was escorted to the desk of the officer in charge.

"Caught shoplifting."

"Evidence?"

One of the men produced the box of cough medicine and placed it on the desk.

"Name?"

"James Bedloe."

"Age?"

"S-Sixteeen."

"Address?"

"901 East Tremont Avenue, Bronx, 10460. Can I ha-have a lawyer?"

He knew from watching TV that people could get a court-appointed lawyer to represent them when they were arrested. That people had the right to talk to a lawyer without delay.

"You watch too much TV, kid. Take off your coat, boots and belt and empty your pockets. Sign here and put your shit in this."

The man produced a box from under his desk and pushed it towards him. Then a phablet followed it. He did as he was ordered placing his keys, his TransiPass, and whatever small amount of money was in his pocket into the box.

"What is this?"

"The arrest record. Sign it, so we can all get outta here."

An arrest record? He scrawled his signature across the screen.

"Holo 'im and put 'im in the back. Maggie's got dinner waiting for me. See you guys tomorrow night."

With that, the cop rose to leave as James was scanned. He was then hustled away and thrown into a cell already filled with eight other men in it. *Holy mother of...*

The

slog back home from the laundry didn't do Bedloe any favors. Of course their laundry still wasn't ready and when he said he'd wait for it the man said it probably wouldn't be ready until the end of the day. So waiting was definitely out. *We can't sleep without sheets and pillow cases another night.* And his girl is coming over tomorrow night. His son would have to pick it up when he got home. He asked the man what time he was open until and his answer was a shrug of his shoulders and a "seven-ish... depending." That meant that James *maybe* could get there in time. *But how am I going to let h--- Idiot! Leave him a note.* Halfway home he had a coughing fit that again brought up some ugly phlegm. It scared him more than a little.

Two women were approaching—each at least an impressively Amazonian six feet in height. *Beautiful!* As they passed he reflexively said "two tall women." Three seconds and five feet later he heard one of them yell; "whoo-hoo!" *Wow, that hasn't happened in years!* He smiled broadly as he kept on. Man, woman, or child, walking alone or with Jane, when he passed someone who for some reason caught his eye; a dress, a pair of snazzy spectators, a kid dribbling a basketball, he usually made an appreciative comment. He wanted them to know their individuality was appreciated. It made them feel good and it made him feel good. It was a warm human connection. Glancing at the clock in the window of a bar he passed he saw that he had two and a half hours before he had to get to work. He stopped abruptly, turned and went back a few steps and stared at his reflection in the window. It wasn't pretty. He was drawn, haggard, hadn't shaved in days. He shook his head slowly at what he was seeing looking back at him. *Christ, I use to be worth a glance. Sometimes even a second look. It happened just like that. A switch went on somewhere and, all of a sudden, the women on the street who once might have given me the sidelong glance...even venture a smile...and on some rare occasions even give me the return turn-around... suddenly they just sailed on by.* He had become invisible overnight. That's what had made him so happy about that return whoo hoo. The strange thing was that he had never given a thought to this situation until now. *Why now? Is it about mortality? Because of this cough that's getting worse by the day? Do I have some condition that I can't do anything about? I can't go yet...my son is too young to be on his own.* He started walking again. *God, I miss you so Jane. All these years and I've never even thought about being with another woman even though I'm sure this life would be more bearable having someone. I miss the comforting touch of a woman. I used to be fairly attractive to women...I think. If I did smile at a passing woman it was understood as a gesture of appreciation of feminine beauty...And, because they could see I wasn't stopping, sometimes it was even returned. And, if I was with Jane, they knew that my smile was just a smile of appreciation—nothing more. I guess I might have been a bit of a flirt...wasn't I? You were so secure in my love you used to get a kick out of it if a woman flirted with me. You'd even tease me about it. You knew that it never went any further than a shared smile in the market, or some harmless banter while on those long lines in places like the Post Office.* His heart ached at the thought of her. The ache that weighed him down and went everywhere with him. This time it would go home with him to leave the note for James to pick up the laundry by seven.

Hail was now mixing in with the falling snow as he trudged on. *I may have smiled at a passing woman a few times since...rarely was my smile returned. And the times when I'd amuse by saying something appreciated as witty... with rare exceptions, gone. I'm well and truly invisible. That whoo*

hoo was fucking great! He was realizing how terribly lonely he was, and *had* been all these years. *Is this rage in me my unconscious mind refusing to recognize how alone I feel…I have James but…*

Bedloe got home and the first thing he needed to do was write the note about the laundry. He could hear the hail pelting the mobile home's top as he searched for a pen that worked—and paper to write on. It took him the better part of five minutes to find the pen but the paper was a different story. He finally settled on tearing a piece off of a brown paper bag from the bodega. He left the note on the table and went back to the bathroom to wash his face. Except that he forgot that the bathroom towels were in the laundry. He went to the front door, opened it, and stood there while the wind dried his face. This brought on a fit of coughing. When it had passed he looked down to see two drops of blood in the snow. *I have to get to work. Fuck this shit.* And still, never leaving his mind for a second; *don't worry punks, I haven't forgot.*

#

That night John got home from work and his son still wasn't there and never came home at all. *Could he have spent the entire night with this girl? I hope that's where he is. Or…Am I being…Has something happened to him? Is he hurt…or worse? Why don't we have fucking phones?* He was worried beyond sick as he went to pick up their laundry, and more so when he returned to find his son still absent. And even more so as another sleepless night wore on.

#

It was now morning and Alexandra Winstead and her family were on another hypersonic jet bound for New York. It had been five days of ocean, sun, sand and great food and wine. None of which she had enjoyed. Now, it would be back to reality. She looked at her hands. *Going with James tonight to meet his father is out of the question. I don't know how long it'll be until I can see him…Going right back to the messenger job is also impossible.* Still on semester break her plan was to hang out at CyScenSec for the next few days while she lost her tan. It was late afternoon when their limo dropped her and her father at the nondescript downtown building and her mother and brother continued uptown to their home. She entered alongside her father both flashing their ID's and, after a hug they split up, he off to his office and she taking the elevator up to CyScenSec. Entering the room, as a matter of standard routine, she scanned the holograms that filled the room and was shocked to see...*James? He's been...What? Arrested? For stealing some cough medicine? In a cell in mid-town? Oh, James...*She immediately picked up a secure MorPho.

"This is CyScenSec code two-two Viperbite, you have a James Bedloe there. He's to be released *at once.*"The voice on the other end knew that this demand was to be taken seriously.

"He's not to be told *why* he's being released. Just do it! Give him back the medicine and then drive him to the East side to the nearest six train."

She ended that call and then called the messenger office to tell them not to dock James for any missing days. *Why did he do something so stupid? My God, he must be scared to death—and his father must be freaked out that he didn't come home last night. What must it be like to be that desperate knowing what could have happened to him?*

"James Bedloe" bellowed the voice as the cell door was unlocked. *Oh Jesus, where're they gonna take me?* He'd spent the night curled up in a corner of the cell afraid to close his eyes for a second. He was rushed to the front of the station, given back his valuables, his coat, and out the door into the back of a waiting car. *They returned the medicine to me? What is happening?*

"Please...W-where are you taking me?

No answer. Siren on, the car was weaving through cross-town traffic. *Are they taking me to Brooklyn? Why did they give me back the medicine? What the heck is going on?* After some time the car pulled into a bus stop at the corner of Lexington Avenue and Fifty-First Street.

"Get out."

They're letting me go? They are. They're letting me go! He didn't waste any time tumbling out of the car which then sped off into traffic. He stood there on the sidewalk as people rushed by him trying to gather his thoughts. *What the heck had just happened?* Whatever it was, the anxiety he felt over meeting the same fate as those men who robbed the Citizen's Market still lingered—and would probably do so for days. *This is bad…I missed a day of work.* Gathering his wits he made his way down to the train. *Forgive me God, I know how worried he is. He probably spent a sleepless night wondering where I was.* As the train approached his stop he was still debating what to tell his father about why he was out all night. *I could lie and say I was with Lacey all night but that would seem really inconsiderate knowing he would worry about where I was. Maybe…I got sideswiped by a cab crossing the street on a delivery and they kept me in the messenger place infirmary overnight for observation. Yeah, the infirmary that doesn't exist.* He walked down the stairs and trudged home through the snow. The front door opened when he was five yards away and his father, who was indeed "freaked out" and had stayed up all night worried sick, was standing there bent at the waist, hands on knees, then looking up at him with relief on his face.

"Poppa, poppa, I am *so* sorry."

His father stepped aside to let him in, closed the door and then hugged him close.

"Jeez ma—sorry…You okay? Give me your coat. Are you hungry? Are you alright? Where the fu—Where the heck were you? And where's Lacey? I thought we were getting together tonight."

"I got you this."

He reached into his pocket and handed his father the medicine.

"Thanks, kiddo…Really. Thank you. But this didn't take all night…and where is she?"

Over some Natasha's he told his father the whole story. His father listened, riveted by the story and as puzzled as his son at the outcome. John, still angry and ashamed of it, didn't have the heart to tell his son about what had happened to him on the train when he tried to buy the same medicine. He did however show him his freshly laundered clothes.

"Lacey will like you even more with clean clothes."

I should tell him. "Pop, I haven't seen her for…I guess it's five days now. Maybe she was in to work today…but, I don't know."

"James, she's probably sick." *I hope.*

That night James could barely pay attention to the BashBall game. He sat there in a sad trance wondering what happened to Lacey. *I dunno if I'll ever see her again.*

# # #

Alex aka Lacey, meanwhile, was fighting back against all the unbidden thoughts that had elbowed their way into her mind while on the beach in the Maldives. Now they were there along with some new ones brought about by James' arrest. *I really cared that he was in custody. For him, not for my case…or whatever this thing about his father may turn out to be.* She knew she had to see him but had to wait until her arms and hands had completely lost their color. *How could I have missed him as much as I did? I'm actually in love with him. But I can't be in love with him. This has to be just some stupid crush. And… I have to keep pursuing this thing with his father. If his father does turn out to be an enemy of the state I can't ignore it. And now I have to lie some more about missing tonight's meeting.* These thoughts kept coming at her - even as she made conversation at dinner while hardly eating - and up until she finally again cried herself to sleep.

What

he was about to try to do filled him with a strange feeling of relief. *Nothing will happen to me anyway.* He walked straight back to the closet in the rear of the mobile home, went into the hidden compartment, and took out his .45 and the extra clip. While he felt bad for his son who was still in a deep funk because Lacey still hadn't been in to work, John had to finally leave him alone tonight to do this thing that had been gnawing at him for days. He heard his son from up front.

"You going out?"

"Yup…A date. You believe it?"

He quickly stuffed the gun into the back of his jeans and put the extra clip in his pocket. *I'll put them both in my coat pocket later for easy access.* He went into the bathroom, flushed the toilet, came back to the front, quickly picked his coat up and put it on as he was going out the door.

"That waitress?"

"The same. Don't wait up." "Have fun."

"I think we will. James, she'll probably be in tomorrow."

"I know." But he wasn't at all convinced.

# # #

Bedloe made his way through the one-foot-and-still-counting falling snow to the train; *what kind of animals do something li—No…No, these monsters aren't animals, they're people. Animals don't attack other animals for fun. They attack for food. They defend their territory. They fight for supremacy. For mating. They don't attack just for the fun of it.* Whether he was right or wrong what he believed deep down was that animals, with too few exceptions, were far better than people. *If that makes me some kind of a sociopath or something I don't give a fuck. If there is such a thing called heaven then I'll bet there are far more animals there than humans. Calling someone terrible a pig or an animal is an insult to both. These creeps are all too human. I'm coming for you motherfuckers.*

He reached the train station, climbed the slippery trash-filled stairs with some difficulty, showed his transi-pass to the eye and went through the stile and up to the platform. As he stood waiting for the train he found himself actually savoring what he was about to do. Adrenaline was pumping through his body. *I haven't had this kind of jumpy twitchy feeling since Iraq. It's like I drank two cans of M.* In the dim light of the platform he turned his back and made sure the gun's safety was on and that the piece was definitely chambered. *Ready to go sweetheart.* He carefully returned the gun to his coat pocket—and waited for the train that would carry him to satisfaction.

As he waited, coughing intermittently, he thoroughly believed that what he was about to do was righteous. *This is what that cocksucker has wrought.* He knew that he obsessed over Conover. *Nobody's going to give a fuck about this. That's what it's come to. It's a fucking wonder every "Associate" isn't wearing a government issued one piece jumpsuit like in sci-fi flicks. Probably the only reason we aren't is these criminals would have to spend money on us. Yeah…that'll happen.*

He peered up the track and saw in the distance the two front lights of an approaching train. In about a minute the ancient train rolled noisily into the station and screeched to a loud halt. The door opened and he stepped into the car. It closed behind him and for a few seconds he stood surveying the car. It was half-filled. *Socees going somewhere exciting and wonderful. Thrilled to death to be alive.* The train pulled away from the station. He took a seat at the end of the car and after a little while he looked around at his fellow passengers. *What a miserable bunch we are. Grey sullen faces. Sick. Coughing…like me. We used to live to 80, 85, now it's probably 65. If we're lucky. None of us can afford to see a doctor, a dentist. We are truly on our own. We eat crap, take crap, and have a life filled morning to night with nothing but crap. I'm going to enjoy this. They said the Clown.*

The train rolled on down the track. It was only three stops from their place to the Jackson stop. As he got out and walked to the stairway to go down into the street he fell into step beside a harmless looking man who had also gotten off.

"Excuse me, sir, but do you know a place near here called the Clown Bar?"

The man responded in a tired raspy voice;

"It's a block down that way and a block to the left just off the corner."

He thanked the man and allowed himself a wry smile; *he didn't say "no problem."* He proceeded carefully down the stairs, stepped onto the street into the snow-piled sidewalk and began trudging in the direction the man had given him. He reached the corner and made the left turn. *Bingo!* A tawdry blinking red neon sign announcing the Klo n B r. He had long ago renounced religion, but he now said a prayer to the Universe that they'd be there. *Please be in there …'N if you're not, I'll come here every night if I have to 'til you are.* As he walked down the empty street he reached into his coat pocket, took out his piece, released the safety, and carefully returned it to his pocket. *I'm sure this joint will be dimly lit…Be there assholes. Be there! No way they'll remember my face. And so what if they do. I'll just leave and wait outside for them to leave. They're not going to be afraid of a harmless old man they've already punked.*

He got to the bar's door, opened it, and silently edged in. As he thought, it was quite dimly lit. A few sad looking people were seated at the bar. He slipped into a seat at the short end of the bar from where he could scope the entire square room. Sure enough, there at a round table in the corner sat his quarry—raucously drinking and laughing. *Got you!* He'd decided that if they were there he would order a beer, nurse it, and wait for them to leave. And, if he had to, he'd order another. *If it takes us all night, you worthless fucks are going down.* He ordered a beer. The barman placed his beer in front of him and he immediately paid him the ten dollars because he knew that when they finally got up to leave he would need to move pretty quickly. *It's worth it.* As he watched them out of the corner of his eye, enjoying themselves so much, so without a care, his anger was building— even beyond what it was before. *Yak it up boys. It's your last night alive on planet earth.* He singled out the creep who'd grabbed his medicine. *You're going first ace,* and the slime ball who punched him. There were five of them and he had seven rounds in the first clip. He knew he could make them count. And, he knew he would re-load whether he needed to or not. *It'll take me maybe three seconds tops. Hold the second clip in your bottom steadying hand as you empty the first clip. You have fourteen rounds to eradicate these pukes.* He also reasoned that the deep snow would keep them from running too far, and too fast, once he began firing. The thought of what he was about to do filled him with the most excitement he'd felt in at least fifteen years. The adrenaline rush he was feeling was equal to the rush he'd felt on patrol in Iraq all those long years ago, when death waited impatiently for him around every corner. *This is…it's perverse but…I fucking can't wait.*

One of them waved to the waitress. *That's it, call for the check.* He watched as she slapped it down on their table. *Yeah, pay with the money you mugged some poor sap for.* He was quickly off his bar stool; *here we go* - and out the door ahead of them while they were still standing at their table. As soon as he reached the street he took his piece out, along with the second clip, and positioned himself flat against the wall to the right of the bar entrance. He was some five or six feet closer to the el in the direction he would have to walk to get back to the train. His mouth was dry, his heart was beating wildly out of his chest. *Come on...Come on.* He stood there breathing hard, his .45 at his side in his right hand ready to be raised. Thirty seconds. *Come on.* One minute. *Come on you moth---*The bar door opened, and all five of them came reeling out and stood on the sidewalk saying their goodnights to each other. He relished the thought that it was the last time they would ever do this. *Goodnight motherfuckers.*

"Hey! Assholes! Remember me?

They turned to him.

"The other night? The deaf guy on the train?"

They stared at him with quizzical looks on their faces.

"Remember? The deaf guy with the cough medicine?"

He waited as they slowly became aware of who he was. The man who punched him spoke.

"Yeah...So? What the fuck do you wa—

He dropped him first. As they were realizing what was happening he dropped the man who took his cough medicine. *Okay, so you went second.* The three others, now in a shocked panic turned to run. As he knew it would, the snowy unheated, un-shoveled, sidewalk made it difficult for them to move too fast. He moved in closer, as fast as they could move away, and in rapid order shot them in their backs. Moving up to the first two he put another round into each of them as he passed. Then, while re-loading, he moved as quickly as he could back to where the others lay, he put a round into each of their heads and began to walk to the el. As he did, he heard one of the first two men he shot groaning in pain. He quickly stepped back to him. *Still breathing? Guy's a roach. And this is the asshole who grabbed my medicine too...*

"Please don't kill me. Please. I'm beggin' you in God's name please!"

"Okay, go ahead. Beg me. In God's name of course. I might let you live."

The man looked at him with a curious mix of hope, fear and supplication on his face. "In God's name..."

"In God's name...Yes? Please, do go on."

"I'm beggin' you...By all that's holy...In Christ's name please don't... Please."

"Aren't you the guy who took my medicine before? Smashed it on the train floor?"

"I didn't mean to. I swear to God!"

"You didn't? You swear to God?"

"Yes, yes...I swear to God in heaven!"

"In heaven? Hey...In that case you know what...I am going to let you live."

"Oh God. Thank you, thank you, thank you, thank you."

He looked down at the man.

"Hey, you know what else?"

He smiled down at the man.

"I'm just kidding."

He raised his piece and watched the man's face slowly turn from relief to horror.

"If you see this gorgeous black woman with a half-up half-down say hello to her for me...You know? Your friend God, asshole."

He waited long enough for his message to fully sink enjoying the terrible look of understanding on the man's face—and then shot him squarely between his eyes. Twice. The whole thing took less than one violent minute. Except for the added pleasure of his dialogue with the last man, it went exactly as he'd pictured it would. *Fuck with a combat vet.* He turned, and calmly began walking back down the block towards the Jackson el station. Remarkably, no one inside the bar had come out into the street to see what had happened—not even by the time he'd slowly trudged to the corner. He reached the uptown el stairs and slowly climbed them. *No police sirens, no shouting, nothing! I knew it.* He flashed his transi-pass at the eye, went through the stile and climbed back up the stair to the platform. He waited there, his heart still pounding. The adrenaline still coursing through his body. *If I have a fucking heart attack right now it's worth it.* About fifteen jumpy minutes later the ancient train rolled into the station. He got on and sat down. He took a few very deep breaths trying to quiet his heart. *Calm down. Calm down. Relax your shoulders.* He took a deep breath. *I need to get another clip or two from somewhere because from now I'm carrying. Nobody is fucking with me again. My guy...He can get it.*

Except for an intermittent cough he sat silently again among the same gray faces. But now, he was sure that, unlike everyone else in this car, his ride back home was different. Now, though he sat quite still, he was silently screaming for joy inside thinking about what he had just done. He was unaware that he had a broad smile on his face. Suddenly he realized it. *Holy shit, except for being stoned out of my mind on M and laughing stupidly at inane cartoons, I haven't smiled like this in years. I'm a stone cold murderer and I don't give a shit.* The train pulled into his station with another ear-shattering screech and he got off. *Oil costs money.*

It was still snowing as Bedloe trudged home. Suddenly, he jumped into a snow bank, jumped out and then made a snowball. *I can't remember the last time I did this.* He threw the snowball at a street sign and hit it! *I can't miss tonight.*

He reached the lot where their home was. As he got twenty feet from the front door he could see that the light was still on inside and he knew his son would be up watching some FAIR show or another. He was almost right. His son was preoccupied with his missing girlfriend. It had now been almost two weeks. *Why don't I know her address? I could go and see what's happening. Is she sick? What?*

The FAIR show James had on, but wasn't watching, called itself America's Puzzle.

"Hey, you're home…so…how'd it go?"

"I haven't had such a good time in years." *Oh Christ, I mean it.*

He couldn't help but stop and look at the TV.

"She's nice?"

"Tell you in a second."

The puzzle that the man was working on was a four word crossword with the common link "BARS." On the board was the following;

?   **T**

P R O T E I N

L   **K**

S A L A D   **I**

The question mark was in place of the missing letter he had to fill in. There was tiki bar and salad bar and after much pondering the man finally asked for…an M. *A bar of mold.* John stood there in awe. Then he turned to go to the back.

"So…she's nice?"

"Very…we may even do it again…Soon."

"That is so good to hear."

He's in a really good mood. He wanted to tell his father how worried he was about Lacey but decided against it. *Why bum him out.* His father went straight to the back. In the back John was quietly wrapping his .45 in the chamois and putting it back in its hiding place to be oiled later.

"There's some stew in the pot."

John came back upfront.

"Thanks, kid, I'm actually still hungry."

James took his father's bowl over to the hot plate and filled it with stew. He placed the bowl on the table in front of his father and sat down. *He's gonna eat it? Rat? He's eating it? Holy…* He crossed himself…*Does he know what it is?*

"You're still bummed huh, kid?"

James couldn't hide what this turn of events had done to him. And worse, he felt powerless to do anything about it.

"She still hasn't been at work."

"James, I'm telling you, she probably has a cold or something. Don't worry, she'll turn up."

Now is not the time to hector him about us not being allowed to have phones.

"I hope so. Two weeks…a cold?"

"Colds last forever these days. You're not going to lose her. She'll turn up you'll see. And I do want to meet her."

I hope she shows up soon. For James' sake and mine.

She's amazing, Dad."

"I'm looking forward to meeting her."

"I hope you do."

He took his son's hand.

"James, I will. Please don't worry, I know she'll show up."

"Yeah, I know."

They watched some criminally cruel BashBall game together for a couple of hours during which they showed four promos for a new morning show: "Breakin' Bredd." And when it was finally time to turn in, and James had said his prayers, John lay there while his son tossed and turned and finally fell asleep. He was still so jacked up he was unable to stop replaying what he had done earlier over and over in his mind. No sleep came to him. He lay there all night staring at the ceiling and, as the light of a new day came, and he had finally come down, he was starting to question his actions; *I stewed over this for days...I planned this...is this what I've become - or is this what I've always been?*

Why did they let me go? For his part James had gone to bed every night since he was released from jail in fear that "they" would discover they had let him go because of an error and would come pounding on the door in the early hours. He also was heartsick about Lacey; *where is she? Is she alright? Will I ever see her again?* As concerned as he was about his fate and his father's health he kept finding himself thinking of her. *I love you so much...Where are you?*

Why

did a lot of things that didn't seem to annoy anyone else annoy me? Was I the one out of step? Was anyone else as annoyed as I was by the constant hyperbole that peppered most people's conversations? By so many people starting a sentence with "I mean?" There must have been others who also thought that the debasing of our language was as serious a matter as I thought it was. The man who wrote that column in the Times did. Did others think that our language was being debased to bad ends? Other than sociologists, why didn't enough people make the connection between language, intelligence and civility? Some people must have also seen the danger in no longer having to bother to add or spell because computers did it for us. The danger in destroying our public schools. John sat there questioning himself yet again. He *had* let his wife go to that abortionist. *So how smart am I? I should have known... should have insisted.* He was chased by that fact. Hounded by it. Everything he felt, everything he believed, was magnified by this tragedy that he had a large part in. He knew that Jane would tell him he was being ridiculous to think this way. That it was her decision and nothing he could have said would have changed her mind. Still... *And what would you think about what I did the other night? You'd be very upset at my resorting to such violence. Wouldn't you?* The thought made him feel ashamed—but he would still get the extra clip.

With this confusion of thoughts swirling around in his head he started to get ready to go to work. *Hey, I got a date wit' a hot dish. Stop it Johnny, you're killin' me.*

#

Besides his own worries about Lacey, James was now deflated over the two hundred and fifty dollars, and also worried that in the past few days his father seemed to have lost the sudden appetite he had. When he asked his father about it John shrugged and said it was nothing. As worried as he was about his father he was even more preoccupied with the missing Lacey. He crossed himself and said a prayer that Lacey was alright and that he'd see her soon. He also decided to tell his father about the clinic when he could give him the money.

#

On Manhattan's Upper East Side, now back from the Maldives, her semester break over, and having finally lost her tan Alex aka Lacey was ready to get back to the messenger office. And, far more importantly, to James. Since she was certain her father had gone through the TV holo-vids and had come to his own conclusions as to whether or not James' father was an enemy of the state, she had decided that she needed to look at the Holi-vids and the surveillance cams also. She had to know if there was hard evidence against his father. So, during this time, alone in her bedroom she checked the Holo-vids on her secure device. And, when she did, she saw nothing that would definitively prove that James' father was an enemy of the state. However, this didn't make her feel any better, she still knew in her now anguished heart that there was no future for her and James. However, because she saw plenty to show that his father was very angry and very dismissive of the country's leaders she knew her own father would expect her to meet the man and check him out herself. She also knew he was depending on her.

She pushed back from the breakfast room table and peeked into the adjoining restaurant-sized stainless steel kitchen. She had hardly touched the breakfast of fresh organic orange juice, organic honeydew melon, fresh wild blueberry pancakes topped with two sunny-side up organic cage-free eggs and a side of heirloom bacon. She did, however, drink two cups of Kona coffee.

"Thanks Maurice...delicious, as usual."

She padded out of the breakfast room and down the hall to her brother's room.

"You had breakfast?"

"Yup...Hey, I'm working on a security test dad gave me. A code insuring the integrity of information. He wants to see if I can make this program complete and tamper proof. I have to make certain its confidentiality code insures that any information gathered will be secure from unauthorized access. Tell me what you think?"

"I'll look at it later. He said something about bringing you in to the office this week.

"Great."

I'm not so sure it is. She almost said it out loud.

"You haven't been yourself the past week sis...You okay?

Oh God, if an eight year old can see it..."

"It's just...female stuff bro." *The all-purpose excuse to men of all ages.*

"You going back in today?"

"The tan's pretty much faded away so...yeah. See you at dinner."

She padded out of her brother's room, down the hall, glancing into her mother's empty office on the way. Her mother had already left for her meeting at the Mayor's office. She continued on up the two flights to her own bedroom. With all of it, she still was anxiously looking forward to seeing James. She showered, put on freshly laundered lingerie, her grungy Socee clothing and checked out her hands one more time. She combed her hair and put on a touch of lip gloss. Satisfied with what she saw, she called down to their doorman to have her personal Andro-car brought around to the front. The car would drive her to a corner five blocks from the messenger service and she would walk the rest of the way.

# # #

She wanted to surprise him. So she was in a doorway across the street and down the block waiting to see him come up the street and now he was. *My beautiful James.* She quickly moved in a few feet behind him as he entered the building, busied herself at the sundries stand, and waited until he got into the elevator to make her move. He stepped into the elevator. Just as its doors were closing a slender pale hand reached in and the doors re-opened. *Oh my… It's her! Thank you lord!*

"Oh, my dear Lord—Lacey, I thought…I dunno what I thought but…"

She laughed and stepped into the elevator. After thinking he might never see her again he couldn't believe she was here and he also began to laugh. In that moment they were the two giddy teen-agers they were always supposed to be. As the elevator doors closed she put her arms around his neck, drew him in close and kissed him between words.

"You look—like you've—seen—a ghost."

The elevator started its climb.

"I—was so—worried. Where were—you? Were you—sick? What?"

They kissed passionately both moaning softly. He thinking; *Oh, thank you dear Lord.* She hearing in her mind an old Edith Piaf song her mother had played for her.

He was indescribably overjoyed. He felt a relief he had never felt before. She explained that she had come down with a bad cold—*Pop was right*—and even as she told him this she felt she was betraying a trust. They decided they would go for a walk after work.

# # #

They were on the promenade leaning on the railing looking out over the water. James was staring at the Statue of Liberty in the distance. Being the kind of a person who didn't wear his feelings on his sleeve, he had been able to mask his disappointment over the news about the clinic from his father. Lacey, however, was a different story; she was picking up on it. She had become used to James being positive and this change in his demeanor made her wonder if it wasn't something she'd said...or done. Was it her? At first, she thought it best not to say anything and see if it was just a passing thing. Had her being away done something that had changed their relationship? Despite her intelligence and all her advantages she was still a somewhat insecure young girl. She knew, at that moment, that wondering about the state of their impossible relationship was surreal. That while she wondered about it, she was aware that there was a high probability that their relationship was doomed anyway. So this moment, as they stood at the promenade railing, they were both off kilter; he was down and she was up in the air. Finally, she had to ask:

"James, what is it? What's the matter? You've been acting differently lately. Is it your father?"

James, of course, didn't want her to think that it had anything to do with her. So it would be a relief to tell her why he was so bummed out. He stared out over the water as he responded.

"This is a heck of a country. That's all I can say."

"I'm not following. What is it?"

She realized with great relief that, whatever it was, it had nothing to do with her. Again, she was aware that wanting them to be okay, while knowing they pretty much couldn't be was...crazy. But she couldn't just stop loving him on a dime, could she?

"Two hundred and fifty dollars."

"Two hundred and fifty dollars?"

"The clinic. That's what they want."

"The visit is two hundred and fifty dollars?"

"Minimum."

"They told you that?"

"When I called them. Two hundred fifty dollars is the minimum. I can just imagine what the maximum could be."

"Why didn't you tell me? Oh my God...that's...It's a clinic. It's criminal."

"And he's *gotta* see a doctor. We have to find out why he's been coughing so much."

Lacey was well and truly bummed out by his plight. Bummed and suddenly angry.

"And by the time I put that much together who knows how bad his cough will be."

He fell silent, still looking at the Statue of Liberty.

Should I offer? Yes. There's no question. This is criminal. Of course you should!

"James, let me give you the money. Please."

"What? No. No way!"

"James, I have it. I told you, I don't have to chip in for rent. Let me help. It would make me feel good."

"I can't, honey. I can't. Thank you."

"Why not. You're being silly."

"I'll get the money."

"Your side job?"

He couldn't say anything. He stood there—fixated on the grey figure rising out of the water.

"James, I'm sorry. I shouldn't have said that."

Oh man, she's just trying to help you idiot.

"You'll come over and bring him some soup. I'll get the money. But I can't take yours. Your family may have an emergency and who knows…"

She knew she couldn't argue with that. She turned him around to face her and embraced him.

"Alright stubborn, I'll bring him some soup."

"He'd like that. Let's pick another night."

He wanted to change the subject from her offer.

"I have to warn you: BashBall brings some crazy stuff out in him. Just be prepared for M induced speed rants where he talks about our 'criminal leaders' and how kids're-kept-dumb-and-poor-so-they'll-go-to-war-unknowingly-and-willingly-to-protect-the-property-and-agendas-of-thewealthy. Right? His latest is that it's the same for BashBall players. And on and on and on."

He may be right James. "Um…Okay. I'm looking forward to meeting him."

James let out a short laugh. Lacey smiled.

"Why don't you ask your dad what night's good for him? I'll bring over a couple of cans of a good soup, or a stew, and we'll watch one."

"I can't wait for him to meet you."

He turned from her to look back out over the water.

"I uh…I had a bit of a strange week."

"I'm sorry, I haven't even thought to ask…how have you been?"

"Well…Strange…Puzzling. I tried to get my father some cough medicine and I couldn't because the law is people our age we can't buy anything that has codeine in it."

"But it's medicine. That is too…That's crazy."

"I got caught stealing it.

"Oh, James." *You liar.* She was draped in guilt.

"I spent the night in a cell, but they let me go! My dad can't believe it. Me neither. But I'm here, right? He thinks I might have run into the one cop in the whole city who still had a heart. Maybe a whole precinct full of cops with hearts."

"But he has the cough medicine, yes?"

"I'm not so sure it really helps."

"Well…Look, it turned out okay. Right? Overnight…your dad must have been worried sick."

"I think he thought maybe I spent the night with you."

I'm not sure we ever will. The lousy way she felt was getting to be a daily occurrence. But she smiled and held his hand as they walked from the promenade. He, thinking how lucky he was to find such a girl; she, thinking how rotten the whole thing was.

#

James was on his way home. *That was so sweet of her to offer to give us that money but…No way I can take it. No way. Come on, let's go.* As usual the train was stalled. *We'll set another night. I hope she can take when pop starts going on about how BashBall players are forced to risk their very lives like soldiers. And why do we suppose that most BashBall players and soldiers are black or Latino? I dunno, why shouldn't someone be willing to risk everything for any opportunity to have a better life? If I was any good I might wanna play too. And join up. Sure, a few really bad people start wars. But it's ridiculous to say all's it takes is a whole lot of desperate kids to have one. He told me someone once said; we should take all the statues of generals and soldiers off of the horses and just leave the horses. Or, if we're going to have statues of heroes, we should have statues of mothers, or nurses. Even conscientious objectors. I dunno, Pop, I'm starting to worry about you more than before. I sure hope you don't worry her too much because she may be your future daughter-in-law.*

FAIR was showing the latest Cyberwar news. The anchors were very solemn. Half of Alaska's power-grid had been knocked out, and the power grids of all our major cities was now threatened. *Darn, this is serious.* The news anchor was saying that Government sources were telling her that, although this was a successful hack-attack, there was no need for alarm and that our best cyber people were hard at work making certain that our power grids on the lower forty-eight were secure. *That's a relief. But I sure wish I could be in the hack room along with all the cyber warriors.* And, in spite of this news, his mind still kept going back to Lacey and how relieved he was to know that she was still in his life.

Now

that they finally had clean laundry he put on a clean t-shirt and briefs and his clean second pair of jeans. *Pop's right about one thing; I have to be clean, I have a girlfriend.* His second sweatshirt also smelled good as he slipped it over his head. Bedloe's mood which, for a short while, had been lighter had darkened in the last few days. James attributed that to the state of his father's health. Whenever James asked him how he felt all he would say was "fine." But he obviously wasn't. She wasn't a doctor, but maybe Lacey could cheer him up. He'd told his father how great she was, smart, loving, kind, and his father actually said that he was looking forward to meeting her.

They were both going to come straight from work and then wait for John to come home from his own job, let him settle in, maybe get him to have some of whatever she decided to bring. She told James that since this was a very important night for her—meeting her boyfriend's dad—that she'd put aside some money for some small gifts for him. Lacey decided she was going to bring him four large cans of the good park pigeon soup as a gift. When he told his father she would be doing that he said that just meeting her was good enough. When James told her what his father said, she replied, "Nonsense, who visits someone's home and comes empty handed?" He began to think of this future meeting, whenever it was going to take place, as a celebration of a sort. His father meeting the future daughter-in-law. He asked Lacey about meeting her folks and she said she would try and arrange it. He thought that eventually the parents should meet and she agreed, saying it should be as soon as it "was possible." Anyway, they soon planned to kick it and really show her off to his father. In a few days there was a real good BashBall game on too, so maybe that would be a good night. The plan was to have some good hot bracing soup while they talked, and then watch the game. He couldn't wait. She was so thoughtful. He knew that his dad would love her.

He spent the day fantasizing about their life together. Yes, things were tough, but they were tough for everyone and he knew that together they would make a good life. Aside from the fact that she was really sweet, she seemed to be very resourceful, and he could see by the way she performed her duties at work that she was quite competent. She'd even told him that she wanted two children, a boy and a girl. His fantasy come true. She would make a terrific mother he thought. Which reminded him that he hadn't asked his father about his own mother and he was determined to find out more about her. He hoped his father was feeling good enough and in a good enough mood tonight to talk with him about her.

# # #

The diner was slammed as usual and Bedloe was doing his best to keep the dishes turning as soon as they came back to him. The job was not only mindless but so shitty that the only way he could bear it day after day, hold on to his sanity, keep him from screaming, was to transport himself back to a better time. He could, and usually did.

At the moment it was spring 2008, and he was on a downtown express with Jane, his best friend Sacky, and Sacky's future wife Hannah, who everybody called Honey. It was their weekly Friday night date and, knowing Jane liked jazz, he thought he'd found a great place for them to go to. Earlier in the week he'd read about a restaurant in the Times

Square area called Child's Paramount that also had a jazz quartet. It was part of a chain of three Child's restaurants in the area but, of the three, this particular one was the only one that featured music. *And* it wasn't that expensive. He figured they could have a burger, or whatever, and also hear some great music.

He could still see her as she opened the door when he called for her. She was wearing a black cashmere sweater over a white shirt and jeans - and a single strand of pearls. She also had small pearl studs in her earlobes. She was a vision. She welcomed him in with a kiss, took his hand and led him through their small foyer to their living room. Her father was watching television and, as he would always do, rose from his easy chair to greet him and shake his hand. Her mother joined them and they made some small talk about politics—they were Progressives—and the beautiful weather. As usual they asked that he have her home by eleven even though it was a Friday and not a school night. Of course he said he would. He remembered that she took his arm and how giddy he felt as they walked the two blocks to the el where they were meeting Sacky and Honey. He had on a black blazer he'd bought at Sid's, a men's store in the neighborhood, jeans and a white button down shirt, which had made them laugh when she opened her door because they saw they were both pretty much wearing the same thing. He remembered asking her if she had another pair of pearl earrings for him which made her laugh some more. He loved her laugh. It was unrestrained and irresistible. He recalled that the weather was glorious that night. A perfect spring evening. All the way downtown the four of them were joking and having a great time.

The train pulled into Times Square and they climbed the stairs to the street. They were at what is no longer called "The Crossroads of the World." Bright lights, the roads clogged with traffic and, since the weather was so mild, crowds of people so thick it was difficult for the two couples to walk together. Since he was the one who knew where the restaurant was, he and Jane led the way. He knew the place was on Seventh Avenue and Forty Sixth Street and they made a beeline for it. As was her habit, Jane put her arm around his shoulder as they walked, and having this lovely creature signifying in this way that he was her man never failed to fill his whole being with joy. He might have only been sixteen, but at moments like that he knew it would be heavenly to be married to this wonderful girl. Up ahead on the next block he could see the bright neon sign that read Child's and he pointed it out to Jane, and to Sacky and Honey, who were walking right behind them. He laughed as he recalled turning around and saying to them all at that time "I think we're gonna hear some great music."

They got to Child's and walked in. There was a man in a tuxedo standing at the head of two escalators—one down and one up. Behind him in there was a large bustling room where people were dining. He didn't see any stage, or piano, or anything that would have suggested that the jazz would be in this main dining room so he assumed that the music was downstairs. Why *else* would there be these escalators? He shook his head and chuckled to himself as he recalled saying to the man; "any room down there?" And he could still hear the man's reply: "plenty of room." He turned to Jane, Honey, and Howie and said triumphantly: "let's go"— as he gallantly waved them on to the down escalator before he stepped onto it himself. When they got to the bottom what they saw was the men's room and the ladies room. That was it. He stood there in shock and embarrassment. Of course they got onto the other escalator and went back up to the dining room. His face was red as he asked the man in the tuxedo: "don't you have jazz here?" "Oh, you want our Fifty Eighth Street restaurant, Child's Paramount. It's on Fifty Eighth and Broadway." He was smiling now as he recalled this but he was mortified back then.

All the way on the walk to the Child's on Fifty Eighth they were kidding him repeating; "any room down there?" And laughing uproariously —and he was laughing too. But he couldn't help feeling really embarrassed. They reached Child's, walked in, and another man in a tuxedo asked him: "do you have a reservation?" Of course, being sixteen and unaccustomed to going to a jazz club or to *any* club, he hadn't thought to make a reservation. At either of the Child's. He was grateful that the man saw how surprised he was at this turn of events, and how let down the whole party appeared to be, that he took pity on them. He checked their ID's, and because they were minors they didn't get a wrist bracelet, which meant they couldn't order any alcoholic beverages. It had just occurred to him—all these years later—that the man must have been a romantic because he led them to a nice table in a corner. Romantic as he may have been he still slyly tapped John on his trouser pocket as a signal to tip him. John gave him a fiver which did make him feel grown up. Of course, he was still really embarrassed at what had happened regarding the escalator to the bathrooms. His embarrassment lasted all through the burgers, fries, cokes, and the music. Jane acted as if nothing unusual had happened and really enjoyed the evening and the music, as did Honey and Howie, which made him feel somewhat better. Until the train ride home.

He felt it coming on around 125th Street. Just as the train pulled into the 135th Street station he bolted up out of his seat saying; "I'm gonna be sick"— and with Jane right behind him threw up all over the platform. Because it was all so sudden, Howie and Honey, taken by surprise, were still on the train and so continued on home.

This was the capper. Or, as he always thought of it, the crapper. He was now officially doubly mortified and no amount of Jane's assurances that it "could happen to anyone," etc. etc. could make him feel better. Still, she put her arm through his as they walked up the platform away from the sick and waited for the next train. He wished he could crawl into a hole and hide. He was so embarrassed at the evening's mishaps that he couldn't bring himself to call her the whole week-end. Indeed, the way he felt the possibility existed that he might have never called her again. Sunday night *she* finally called *him*. He could still hear her words as if it were yesterday.

"Johnny, why haven't I heard from you?"

He laughed. Thinking of Jane saying that always, *always* made him laugh.

James

and Lacey had lunch together, mostly at the auto-café, for the next few days and though he could see she still hadn't gotten her appetite back she said she felt great and was finally over her illness. They made the plan to get together with his father early the next week. There was a good game Thursday. Mostly, they exchanged loving glances and smiles as their paths crossed during the rest of the day.

#

John was nearing the end of his shift in the diner where he washed dishes—and he was coughing and trying hard to stifle his coughs. As happy as he was for his son, and looking forward to soon be meeting Lacey, he had become conflicted, and saddened by what he'd done a few nights before. Still, the gun in his coat pocket was now going with him wherever he went. Life had become humiliating enough and he didn't want to get taken advantage of again. But, he had to somehow get another clip or two —and he knew it would be a problem. Of course, he never saw anything on FAIR News about the massacre. *That's what it was John.* A Socee on Socee massacre, and as he had figured, who gave a shit about that? Not FAIR. For days the night's movie had been playing on an endless loop inside his head. *The freaky thing is that it played out almost exactly as I visualized it on the train going there. I saw how it was going to go down over and over in my head and that's how it went. You always did go on about visualization Jane. Maybe I should start visualizing a better life.* He let out a short laugh. *Yeah… that'll work.*

# # #

By now, just as Alexandra Winstead suspec—no, *knew* he would do, Arthur Winstead, the head of domestic security for The United Oligarchy's sector one, had indeed looked at all the TV holo-vids of everyone who worked in the messenger office where his daughter was on her first field trial. He'd checked those as well as all the security cameras in the Financial District. He was quite aware there was a *possibility*, as yet unconfirmed, by the TV holo-vids that James' father posed a threat, and that he could *possibly* be a part of the underground. It was clear that this fellow certainly *hated* FAIR—and the Servers. However, the evidence wasn't as compelling as he thought it would be. He could see the man was angry. He also could see the infatuation that existed between his daughter and the man's son. And, though he fully expected his daughter to carry out her mission, as a prudent man, he nevertheless had to hedge his bet. So, he somehow forgot to alert CyScenSec and, instead, did this scan securely at home on his own.

# # #

Bedloe was navigating the deep, still falling, snow to the el—the same one that had carried him to and from the Klo n Bar. He was going to their M-POW!-r connection. *He can score me a clip.* As he walked he kept telling himself that he was doing this for self-defense. *What I did was an aberration. I snapped. I did something terrible.* In the days that had passed since he gunned down those men the high he'd felt from it had turned into something close to recrimination. *I took a stupid chance. I have a son, and if something happened to me what would James do? I'm going to score another clip, but I hope I'll never have a need to use it again. If my guy can get a clip for this I wonder what it will cost. It's an older piece…probably tough to find. Probably expensive. If he can hook me up I have to go for it.* He opened the C-Coff and took a healthy swig. *Ugh. Shit better help.* And he coughed.

It was a short train ride and, as he carefully descended the litter filled stairs, he reminded himself that this was a dangerous neighborhood. His right hand curled around the gun in his coat pocket. It was still a heavy, reassuring feeling. He knew his last two rounds would be enough for any problem he might encounter. *If it's more than one person I'm certain that the other—others, would run as soon as I put the first—Stop. Stop it! You're just getting another clip as a precaution. That's it. You're not a fucking murderer.* Thankfully, no one was on the streets. He got to the building and pressed the downstairs buzzer. He could hear the voice through the static:

"Y***?"

"It's Straddling Bus."

The buzzer sounded and Bedloe pushed open the heavy door and stepped inside the dimly lit trash-filled, smelly hallway. He began the climb up four flights to his connection's apartment. This time he wasn't there for M-POW!-r. He reached the fourth floor and knocked on his man's door. The peephole slid open and then closed. As was always the case he heard the old door-jammer police lock removed followed by the cacophonic succession of chains being slid open. The door opened just wide enough to allow him to step inside the dark apartment. The man closed and locked the door behind him.

"How many?"

"I'm here for something else. I don't want to spook you. So just know, I'm going to show you a gun that's in my pocket because I want to know if you can get me a clip for it."

Slowly he removed his gun by the barrel and handed it to the man.

"The safety's on."

The man looked at the gun carefully.

"Old huh?"

"It works just fine."

"Browning .45? I cou' geh you a smar' gun."

"Thanks. I appreciate that...But this'll do me just fine."

The man handed the gun back.

"Sui' yourself flaco. Not a lotta these around...a clip'll prolly cost."

"How much?"

"Uh...sixty-five, maybe seventy...an' thass a deal ese."

"When?"

"Umm...Gimmee a week."

"I'll see you in a week. Listen, *just in case* - if I don't show it's only because I need a few more days to put the bucks together. But, I *will* be back to get it. Okay?"

"Okay. It'll be here. Yo...I wan' you ta know I don' do this for jus' anyone...comprende?"

"Comprendo. Thanks man."

"So you wan' any juice?

"Not this time...thanks again."

He turned to leave. The man unlocked the door and closed it behind him. Bedloe heard the now familiar symphony of bolts and chains as he began his walk down the flights careful to avoid the garbage. *Ahh...the ever barking dog and the always howling baby...The garlic and onions frying in rancid oil...How did I miss them when I walked up. That's how fucked up I am. Man...*

It was now snaining as he made his way back to the train that would take him home; *it'll be seventy. I'll set seven bucks aside each day for ten days —that'll swing it.* He shook his head. *John, it was an aberration! Okay?* He then continued gingerly to his train.

#

Their place was dark inside. No lights on inside was a bit unusual. *The kid's with his new girl? Man, I am so glad she's back.* He let himself in and took off his coat and boots. *Johnny…how about a nice cup of virtual coffee- with a K? At least I don't have to see or hear FAIR. It's nice to have a little alone time. Enjoy it—the kid'll be home soon and the TV will go on.*

Just then the TV turned *itself* on. It was the ubiquitous Kaw-Fee commercial featuring Caw-Fee the Krow. "Caw, Caw Kaw-Fee, It's virtual—"

"FUCK YOU! FUCK YOU! YOU FUCKING…"

Once again he fairly leapt for the remote and turned the TV off almost as soon as it turned itself on.

"You fucking brain-dead robot motherfuckers!"

He took another swig of the cough medicine and sat sipping his Kaw-Fee. All he could think about was what he did a few nights before — but he was now seeing it in a different light—and it was harsh. *Did any of those men have wives? Children? They were young…probably in their twenties. They maybe had parents. Loved ones. Jane, you know…Did I have the right to be their judge and jury? Wait a minute… I was wronged…Me…They attacked me. But…did they deserve to be killed?* The trade-off; some cough medicine for a life—for five lives—now seemed far from a fair one. *Their lousy luck came up against mine and they pushed the wrong button of the wrong person.* All the rage he'd bottled up for so long had come spilling out with that medicine. *They just happened to be at the end of my last straw. Now I'm sitting in a cold broken down mobile home in a run-down neighborhood in the Bronx, a murderer — without you. Was what I did uncalled for?* He felt himself disintegrating. After some while he clicked on the TV to see the time. 6:55—and then he clicked it off. *He's probably with Lacey. This can't be another incident. Don't freak, he's just a little late. He's with her. God, I hope she's for real. Please let her be real…It's…It's crazy but…she could save him… Save us.*

###

They had indeed lingered over their "coffee" because besides both of them being oblivious of the time, and the fact that they were in love and enjoyed each other's company, maybe it had something to do with neither of them wanting to go home. James, who, consciously, or unconsciously, needed some respite from his father's ranting and coughing…and preaching…and Alex-aka Lacey, because she knew that her father could see right through her.

Bedloe

had sat up for hours waiting for James and hoping his son was with Lacey. When the boy finally showed up John was over-the-top relieved to see him. It actually made James feel a bit guilty about staying out so late. Explaining that he was with Lacey really made John happy. As happy anyway as John could get.

Now John was on the train acting on an urge to go further uptown to the neighborhood he grew up in. He suspected it wouldn't amount to much but it was such a great neighborhood maybe it was still pretty nice. *I can't be hoping for some kind of time machine that will transport me back to what I know was a far better time. I don't know...Maybe being on those streets can make me feel better. It's been twenty five years.*

He'd grown up in a neighborhood of six square blocks bordered on three sides by parks. He'd spent the first nineteen years of his life there. Everybody knew everybody. When he grew up he had ten mothers on each and every one of those blocks. In the winter the women of each block got together and played canasta and mah jongg. In the summer they sat out front of their six story apartment buildings in beach chairs, knitting, gossiping, sharing watermelon, and the lemonade and iced tea they'd made and, in general, just keeping an eye out. And, woe was you if you did something bad because your mother had already heard about it and confronted you with it the *second* you walked through the door. *And*, if something bad happened *to* you—a fall, or whatever, they immediately sprang to help you before you even *got* to your mother. He remembered the time when Donny Cale threw a stick at him and its pointed end caused a one inch gash on his cheek. It was bleeding profusely, and as quickly as it had happened, their next door neighbor in apt 3J—Mrs. Goldfarb—had rushed upstairs and rushed back to him to apply the alum she'd grabbed from her medicine chest. It burned like hell, but it stanched the blood flow. He liked that he still had the scar to remind him.

In his old childhood neighborhood no one locked their door because everyone trusted everyone else. You went to the bakery to buy a dozen of anything and if you didn't have enough money you'd ask the counter person to "trust" you they'd say "sure." They knew you, they knew your parents, and they trusted you to come back tomorrow, or the day after, to pay them. *What a drag that my son will never have that experience.*

The kids in the neighborhood all knew each other. They went to the same public school: kindergarten right up through high school—only separating when they each went off to college. They played in the same streets, in the same schoolyard, and on teams that represented the different blocks they lived on. He played football on the Rockets. Money being a little tight only a few of them had shoulder pads—and a few had helmets. He wished he had one—and a face mask— the day he broke his nose. Or, to be more precise, the day Gerry Katz's "flying" tackle broke it for him. And when he was fourteen he played third base for Louis Barber shop. And like all kids they competed for bragging rights in the friendliest of ways. He, like many of them, was a delivery boy, and a soda jerk, and a busboy/waiter for the businesses in the neighborhood. So, they all had some pocket money for the movies, a rack of pool, a pizza, and whatever. On his way uptown he was thinking about all these childhood memories... the time he watched he and his best friend Sacky's favorite big league team win the pennant on the last day of the season after being *thirteen and a half games out* with a month to go. He ran giddily down the block to Sacky's apartment, which was on the ground floor, and knocked so forcefully on the window that he broke it. Big Moe, his friend's father, who was also one of the neighborhood scoutmasters, just pooh-poohed it.

And then there was the magical way every kid in the neighborhood automatically knew when it was the season for marbles, or card flipping, or stickball...because there *were* seasons, and we *all* knew when one season was done and another was upon us - as if we were all linked by one divine consciousness. On week-ends getting to the schoolyard by seven AM so he could be in the first softball game. He treasured the memories of the years spent growing up in that wondrous place. There were two movie theaters in the neighborhood and one of them was this throw-back vintage movie theater called The Globe, and every Saturday beginning when they were about nine or ten and continuing on until they were seniors in high school they would all go there in the afternoon. Boys and girls, and they'd all sit together. When he and Jane met she joined them. It was half the price of all the other movie theaters, three dollars, and there would be three or four cartoons and then two features. And, you could come in any time, even in the middle of a movie, which he knew was where the expression "this is where I came in" came from. That thought begat a rare smile—however small, however rueful. "This is where I came in," an expression whose derivation was now lost in the passage of the years—along with so much more now sadly lost in that same stormy passage. There was the "big" rock in the park where they played hide-and-go-seek when they were in grade school but was, when they passed it on the way to high school, not so "big." And the other rock, opposite the grade school yard, on which they played "king of the rock." And the corners where they hung out. And the stores; Max's candy store and luncheonette, where they lingered over a coke and checked out all the magazines and comic books—and Max or Trudy never chased them. And the two supermarkets in the neighborhood—though his mother preferred they shop in the remaining mom and pop stores. The Diamond bakery, Marty's butcher shop, Yoshky's dairy, Falco's fruit and vegetable store, Ray's hardware. And every proprietor in each of those stores, and all their help, knew you by name—and you knew theirs. He had also worked for many of these stores. He delivered prescriptions for Sal and Ben's Pharmacy, delivered groceries for Yoshky's, jerked sodas at Max's and C & R's Luncheonette, and peeled potatoes at Sonny's Delicatessen.

And then there were all the other places that he and Jane had frequented. The other movie theater, The Pelham, where they went to see *Match Point* on that first date, and where they went many more times after that...and Sterling pizza where they first had pizza together. She said that Sterling had ruined pizza for her because no pizza ever tasted as good again. The days he walked her home from high school, and the nights they kissed in her hallway before she had to go in.

And the park that ran the length of the neighborhood and kept on going way, way up and where on so many of its benches they would sit for hours and talk...and plan...and invariably neck... Back then, when it only snowed in the winter, they would belly-flop down Brady Avenue which had the steepest hill in the neighborhood. And, though the hill ran through an intersection at Wallace Avenue, they worked out a system in which they took turns holding any traffic that might have caused a serious accident. There never was one—and nobody minded the delay.

He smiled again, this time broadly and nostalgically, remembering the day when he was about ten and Ronnie Cogan clanged into a lamppost when he looked up distracted because his mother had called him to dinner from their window on the third floor. *The clanging sound was because he knocked out a front tooth—and all us boys were doubled over howling with laughter*. He realized he hadn't heard a kid laugh in years. Nor had he himself laughed at anything that occurred in the present. At least not when sober.

He was being drawn back to this most dear place of his childhood. Could being there again, walking down its streets, somehow magically transport him back to that sweet untroubled, unburdened time? Would he somehow feel what it felt like to have the hope of youth again? Would he have a future again? Feel free again? What was he expecting to find on those innocent streets of his youth? Could his childhood Shangri-La melt away all the indignities, the anger, the despair he now felt? Of course he knew the answers to these questions. Still, he was aware that he was being ineluctably drawn back to these streets because they represented the carefree happiness of youth, and on a subconscious level the glimmer of hope that walking these streets again might offer him some small measure of comfort. He was also curious to see what they looked like now.

He stood at the train window looking down on the passing snowy Bronx streets, seeing the years rolling back as the train carried him back in time. As the train approached his childhood station he saw the schools he went to. There, in the distance, was P.S. 86, the middle school he attended before high school from the age of twelve to thirteen. Now below him up Brady Avenue, P.S. 105, the public school he went to from kindergarten to the sixth grade, and its schoolyard—the one he played in, now shockingly overgrown with weeds. *There's a cross on its roof?* He had to laugh though, because the cross was in almost the exact spot on the roof ledge where Moose had parked a colossal home run some thirty five years back in time. He almost said "unbelievable." From up above, the main street, Lydig Avenue, had looked the same as the train pulled into the station. He got off at the stop he had gotten on and off of so often for so many years before and made his way down the old slippery metal stairway to the street. Had he not seen all the people laying in the doorways because he was distracted by seeing the cross? Now, he saw the people begging in the street. The rotting garbage piled high. The gamboling rats. *They look like they eat better than us.* All the stores with "for rent" signs. What was he looking at if not something that no longer existed—save for in his mind?

What glimmer of hope? *What* melting away all the indignities? What was he even *thinking*? These already answered questions now had no reason to even be posed. *Question is the answer Johnny boy. Don't ever ask if you don't ever want to know.* He knew this long before the expression "garbage in, garbage out." And now, besides taking everything else, they had taken all the questions away from him. Now there were only terrible answers and the questions were meaningless. *Along with whatever else had been meaningful to me they had also stripped me of my philosophy. These people who never look inward, whose philosophy is power and nothing more...* It was unbearable. *My idealistic young world has completely vanished in the span of some thirty five years. Go home old man. Old man...Forty eight...I feel like eighty eight. I must—I am crazy to have come up here.* He returned to the slippery ancient metal el stairs and slowly climbed upward. *I'm an Associate. I'm a disassociated Associate.* That *almost* made him laugh. Almost. Instead, he suddenly started to cough violently.

Alex

knew it was impossible not to engage with her father at home. She knew he would be questioning her about her assignment any day now and she also knew it would be impossible to try and avoid the conversation. Conversely, the best approach would be to go to him immediately, before he summoned her, and reassure him that she could carry out the job he had tasked her with. She took the first opportunity she had to do this.

Her father waved her in when she appeared at the door of his office and gestured she should sit while he finished what he was doing. She sat there for the minute it took for him to turn his attention to her hoping she would say what she had to in the right way. While she believed the Bismarck quote "when you want to fool the world, tell the truth" held true for most people, she knew that in her father's case it was tell the truth or else. That only her truth would do. What also factored into this decision was the knowledge that her father could A. smell a lie a mile off, and B. no doubt already knew the truth. She decided she would speak plainly.

"Father...do you think I would be crazy to marry an Associate?"

He stared at her while turning this absurd question over in his mind. After about fifteen seconds, during which she never took a breath, he responded.

"You want me to tell you how terrible your life would become…don't you?"

"Well, wouldn't it be?"

"Alex, as much as I might like to - *We*…might like to…fix things, it's just too late."

"It's not right father."

Now he turned how he should respond to *this* over in his mind.

"Okay…Alex…Sweetheart, let's say we wanted to, shall we say, level the playing field. It would take at the very least a generation of education to get people up to speed—"

"The internet educates people very quickly."

"As fast as the internet might do that, in the time and money that it would take, too many problems would arise that there would be no resources to combat."

"Why can't Associates get the services their taxes could pay for? Daddy… I know there's more than enough money in the world to do this."

"Alex…you are…you are noble. You're right…and if it were day one and we were at the beginning we could do it your way. I would want that also. But we aren't. It's too late. You know the expression: power tends to corrupt, absolute power corrupts absolutely."

"Are you saying that we are corrupt?"

He studied his wonderful daughter. It was a strange feeling to be challenged this way and even more strange was that he was actually proud of her.

"No Alex, no. We are not corrupt. We are servants of the law."

"Shouldn't some laws be changed then?"

"I suppose they should but..." His gesture was the universal sign for resignation.

"But it's too late." She stared at him.

He nodded. They sat looking at each other.

"You're in love with this boy?"

"Yes."

"Even though his father is most likely a criminal and a prime candidate to join the underground? Maybe even be an underground leader?"

"He's just a protestor."

"Who has expressed some disturbing ideas."

"Words father. Just words."

"So what do we do...wait until he shoots one of us?"

"Due respect, is it alright if he shoots one of *them*?"

"Of course it isn't. Alex, this seems very painful for you. Would you prefer I take you off of this?"

Now, it was her turn to ponder what she really wanted...because whatever it was she knew her father would make it happen.

"Alex?"

If I ask to be removed they won't allow me to see him anymore for fear I might warn them and John would escape to the underground. And that would disgrace my father.

"Father, I can see this through."

"Can—or will?"

"Both."

"To be with James as long as you can."

Of course he knows his name. "Yes."

"I can understand Alex. You know I love you dearly—and I only want your life to be free of want. You're sixteen…there will be other boys…One will be the one for you. You'll see. I promise that's how it is. The way you feel now…this too shall pass."

She listened to him and knew that, even as he believed what he was saying, none of it was true. None of it meant anything to her. None of it was how it was going to be. She would do this thing which would destroy the boy she wanted a life with. The ache she felt, the guilt, it was as if there was a hole in her center as large as the Universe itself. What she felt building up for the last month was now fully formed; an inescapable black hole of emptiness. She rose and turned to leave. She may have known the Bismarck quote; but had she the advantage of any factual world history at her disposal she might have been aware that her burgeoning feelings regarding the plight of the Socees could be likened to Benjamin Netanyahu's daughter being sympathetic to the plight of the Palestinians.

"Alexandra, I'm fairly certain I don't have to say this, but I would be derelict if I didn't—

I won't, Father. Don't worry.

"If you warn him it will go badly for us."

"Father, I could never do something so selfish."

She left his office, went up to her room, and lay curled up on her bed in a fetal position, sobbing.

"Lacey,

what's wrong sweetheart?"

They were in the auto-café after work. This afternoon, whenever James saw her going in or out, she didn't look like herself. The smile seemed forced. Though he could tell that she still was happy to see him, be with him, he sensed that something was off with her. They already possessed that ESP that all well-matched couples developed over a period of time.

"So…are you gonna tell me what the matter is?"

I have to get out of myself. At least try to enjoy these days with him. It isn't fair to make him worry about me. Say something. Anything. Just get him off of worrying about you.

"It's…my mom is sick."

"Oh, sweetheart…I'm so sorry."

"It'll be alright—*Give him a bright side*—the building he works at has taken up a collection and we can afford the medical care she needs."

"Can I ask…what it is?"

"Shingles—*Just get off this*—It's just that sometimes she's in such pain that it affects me terribly. But she's getting treatment and she'll be better soon." *But I won't be.* She smiled.

"I'm sorry I've been such terrible company lately."

She felt love and concern for him and her smile was warm and genuine. Seeing her smile reassured him that everything with her mother would be alright.

"What about your father…How is his cough?"

"It's getting worse. I still can't believe that a public clinic can cost so much."

"I can't either. It's criminally unfair."

"Like we're supposed to have two hundred and fifty dollars. I wish he worked in a place like your father does."

"I know. I do too." *I really do.* She reached across the table for his hand.

"Anyway, I can't wait to meet him tomorrow night."

"He's looking forward to it. I've told him all about you."

Oh, James, I wish you could know all about me too. She felt sorry for the life James and his father had to endure and was aware that she would soon know what home life as a Socee was like. Was it as bad as she believed it was? Going to where James lived would tell her a lot.

"James…let me help. Please."

"Say a prayer for him every night."

"I will." *If only that would help. Sixteen…the gene for stubborn male pride must be present at birth.*

# # #

She was on her way home almost certain James' father wouldn't be in the Socee underground. She knew she would be expected to find out if his father *knew* of the Socee underground, and she hoped that John didn't. Even in this hope she was conflicted. If he did, and somehow decided out of the blue to join them, she might possibly be blamed—even though there could be no evidence of her having a part in this. She also had to remind herself that her father would be blamed for his poor judgement in choosing his own daughter for this job. As it stood, there was still a chance that James' father's words would be seen as harmless. A small chance perhaps but still a possibility. And, if it did turn out that James' father *was* a legitimate danger to the government, he'd be arrested, disappeared, and his son would be crushed. There would be no returning from a political arrest. She—they, were damned in any event. The only hope she had for James' sake was that his father was only about some idle words and maybe it could somehow be smoothed over. *Please, let it be so.* Whatever his father's fate was, her love for his son was doomed.

#

As usual the diner was busy. Dishes were coming in as fast as he could get them out. During his entire shift all Bedloe could think about was that tomorrow night he would be meeting this girl Lacey. They had straightened out their home as best they could trying to make everything as neat and clean as possible. Off of what his son had told him she sounded perfect, and he couldn't help but again wonder if the boy hadn't found his own Jane. That would be all he could ask for. Now, on top of all the other things gnawing away at his psyche, he felt as if he was betraying Jane's memory by finally admitting to himself that he would welcome a female presence in his life—however long he chose to continue to endure his life. He still hadn't completely discarded the notion of suicide if his son had indeed found a life partner. Of course, he would wait a year or two to see if James and Lacey were truly a loving couple. He would only either take himself out, or take his gun to the underground, if he was certain that together they could afford to keep the mobile home and pay the monthly. From what he gathered she didn't seem to be someone flighty or trendy or

any of that stuff, but a well-grounded person with a good mind. He hoped
that the boy's assessment was on the nose. His son had intimated that
she might agree with some of his own positions regarding the inherent
unfairness of the system…that her father held some of the same opinions
and grievances that he did. Which reminded him—he had to reinforce his
admonishment to James about saying things he shouldn't to *anyone*—not
until he was one hundred and ten per cent certain that the person could
be trusted. Lacey was probably one such person, but he had to make sure
that James did not say anything further about his thoughts regarding the
government to *anyone* else. It was dangerous and almost anyone would turn
around and collect a few bucks for turning him in. He'd heard stories about
small rewards being given to people who, overhearing someone utter the
slightest disparaging word about the leadership, turned them in. And even
for a *small* reward! Ten dollars small. And, there were too many Socees who
would do such a thing for, what now, *wouldn't* be considered a pittance.
People needed every dollar they could lay their hands on to pay the rent,
put food on the table. Those basic necessities were justification enough to
act in such a way. The overwhelming odds were that she was not such a
person so he wasn't really that worried. This will be interesting he thought
and, despite thinking of himself as nervous as a hermit expecting company,
he was actually looking forward to meeting this Lacey girl. A game, a little
sip—a *very* little sip—some good talk—what could be bad? He wanted to
pick up some M-POW!-r that evening but his boss had asked him to work
late. *I'll do it tomorrow after work.* He figured his connection had already
laid out the money for the clip and, if he wanted the M, he would have to
explain about needing more time to get the seventy together. Now, part of
him regretted even ordering the clip.

# # #

Lacey had been going over the way she would go about tomorrow's
meeting for days. *I have to let him talk. Certainly during the game and it'll all
be on camera. I feel sick.* Since James had said that his father had little or no
reservations about speaking his truth, she was dreading seeing him hang
himself. And she being the catalyst. James had mentioned that he and his

father had a connection for M-POW!-r and like to, as he put it, "throw back a few" and watch cartoons, so the M-POW!-r she was bringing could turn out to be the loaded weapon. *I have to bring him M- POW!-r. If I didn't, CyScenSec would wonder why I'd overlooked such an obvious play.* Whatever the outcome was going to be, she dreaded the upcoming evening. *This could be one horrible party.* She was trying unsuccessfully to cast aside any pre-conceived notions that James may have led her to harbor. *He could be harmless. But, maybe not. Please don't let his father be an enemy of the state... Oh God, if you ever had an ounce of mercy...* Still she reminded herself that this was her career. A thought that was becoming less and less attractive with each passing day. *But it is Alex...It is.* And if she wanted to do her job and make her father proud she had to be thoroughly professional. Objectivity. Look, listen, stay in tune. *As difficult as it's going to be...*From what James had said she knew he was an intelligent man capable of sharp observation so she could not throw off *any* false signals. No missteps. Not to his father but, even more importantly, not to the watchers. If he was a danger to the system she needed to make the case. But only *if* he was. She unenthusiastically requisitioned two four-paks of M. *Please let him turn out to be harmless. Please...for James' sake.*

On

the train coming uptown after his shift at the diner Bedloe was hoping his man would be home. He was also hoping his man wouldn't be pissed off that he didn't as yet have the money for the clip. He did, however, have just enough cash to pick up a four-pak of M-POW!-r, and maybe that would help in the matter. This was going to be a big night. He couldn't wait to check out this girl Lacey that his son was nuts about. Could she be anything like Jane? *That would be close to impossible. Just let her be sweet...sincere... someone who truly cared for him. That would be enough.* The train reached his station and he got off. He gripped the railing tightly as he walked carefully down the stairs to the street. He plodded through the dirty snow to his connection's building. He was glad that, except for the random person walking here and there, the fact that it was cold and icy kept the streets pretty much devoid of people. The snow covered garbage had created walls that people had to climb over. It didn't help the walking in this neighborhood, his neighborhood, or *any* of the poorer neighborhoods. This particular neighborhood was a dangerous one and his hand gripped the gun in his pocket. He reached his man's building and rang the downstairs bell. After a short while he heard the man's static covered, but still unmistakable, voice on the intercom:

"W*** Th***"?

"It's Straddling Bus."

The buzzer croaked and, as he had done so many times before, he pushed open the heavy door and stepped inside the dimly lit hallway. He looked around, took out his money and counted out enough for a four-pak. He began the climb up four flights to his connection's apartment. The trash still had not been cleaned from the stairs or the hallways. It fairly reeked. The baby was howling and the dog was howling along with it. *If I had to live in this building I might have already killed myself.* He reached the fourth floor and knocked on his man's door. As always, the peephole slid open and then closed. Then the door-jammer police lock was removed followed by the symphony of chains being slid open. The door opened just wide enough to allow him to step inside the dark apartment and just as immediately closed behind him. All the chains were then slid back into place.

"Stay here, I got your clip."

He started to walk down his hallway.

"Wait…wait…I uh…I don't have the money yet."

The man turned, came back, stared at him for a second and then pushed him forcefully up against the wall.

"You fuckin' kiddin' me?"

He had gone over this in his mind on the train. Whether to just tell the man the truth or not.

"I had to spend the money on doing our laundry…and medicine."

"What?"

"I'm giving you the respect of not lying to you about why I don't have your money."

"Respect? Dat shit don' gonna pay my rent muthafucka."

"I prolly should've just lied to your face—yeah?" The man stared at him.

"The fuckin' laundry?"

"I'm still gonna get you your money."

"Damn righ' you are."

"Can you let go of my throat? Please."

After a few seconds in which the man stared at John he relaxed his grip on John's neck but still kept him pinned.

"I heard a lotta reasons someone don' have what they owe. Laundry's a new one."

"Like I said I could've lied. Look, I will get you your money. I promise. I had it…I'll have it again."

"I fronted this fuckin' money for you because I like you. I trusted you."

"I know. I had to buy medicine. And I was mugged. On the train… and they broke it. The medicine. Look, I'm…I'm gonna ask you something crazy."

The man stared at him debating whether or not to punch him in the stomach.

"Let me have the clip so it can't happen again and I promise I'll be here in three weeks with the money."

"Now you *are* fuckin' kiddin'." He made a fist and drew his arm back.

"I used the two clips I had outside a bar dropping the five guys who did it."

The man stopped and stared at John. His eyes narrowed as he kept staring at him.

"Tha' was you?"

John hoped he would have heard about it.

"You heard about that?"

"Uh...Yeah!" Five bodies layin' in the street? The Klown?"

"The same. I only got two rounds left"

After a few seconds he dropped his arm, relaxed his grip, and let John move away from the wall. "You some piece-a work huh flaco?"

"I used to be."

The man shook his head and laughed wryly.

"Not too many speakin' truth these days."

"You know what...it feels...I feel a whole lot lighter."

"Been carryin' it around?"

John nodded.

"Feels good tellin' someone?"

"Confession."

"Yeah...confession."

"Better to me than to your kid."

Again, John nodded.

"I have enough for a four-pak."

The man laughed again.

"You got big balls ése...I'll gi' you dat. But I'm cuttin' you off—and this here's goin' to interes' on your debt."

He took John's cash out of his hand.

"Will you trust me for the clip?"

"You mean I shou' let you have it?"

John's gaze was steady. His connection stood there...staring back at him. Then the man turned, went back into the dark and after maybe thirty seconds returned with a brown bag. In it was the clip.

"Tree weeks righ'? Don' make me a fool."

John shoved the clip into his pocket.

"I'll be here. Thanks."

The man nodded, went to the door and undid all the chains. He opened it and as he let John out:

"I figured dose guys did somethin' to someone."

His smile was brief.

"See you in three weeks."

He closed the door behind John who started walking down the stairs. *I'm glad I told him I still had two rounds left. This is his neighborhood...He knew there were twelve rounds in those guys so I had to have had two clips, fourteen rounds...So he knew I probably had two rounds left.* As he began to plow through the snow to the el he was thinking how sometimes people can still surprise you. The rest of the way uptown was spent looking forward to meeting the girl he hoped was the real thing.

She

had put her left arm over James' shoulder on the way to the train, and whenever she did that he loved the feeling it gave him that she was making him her possession. His father had once told him that his mother would do that also and he considered this to be a very good omen. Now, on the train uptown she sat very close to him. He could feel the heat coming from her left side. Feel her left breast against his right bicep. He was openly thrilled and she was doing her best to hide her shock at what she was seeing. This was the first time in her life she had ever traveled so far north on one of these ancient trains surrounded by Socees. Now, she saw the missing teeth, the shaking hands, the raving out loud, the coughing and sneezing. More than shocked, she was appalled. He had taken her hand when they sat and despite the distress she was witness to she still kept it together. Better even than her word she had met him carrying a large bag; the four cans of park pigeon soup, and two four-paks of M-POW!-r. *And,* she told him she had a surprise for them. *She is amazing! She's the surprise.*

He was as high as the moon. By the time the train reached the West Farms Square station she was back to enjoying just being with the boy she loved, and they clambered giddily down the ancient trash-strewn stairs to the street. There was no one on the street. Now, she was stunned at the state of the street they were walking, rather slogging, through. This little trip to another world was an eye-opener for her to be sure. The slush was ankle deep and the trash was piled chest high. Still, on that short walk to his home she stopped, turned to him, and they kissed passionately. *Oh James...I love you. Forgive me. Forgive me.* Taking her by her hand he led her as they fairly skipped through the slush and over the wet garbage walls all the way to the junkyard and up to the mobile home, both out-of-breath and giggling. She kissed him again. His feet were soaked and he couldn't have cared less. Once inside he took her coat, bade her sit, and headed for the rear to lay her coat on his bed.

"Have a seat."

"I will—*No one should have to live like this. And it's freezing cold. No wonder his father has a bad cough*—but you have to give me the tour."

He stopped and turned to her.

"This is it...There's really not much more to see."

"I want to see where you sleep."

He never imagined he could feel the way he now felt as he led her back to his single bed. "I guess it's not much."

He carefully laid her coat down on his bed.

"Is this one yours?"

He nodded "yes." She stood looking at his bed. She moved her coat to the foot of the bed and then slowly lay back on it. All she wanted to know was this exact moment they were alive. No past, no future. Now. Only now. She was determined to be as close to him as she could while she could. With outstretched arms she motioned for him to come on top of her. He gently lowered himself onto her and they kissed. He was lost in her...in her soft lips, her sweet hair, her loving arms...lost. She was moaning softly, almost as lost as he was. After about a minute or so:

"James...love...we'd better get up now or else we'll never get up."

Reluctantly, but realizing she was right, he lifted himself up, reached down and pulled her up to him and together they headed for the front.

"Would you mind terribly if...if I changed my socks? My feet are soaked. I haffta get new boots."

"Of course I don't mind. Let me help you...sit down."

He lowered the seat on the toilet and did as she asked. She unlaced his boots and pulled off his socks. *He's wearing boots with holes in them. Oh, James...*

"Do you have a towel?"

"In the bathroom - over there."

She went to the bathroom—*this is their...it's—I don't know, four by eight?*—and returned with the dry socks he'd hung on the towel bar, and the towel, and dried his feet as if she were his handmaiden. He couldn't believe she would do this.

"I think I love you."

He heard himself saying the words as they rushed out of his mouth. She looked up and smiled at him, her eyes were misting.

"And I love you, James. Very much. Always remember that."

This was more than he could have ever hoped for. They *would* be married. His dream come true. Hand-in-hand they went back up to the front. *They'll wonder if the TV's not on.*

"Shall I put the TV on?" *Shall I? Alex, should. Should! CyScenSec could interpret that as you're trying to tip them.*

"Sure."

She pressed the remote and the TV came to life. It was on to one of the FAIR news stations.

"I wish we had something I could offer you…a beer…Hey, let's put your M-POW!-r outside in the snow."

"In the snow?"

"It's our fridge."

"What a brilliant idea!"

He put the four-paks in the snow next to the stick they used as a signal that there was something in their "fridge." Eight cans! This was gonna be a par-tay. The clock in the corner of the TV read 8:14 PM. *He said he'd be late but...* He hoped his father would be home in time for some soup and the game - which didn't start until nine thirty. Still, all was right with the world. The local news was reporting that the promised street cleaning of trash piled high beneath the snow would be happening in a matter of days. FAIR then switched to Chairman Jeffers who was speaking to the country regarding the ongoing threat of an invasion by Canada. Specifically about the need for beefed-up forces along the Canadian-American border. He and Lacey held hands as he watched intently. He turned to her.

"Wow…Canada. Who'da thunk it? You know. I was thinking about joining up but…"

"*But* is right…You're not joining anything. I would die if anything happened to you!"

This emotion actually took her by surprise. She kissed him on the cheek.

They heard his father cough outside the front door. Lacey felt a tingle of excitement—or was it a twinge of fear—run through her body as John opened the door. James couldn't wait for his father's reaction at meeting his sweetheart.

"The flag was up. When did you get two four-paks?"

"Lacey brought them as a gift for us. And four cans of park pigeon soup. And a surprise."

"Soup *and* a surprise…That's…It's very thoughtful. Thank you."

"Pop, this is Lacey. Lacey, this is my dad, John."

Lacey held out both hands as she rose to greet him. Holding out her hands she stepped forward to him. All he could think was; what a lovely smile…And those eyes!

"Your son told me what a devoted father he has. I am so very glad to meet you at last." He took her hands in his.

"John, give me your coat. I'll warm up some soup and I want you to wash up and then come sit with us and we'll all have a nice bowl. It's the best park pigeon soup I could find."

He let her take his coat and she took it to the rear and laid it on James' bed. John proceeded to do as she asked—and as he went back to the tiny bathroom he was thinking that it gave him a long forgotten pleasant feeling to be asked to wash for dinner by a female. *There's such kindness in her voice. Comforting. Warm.* As he returned to the front he heard sizzling and smelled something very familiar.

"Sausage?"

"I got three sausages at WWB. I thought we'd have them with the soup."

"Huh, Pop? Huh?"

Holy… That's twenty five bucks worth of sausage!

"Well, I am really going to enjoy this. Thanks again, Lacey." *I guess you can do it if you don't pay rent. Still…*

It was nice to smell sizzling sausage outside of the diner. She fished them from the bottom of the pot, set them aside, and opened two of the large cans into the pot to begin heating the soup.

"James. I'm putting two more cans of soup on the shelf for another time, yes? Will you please set out some plates, bowls, and utensils?"

James got three small plates, two bowls and a cup from the shelf, set them on the small table, and then rummaged through the drawer for three forks and knives.

"John, please sit, relax…Let's all have a nice meal together. I'm sure it's been a long day."

John sat down. *I like her. She seems kind. And definitely nurturing.* James scrambled to find another thing to sit on. There were only two chairs so he sat on the wood crate they used as a cupboard. On the TV Jeffers was going on about the threat from Canada.

"Lacey, can we please shut the TV off so we can talk. It isn't every day I meet my son's lady friend."

Lacey knew they'd see it was his request. James turned the TV off.

"How come you got home so late?"

"The diner got busy…This soup is good. Which is it?"

"Apex. I figured it's a celebration so…"

"It's very tasty. And this sausage is delicious."

James was really enjoying it. "It sure is hon…We haven't had sausage in forever." Silence as they ate.

"So…Lacey…James said you live down near Chinatown?"

"Her dad used to be a jazz musician."

"Really. And now?"

"He's a doorman at a swanky building on the East side. James tells me you work in a diner not far from here?"

"I wash dishes."

"Chop wood, carry water." *Should I have said that?*

John looked at her. *She's familiar with Zen?*

"How do you come to know that saying?"

"My father always says it when we don't want to do something... essential. Like washing a dish." She smiled. John did also as he took a spoonful of soup. James was on cloud twelve.

"Her mom is a waitress in a corporate dining room."

"Oh? What company?"

"SpiraTec." She knew her story.

"Some executive there gave her a picture of his family as her Christmas gift."

"We burnt it." Followed by a small laugh.

John's brief laugh gave way to a cough into the sleeve of his bent arm. He coughed again.

"Excuse me. I'm sorry kids...I just can't seem to shake this damn cough."

Lacey rose.

"I'll be right back guys. Eat...please."

She went back to James' bed and fished a box out of her coat pocket.

"James, she seems...really terrific. I can see why you like her."

"I still can't get over how lucky I am that we met."

Lacey returned, sat down and took the bottle out of its box.

"James told me you needed this. Here, it'll help. Take a spoonful now.

She poured a spoonful of the cough medicine and held it for John to take.

"It's good stuff. Open wide."

As he did, he experienced a surprising feeling of well-being which almost brought him to tears—it was the nurturing female energy he didn't even know he had missed for so long.

"You bought this too? Thank you, sweetheart."

"We're going to take good care of you, James and me."

"I'm fine, Okay? Fine. Please stop fussing. Let's finish our soup and put on the game." She nodded. *Yes, let's put the TV on.* They went back to enjoying their soup and sausage.

"So…Lacey…James tells me that your father and I might agree on some things?"

"I think so."

"For example?"

"Well… He says we're all pretty much wage slaves."

James looked up from his plate at his father.

"I told you."

"I hope I'm not telling tales out of school, but James told me you call Jeffers jerk-off."

She was on painful, probing auto-pilot. And, she had to continue.

"My father may not use that expression but I know he would agree. Heartily."

He'd never admit it, but that's not such a lie.

John dipped his spoon into his soup. "Well... I don't believe I ever said that...but it *is* clever."

For a split second he stared hard at James who said nothing. Lacey, of course, didn't miss it.

They finished their soup and Lacey took the dishes and the utensils to the small sink to wash them. *Thank goodness he didn't admit to calling Jeff— This water is...a murky tan. Oh God. How can people be expected to live like this?*

"Is there any dish soap?" *Or dishwashing gloves?*

She's going to wash the dishes?

"Hey there, lady, that's my job." John laughed.

"Well...Not tonight sir. Ah, I found it...Where *else* would it be but under the sink? Duh!"

But no gloves. You're a Socee, shut up and do it. As Lacey finished washing the dishes James switched on the TV to one of the twenty-two domestic FAIR channels that would be carrying tonight's BashBall game. It was just starting. *Good, it's on.* She was at the door ready to get the M-POW!-r they'd buried outside in the snow.

"M-POW!-r anyone?"

"You know...I'm just gonna skip the M-POW!-r tonight. I hope nobody minds."

"Pop...she bought it as a gift for you."

She turned immediately and sat back down.

"James, it's okay...It'll keep for another time." She couldn't help feeling disappointed and glad at the same time. While her outward demeanor was calm, her inner conflict was painful.

The game began and the usual violence ensued. She waited for the derogatory comments she hoped she'd hear from John but he sat and watched commenting along with them on some good plays while refraining from his usual put-downs. There were none. At the game's end he stood;

"Kids, I think I'm gonna turn in. Lacey, it's been a pleasure meeting you. Thank you for the soup and sausage, and the M. And, at the risk of being presumptuous, for caring for my son."

Lacey and James both stood.

"It's not a presumption. I do care for him."

As she was saying this she moved close to James and stared up at him. He held her gaze a few seconds before he turned to John.

"We're for real, Dad. It's like you and Mom."

"It's a little late, so I think I should get home."

"I'll get your coat." James went to the back to get Lacey's coat.

"John, this was fun. I look forward to many more evenings together."

"As do I."

She went to him, hugged him—and kissed him goodnight on each cheek. James returned with her coat and helped her on with it.

"We'll have to get together with your folks soon, yes?"

"Absolutely. I'll speak with them and we'll figure out a date."

"Be careful kids."

"Always. Goodnight again."

And they were out walking arm in arm over the garbage and through the snow to the el. James thinking how wonderfully the evening went and she thinking what a liar she'd become and how less than incriminating the whole thing was. *He didn't make any snide remarks…or rant. Or even take one small sip of the M. He didn't disagree with the wage slaves remark and he flatly denied the Jeffers jerk-off slur. He gave nothing away that would lead anyone to have any suspicions of sedition.*

She wouldn't embarrass her father by putting in a request for CyScenSec to check a TV which could very well show little or nothing. She was certain her father had already seen enough at home to warrant her continuing. But if she was to do this by the book and not embarrass anyone she would need to see the proof herself. Was James exaggerating his father's anti-government statements…his discontent? She was going to ask her father if they could watch the TV holo-vids together. They reached the el stairs and she kissed him passionately. He watched her as she ascended the stairs to the train. *What are you doing you idiot? You can't let her ride a train alone at this hour.*

"Lacey…Wait up."

As she turned around, he bounded halfway up the slippery stair to where she stood. "I can't let you go home alone at this hour."

"Oh…silly, I'll be fine."

"You probably will be, but I'm seeing you home."

I can't argue with him. He's doing what he should. But is he going to walk me to my building? In Chinatown? I don't even know how to get there on this train. Okay, you're smart…figure it out. There's a subway map there. She stood.

"James, I'm completely lost up here. I've never gone home from here. I have to check that map."

She walked over to the map and, as she stood peering at the old graffiti marked and discolored subway map, James came her side. She managed to figure out that they had to change from the two train to the Q at Forty Second Street and take the Q to Canal Street. *I hope I can find a building down there that I can walk into. This is dicey. James, why do you have to be so sweet? A gentleman. I guess I wouldn't love you if you weren't.*

"Okay, I see what we have to do."

She took his hand and they returned to their seats.

"James, I love you."

He pulled her in closer to him. His smile could have lit the entire dingy car. As the train descended from the elevated into the tunnel she lay her head on his shoulder. If she weren't so sad she would have been bursting with happiness.

They got off at Forty Second Street and waited some twenty minutes for the Q train to Canal. When they emerged from the subway she knew from looking at the map that they had to walk southeast. *Oh God, let there be a building that someone is walking out of and I can stand in the open door while say goodnight. Please.* They walked two blocks east and then turned right down a street that she could see had a bunch of what looked like residential buildings. The street sign said Baxter Street. *Let there be someone coming out of one of these buildings...please. Good thing I didn't tell him we lived above a warehouse. That would have been great fun.* They had walked almost to the end of the block. *Someone, anyone. Please.* And just then a delivery person opened the front door of the last building on that block. A building they were maybe ten feet from.

Hurry Alex.

"This is me."

She just managed to get there just before the door closed.

"Wow Lacey! This is a pretty nice building."

Oh no. It's a vestibule. There's another door to the inner lobby. She pulled him to her and they kissed. She kept one foot planted firmly against the door.

"Thank you for getting me home, James."

"No way was I going to let you go home alone at this hour."

"You have a long ride home. I could stand here kissing you all night, but I think you'd better get moving mister. Go! And I'm going to watch until you turn the corner."

He smiled. "Tonight was great. "

They shared one quick kiss and then he reluctantly backed away. She stood in the doorway and watched him as he walked to the end of the block. He reached Canal, turned, waved, and made the left onto Canal Street and back to the train. She let out a huge sigh of relief. *That was way too close Alex.* She waited a full five minutes wedged into the corner of the vestibule praying he wouldn't decide to come back. Come back for some crazy reason—on this craziest of nights—before she allowed herself a peek out of the front door. Satisfied she was in the clear she called for her Andro-car to take her to her real home.

As she waited for her car she was thinking about the people she saw on the train. They looked terrible. *It isn't right that we have so much and they pretty much have nothing. It is so wrong!* She also thought that while it was no surprise that she enjoyed James' company what *was* a surprise was that she also enjoyed his father's company. *He's nice. Cool. Please, please let him not be considered dangerous.* Her car came. She slumped into the back seat. She was tired.

#

John Bedloe was laying in his bed thinking that Lacey was, as advertised, indeed terrific and that his son was a lucky kid to have found her. This was quite a stroke of luck. She seemed very special. Bright, articulate, sweet…a complete package. It would be a miracle for James if he had found his soulmate—the one girl perfect for him—as it had happened for him those long years ago. And, a miracle for him as well because it meant his son might not be alone and thus, morbid as it may seem, it could make his decision to put a bullet through his head possible. She seemed truly enamored of him but it could just be a young girl's crush. James, after all, *was* handsome, and a kinder sweeter boy would be hard to find. He quite liked her, and he would ask James to invite her to their place again. He finally turned onto his side and shut his eyes.

#

As he made his way back home James was reflecting on what a success the evening had been. His father had been on his best behavior. Amazing how he held his tongue at a couple of moments which would normally bring some kind of anti-whatever-it-may-be response ranging from sarcastic to vitriolic. They seemed to get on quite nicely too. He was pretty sure she liked his dad and definitely sure that his dad was impressed by her. And, she had brought all those gifts...she was thoughtful, and he knew that went a long way with his dad. *The look on his face when he saw she'd even thought to bring him that medicine...it was priceless.* It was as if an angel had appeared before him. *He* already *knew* he had found himself an angel...*Well, she found me.* Now his father knew it. Goddam, he was high - and M-POW!-r had nothing to do with it. *Hey, maybe tonight means pop will be drinking less of it - which would be a very good thing.* He finally got home and saw that his father had gone to bed. Tip-toeing back to their sleeping area he was glad to see that his father was already sound asleep and snoring lightly. Maybe meeting Lacey also put an end to the nights - which were occurring more frequently lately—that he'd been unable to get a good night's rest. He hoped this was the case and, if it were, they would have to get together again soon.

#

Having reached her real building her doorman helped her out of the Andro-car. *I'm going to see this through. And I only hope and pray that the evidence on James' father won't be enough to mark him an enemy of the state.* Though this flicker of hope was small, it burned fiercely as she rode up to the sixty fifth floor. *That cold horrible place they have to live in... Should I bring them a small heater?* She opened the front door to PH-A.

Her

arm was again draped possessively across James' shoulders as they were walking to the auto-café.

"I've been meaning to ask; how's your mom?

My mom? My mom? Oh…Oh!

"She's still in a little pain, thanks for asking."

"My pop said that shingles are real painful."

"They are." *Having trouble keeping your lies straight liar? Change the subject.* "So, next tuesday night? I'd love to."

"He really likes you."

"I like him too. But I like you more." She pulled him closer. He laughed.

"Our treat this time."

"Sounds good." *One more time. Let it be as harmless.*

She was pleased to hear that his father wanted her to visit again. She was hoping that it would once more show that James' father was harmless.

At best it would be another chance to show her own father he was right in trusting her with this job—however distasteful she was now finding it. And, it would be another evening with James. *I have to dress very warm.*

"He said you remind him of my mother."

"No...I...He said that?"

"She was also sixteen when they met. So was he."

"Like us." She leaned into him.

"I think our folks should get together soon too. I know my pop would like to meet your mom and dad. And so far he's been off the M so he'll be quite presentable."

She realized it was far too soon to beg off, or make any excuses relative to this meeting.

"I'll ask them what's good."

Anyone watching them walking so close together, looking at each other, laughing, would say to themselves; there goes a couple truly, madly in love. He thinking he had never been so happy, nor had he ever imagined such happiness could exist, and she thinking; I shouldn't be enjoying this so much? Why have I allowed myself to fall in love with him? *It can't go anywhere, Alex.* She hoped he hadn't noticed the sadness that briefly darkened her face. *His father seems sweet...like him. He says he's angry...I haven't seen that yet. He could have been my father-in-law in another reality. This sucks. And, as far as my father is concerned, I'm trying to trap him. I hope John's too smart for this. It sucks and it's crazy. But they're watching all of it. Daddy is watching all of it.* She made an effort to put her mind on the job she was tasked with. *James said the two four-paks would still be in the snow. Would he drink this time? Should I lead a bit more?* She felt as if John had gotten completely comfortable with her...*It's terrible that he feels like he has a new daughter. But is James exaggerating a lot of this? Oh God, I hope so. And now I'm on the TV record of being there.* So, once again, the painful conclusion was that she had to see what she'd started through to its end. She hugged him close as they walked on.

At the restaurant he stared at her with stars in his eyes as she barely ate a quarter of her fern soup. He never noticed.

#

Tuesday was his early day at the diner, so he'd asked James to invite Lacey to dinner and the game for that night. Bedloe was glad they still had the two four-paks in their "fridge" even as he was thinking maybe he would lay off of the stuff just a little while longer. Maybe he'd allow himself one Tuesday night—it being an occasion. *I'll see.* He'd won the last four BashBall bets so he had the seventy he owed his connect—but until he could settle that debt there'd be no more M.

He was eagerly looking forward to being around Lacey again. About that he was certain. He realized he'd just met her, but it seemed as if she and James were truly in love. *You'd like her Jane. She's nurturing. Like you were. And thoughtful. She brought me medicine, and made sure I took it. Sound familiar? James will need that kind of nurturing when I'm gone.* Meeting Lacey had not only made Bedloe happy for his son but, at the same time, had made his choices of joining the underground a possibility, or his morbid plan of suicide another possibility. It had also helped him to divert his mind away from what he'd done some weeks ago. It was amazing how meeting one person could change so much. She was a Godsend.

He had picked up two cans of the ReelGud Fish Stew figuring Lacey would think it healthier for them. He won five BashBall bets and had managed to set aside all of what he owed his guy and hoped that he'd win his bet on The NutKrakkers so he'd have a little more than the seventy he owed. He felt good about it. The kids would be there before him already preparing dinner and he was anticipating another relaxing evening once again in the company of this terrific girl who *might* be his future daughter-in-law. *You know Jane...seeing them together is like looking back in time at us honey. They seem to only need each other to make them happy also.*

He remembered how giddy with happiness they were the first night he and Jane had dinner in their new apartment. They had bought the bare essentials: the one large pot that they cooked the pasta in, the sauce pan, a set of dishes for four, utensils and wine glasses for four—and a salad bowl. They ate at a card table sitting on folding chairs. *Was it a real thing that wine never tasted as wonderful as it did that night? Am I romanticizing that night in my memory? Was it true that I swooped you up in my arms in the middle of dinner, you laughing and breathing "you lunatic" into my ear as I carried you into our bedroom and down onto the floor where we christened that new foam mattress. It seems like eons ago...I only hope our son and this sweet, lovely girl can experience a fraction of what we had.*

He coughed - and the present came rushing back. The train was stalled again. He looked around him at the decrepit people sitting in the decrepit subway car. His son still believed they would be extending either the Centipede or the Straddling Bus into The Bronx. Still believed the future was something to look forward to. He hoped with all his heart that together he and Lacey would be able to brave what he knew the future would actually be. *If they could have what we had it might inoculate them against this life.* Selfishly, he also wanted this girl to be real because, if she was, she would be making it possible for John to put himself out of his misery in a year or two. This life was no longer for him. It had emptied him. Everywhere he looked, everything he saw, or heard, or had experienced in the last twenty years had wrung his life out of him. *It's the resistance or death.* Except for his insane act of massacre he was now rendered defenseless in the onslaught of this existence. Now, his only slice of pleasure was his son's new relationship.

The train started up again. Just a few more stops then out into the slush. Tuesday night would be another good evening. *Good company, a nice dinner, a game, maybe I'll have one - or maybe not...I'll see how it goes.*

Tuesday,

and it hadn't been a particularly tough week at work. Bedloe had all of his man's money and they had this wonderful girl in their life who was coming over again tonight. They also still had eight cans of M-POW!-r in the snow. He felt like celebrating.

# # #

In the trailer James and Lacey were necking on his bed.

"Sweetheart, your dad will be home in a little while. We…should…get dinner…ready."

The words came breathlessly hot into his ear. Slowly untangling themselves, they rose from the bed, straightened their clothes, and walked hand in hand to the front of the trailer. James switched on the TV. She thought; *Well…we're on.*

"I can't believe you bought tomatoes."

"Why don't you set the table James? I'll make the salad and start the stew."

"This salad must have cost."

"Growing men need greens."

"I haven't had a salad in forever. Have you ever had the ReelGud before?"

"No, but…it's probably pretty good."

I can't believe the food they're forced to eat. She wanted them to eat something good for them so she'd bought the pre-washed salad.

"We'll eat the salad first so then I can just rinse the bowls for the stew."

In that terrible water.

James, is there any clean water?"

"I…I couldn't buy it. Sorry."

"Don't be sorry silly. I'll put some on the boil."

"Good. I'll put it out in the snow to cool."

She filled the small pot with the brownish brackish water and set it on the hot plate to boil. The slightly larger pot would serve for the stew. He set out the three bowls, utensils, the two glasses they had, and a cup for him. That was what any good host would do. As he was doing this, all she could think of as she was making the salad was: *the flag is up so the M is still out there. Please don't drink any tonight John. Please. Wait…they're watching. If he doesn't it'll look funny if I don't lead him on. I guess we'll cross that bridge when and if.* The water had boiled and James took the pot outside to cool in the snow. She opened the first can of ReelGud to put it in the pot. *It's not right. What fish is this?* She wanted to read the can's contents but stopped herself.

James came back inside. "Look's good?"

"Yeah, I'm glad your dad bought two cans. It'll just be enough."

*How can I eat th—Hey! Privileged jerk. Count your blessings. Eat! There but for the grace…*She emptied the two cans of fish stew into the pot, set the hot plate on low, and brought the salad to the table just as John, feeling uncommonly good, was opening the trailer door.

"Hee-eere's Johnny!"

"Well...look who's home."

"None other."

"Let me have your coat."

She moved to John and held his coat as he slipped out of it. He turned and, as she did before, she kissed him on each cheek.

"We're so continental tonight."

"Aha...too bad I didn't bring wine. Next time."

I can't afford a bottle of wine. Why did I say that?

"I can bring wine next time."

"Lacey, wine is expensive." *Oh...wait, the rent thing.*

Glad that the TV was miraculously off, she said, "John, do you mind if we eat? It is a bit late."

"I could eat."

Jane, this is crazy. For a second I imagined I'd come home to you. Jeez... John had to catch himself to keep from falling down that rabbit hole.

"How you feelin', Pop?"

"Well...gettin' old, but good...good."

"You're far from old John...salad?"

She took his plate and served him and did the same for James.

"If you want more ranch let me know."

"This is a treat. We haven't had a fresh salad in quite a while eh, James?"

"It's a good game tonight, isn't it, John?"

"The NutKrakkers Lacey. Very tough."

"Who do you like?"

"Well…I'd like the NutKrakkers to win."

"How was your day, John?"

Should I really say?

"Easy. Pretty good as it goes."

"How's the cough? Any better?"

"Yeah, there's been a definite improvement. Thanks."

"You need to wear a scarf. Do you have one?"

Thank whoever she didn't say "no problem." "I do…I should wear it. You're right. I will."

They were enjoying the salad. *What a treat. Rent free is a good thing. James is even luckier than I thought.* Bedloe got up from the table and headed for the back.

"John, where are you going?"

"I'll be right back."

He went back to the bedroom and returned with a ten dollar bill and tried to hand it to Lacey who refused to take it.

"Please don't be insulted. James told me your rent situation, but it's only right that we chip in."

He's even got principles. I cannot take this. And, it isn't an insult, he'll appreciate it.

"John—look, I am not going to take this and that's final. Now, please put that back in your pocket and finish your salad. Go on, eat up. I brought this food to be enjoyed."

John could see that she meant what she said. *Stubborn. Just like you, Jane.* His smile was somewhat sad as he shook his head slowly and put the bill in his pocket. *This sweet girl is a keeper.* They proceeded in silence to finish their salad. The TV turned itself on.

"James, will you get the clean water?"

James got up and went outside to get the pot of water jammed into the snow.

"You bought water Lacey?"

"We boiled some and set it out to cool."

We? You mean you. "Beats buying it for—what is it now twenty?"

And we just open the tap.

James returned with the water and Lacey proceeded to rinse their bowls in the sink.

"James, while you're up, please turn that thing off."

Good for you, John. "Are you two ready for some fish stew?"

She's very together. The way you were Jane.

James turned the TV off and sat back down.

"The salad was a treat, eh Pop?"

"Been a long while."

Lacey was at the sink drying their bowls.

"You two will be eating more greens from now on. Something like frozen peas doesn't cost that much money. And they'll stay frozen in your fridge out there. I'll try and bring some next time." *What am I talking about?*

Lacey served up three bowls of stew, set them down on the table, and sat down.

"Bon appétit."

Before the words were completely out of her mouth she realized that she might have broken character by saying them—but stifling them three-quarters of the way through would have been worse. As it was, it went unnoticed. *I'm glad the set isn't on.*

"Bon appétit."

John hadn't said that in over twenty years. It felt so familiar and quickly rushed him back to the hundreds of nights of dinners with Jane. *This sure doesn't taste like anything you would have made. You always said stew was a complete waste of good animal protein.* He smiled to himself at the recollection. But, he emptied his bowl as did James.

"Why is this better tasting than usual?"

"I scrounged some tarragon, John. There's a touch more in the pot."

"Um…James?"

"You finish it, Dad…please."

Lacey rose, got the pot from the hot plate, and spooned the rest of the stew into John's bowl. She sat back down and watched as he ate—much the way a doting daughter would. She almost forgot where she was—and why she was—as she reached across the small table for James' hand. They held hands as they watched John finish the last of the stew. When he was done she gathered up the bowls, went to the sink and washed them in the rest of the boiled water. James grabbed the remote and switched the TV on.

"Lace, the game's just starting."

"Be right there—*I have to*—You know what, I'm going to have an M-POW!r...anyone else?"

"You wanna split it Lacey?"

"Sure. You want one, John?"

"Uhh...maybe I'll have a sip of James'."

She went outside to get a can of M-POW!-r from the snow. *I hope he never takes another sip of this swill again.* She returned with the one can of M and poured some into James' cup and then into her glass. The little that remained she gave to John saying as she did:

"I'm glad we missed the anthem."

He almost said something but thought better of it. *She feels the same way about the anthem as I do..*

He couldn't believe it. He wondered how deeply her animosities ran. Lacey was wondering if what she said was too on the nose. *Thank God that didn't get a rise. Please let there be nothing in this after all.* James having heard his father's diatribes against flags and anthems many times before, finally breathed—relieved that his father had let Lacey's remark go without going into a mini-rant.

The game was the usual bloodbath. Players were carted off the field perfectly still or writhing in pain—either of which was not good. During one particularly brutal stretch, knowing this would be reviewed, she tried one more gambit:

"God...this...it's barbaric. These people in the stands. In the suites."

"It's business."

"Business?"

"The Money."

"I'm not following." *He's right of course.*

John thought better of going any further on that tack.

"Well…at least they're making *me* money also."

"How much, Pop?"

"A tenner tonight."

"Aww-right… I thought it was a deuce."

But, something in that one small comment "The Money," and the animosity mixed with sarcasm in his voice when he said it, now led Lacey to think that James might not be exaggerating his father's resentments. *Okay, he's angry about the iniquities. I think it's unfair too. But that doesn't prove he's dangerous. He seems anything but.* As the game ended she rose, rinsed the cups, and was thinking about what she should do next. *I have to be seen trying.*

"I don't know, John. How do those people in those luxury suites sleep at night?"

"I guess pretty good. I would."

No anger. Push it. You can clear him right here. "They're pigs who should be hung." John rose from the table. *She's right about that but…just keep your big mouth shut. There'll be time for that later.* He stretched.

"I'm beat. I'll say goodnight children—

Nothing. Nothing. Oh John…You don't know how happy you've made me. "Well…I should get going anyway. My mom is still a little under the weather."

"James, why don't you see Lacey home again."

Oh! No! Oh God…I forgot. We can't go through that charade again. What happens if no one comes out of that door tonight? I can't let him come with me.

"James, I'm just going to let you walk me to the train. You are *not* going all the way down to Chinatown again."

"James, will you please get our coats?"

James rose and went to the back to get their coats.

"This was so enjoyable. Why don't we do it again for the KneeKapper's game, John? It's next Tuesday."

"It's a date. You might be my good luck charm."

James returned with the coats and helped her into hers. She moved to John with open arms - kissing him on both cheeks.

"James, did you hear what I said? I mean it, you are not going all the way down to Chinatown tonight."

"Lace, you can't ride t—"

"I can and I am going to. And if you insist you will make me very angry,"

Holy shit! She is Jane! Jamsey my boy, if I were you I'd do what the lady says.

"James, far be it from me to butt in but....My fatherly advice is; if you know what's good for you, just walk her to the train."

He laughed. She was off the hook. *Oh... Thank. You. John!*

"Goodnight, sweetheart. I hope your mom feels better soon so we can all get together. And thank you for the salad. It was a treat."

He opened the trailer door for them.

"Why don't we make it next Tuesday?"

"Great. And I'll bring those peas."

James opened the front door.

"I'll be right back pop."

Dodged a bullet there Alex.

"Peas would be a treat. But please don't buy wine."

"Alright. Just the peas.

"Safe home. And no sausage either, okay?" He smiled. "It's delicious, but it's way too expensive."

And they were out into the street. He closed the trailer door and shut the TV off. The cough he had been stifling appeared. *James, don't lose this girl...she is a rare gem.*

Arthur

Winstead had called his daughter Alexandra into his office.

"Alex, sit. Please."

Have I done something wrong? She moved to one of the two leather chairs opposite her father's desk and sat there waiting for him to speak. Finally;

"I'm not convinced we have enough on him."

Had she been drinking anything she would have done a spit take.

"You've seen what I've seen?"

"Especially the two nights you've been there."

She sat there calmly—while wanting to leap into the air and scream with joy. *Oh God, I so hope this is true.*

"Should I drop it?" *I didn't think we ever needed enough to get someone.*

"Alex, I know how you feel about this boy. It's evident from the Holo-vids. Are you planning on continuing to see him?"

"I want to. But…The more I think about it…I don't see as how I can."

"Well…Of course he could be moved out of the Associate class."

What? She sat there stunned into silence by this turn of events.

"He might even make a good mole—

Wh---My god…This…It's a miracle.

"From what I can see I'm fairly certain he would like to work with you."

"Um…Yes, he might…Yes, yes, I think so too, but… I mean I am all for this…"

Her mind was racing a thousand miles a second.

"But there are so many…Where would he live? Could he still live with his father?"

"We could subsidize a small apartment for him somewhere."

She couldn't believe what she was hearing. Was this at all possible? Did this mean they could be together? Eventually be married? This was everything she could hope for and everything that had seemed utterly impossible.

"And he would be on the payroll."

"Daddy…I…I want to kiss you. This is…you have made me so happy today."

"Alex, I love you. Your mother loves you. You're our baby girl. We only want for you what you want for yourself."

"How will we do this? I mean we can't just separate him from his father without some kind of an explanation."

"I think his father would be relieved to hear the truth…That you are who you are, that he's in the clear, and that James will be elevated out of the Associate class. And that all this has made you so uncomfortable that you are quitting the service. Isn't this the truth?"

She knew it was… and that it was an amazing turn of events.

"I am certain that if this man John feels about his son the way we feel about you he would want all this to happen. He would be glad to see his boy leave under these circumstances. They can still stay in touch. James will be making a good living, he can help his father out, you'll finish Briarleigh, go to college and decide what you'd like to pursue. You do have connections."

But will James hate me for tricking them? I've told him so many lies.

"I know you plan on meeting again this coming Tuesday."

"I was going to try one more time." *To clear him, but now…*

"Yes, we have to be absolutely certain before we do this. It is on record."

"Could we elevate both of them?"

Now it was her *father's* turn to give *her* words some thought.

"It would really help them to get over the fact that I told them so many…stories. And make it possible for his father to get some needed medical attention."

"Well…I applaud your empathy Alex."

"It's more than that, Daddy, I genuinely like the man. He needs medical attention and he can't possibly afford it. I offered James the money, but he refused to take it."

"Admirable. Look, Alex, can we just hold that idea in abeyance?"

"Can I mention the possibility?"

Her father turned this request over in his mind.

"Can I ask James' father how he might feel about it? If he would he want to be moved out of the Associate class?"

"Of course he would."

"Daddy, I'm going to marry James one day. I know this. And I know that we will give you and Mother beautiful grandchildren." She looked at him earnestly. "Let me give his father this gift."

He sat back and looked at his daughter. She sat there quietly hoping, praying, he would say yes to this request.

"The third time's the charm. So go there this one more time, and if it goes the way it's been going, then okay, I will consider getting both of them out of the Associate class. And the father will receive the medical attention he needs. Fair?"

"More than."

"Now go and get ready for dinner. Pick us out a nice Montrachet to pair with lobster. Go."

She got up, went to him and kissed him on his cheek.

"I love you, Daddy. You're a good man."

As she went up to her room she felt as if all the weight of the world had been lifted from her shoulders. She felt certain that she would be able to explain all of it to John, and especially James, in such a way that their happiness at what was about to happen to them would counteract any bad feelings they might have at her subterfuge.

They

had left work together and were on their way uptown. True to her word she had bought a package of frozen peas for tonight's dinner. Though traveling on this dirty old train was something she didn't particularly enjoy, the knowledge she had, the knowing that she could be with this boy forever filled her with an elation she had to share soon or she would bust. *Just let it go well tonight.* At that moment she felt as happy as any girl who was ever in love has ever felt. The pleasure she felt in being with James was transcendent.

# # #

"**** *****?"

"It's Straddling Bus."

The buzzer sounded and Bedloe pushed the heavy door open. He reached the fourth floor and knocked on his man's door. As always, the peephole slid open and then closed. Then the door-jammer Police lock was slid open, followed by the door opening, with his man standing behind the door as he opened it just wide enough to let John slip in. And, also as always, the door was shut and locked behind him as John moved a few steps past the man and then turned to face him.

It was their pas de deux. John took the money he owed out of his pocket, and held it out to the man.

"I also want a four-pak."

# # #

"Delicious. Lacey, did you get these peas from a World Wide?"

They were all seated at the small table dining on the Meet-U stew and peas. She had happily eaten most of what John had served her.

John was even enjoying it. "I was just in one of them to buy the stew."

"Well John, now you know you can get a nice fresh vegetable in there as well."

John, in an expansive mood, had insisted he serve them tonight and, in a real surprise to him, he actually thought the stew tasted good. Perhaps it was the M-POW!-r they each had with dinner which she and James sipped and, alarmingly to her, John finished. It had been her turn to be surprised when he said he'd put a four-pak in the "fridge" and brought three cold cans to the table saying, "let's celebrate." She, of course, definitely wanted to celebrate for completely different reasons. Although tonight had to go as she hoped it would. So she was understandably nervous as she watched John gulp down the can of M. *Please don't let anything go sideways tonight. Please. I think there are eight cans of M out there. Was it this cold in here last time? You men are going to be so happy to leave this thing and live in a warm apartment. Let it happen.* John, being ever the good father topped off their bowls. *He's actually a very nice man. God, I'm glad Daddy hasn't seen anything on the TV vids.* James, meanwhile, looked on the whole scene feeling as if he finally had a real family. They finished eating and Lacey took the dishes to the small sink to wash them. She also took her can of M with her. *Stay cool John. Please.*

"That stew was delish, John, thank you."

"Your welcome sweetheart. Yeah, it wasn't bad. It wasn't rib-eye, but it wasn't bad."

She had washed the soup spoons and was now washing the last bowl in the water that James had already boiled and cooled for her. *If you want rib-eye just please behave.*

"Who knows, John, maybe we'll have rib-eye soon."

"Lacey...From your lips."

He rose from the table and went to the front door.

"Anyone for another?"

James held up his M. "I'm good for now."

"I'll have one, John." *One less for you.*

She was still at the sink drying the bowls. *Don't forget, you're still being watched. As soon as that TV goes on.*

John went outside and returned with two frosty cold cans of M-POW!-r, popped them open, he put one at Lacey's place at the small table and sat back down.

Damn, there's still six out there. I can't let him drink them all. "John, did you wipe your feet?"

Holy shit...She is Jane all over again. He rose, opened the door, quickly swiped his boots across the worn doormat, closed the door and sat back down. She took a small sip. *Don't drink all the the M, John. Please. The TV isn't on yet. Say something. Say something now!*

"John, I have to insist you slow down with the M. It really isn't healthy."

"Lacey, I know you're looking out for me, but I have been cold sober for two weeks and tonight seeing you two together and knowing how great you kids are together I think I want to celebrate a little. It's sweet of you to care but don't worry, I'll be okay."

You better be, John, or this whole thing could go up in smoke.

John sat down and took another pull on his M as James grabbed the remote and put the TV on. Lacey sat down between the two men as both teams ran onto the field amidst the cannon fire and smoke. The players stood at attention—as did the crowd—as the anthems of China and America played. The New York KneeKapper's were hosting the Beijing Bloodlust. John loved the fact that, as a rule, the well-heeled in the strato-boxes didn't even bother to get up for this ritual. The anthems played as the words 'Dissent Equals Descent" appeared on the screen. Now, a bit euphoric, he couldn't help himself;

"God! What moron coined *that* asshole propaganda saying?"

Oh no…No! Shut up John.

Please shut up! I don't think daddy is the kind of man that would come down on someone just because they insulted him.

However, John, feeling *so* good, continued: "Can we just mute this nationalistic swill until the game starts? Anthems are really stupid. Anyone mind?"

She pressed the mute which didn't interfere with the sound being captured on the holo-vid. *You have to let this go where it's going. You have to appear to be trying to trap.*

"John, I am so on your side with the anthems."

This girl is too good to be true. The anthems were over, as were the TV introductions of the players and the game was about to begin. She unmuted the TV. James was happily watching the both of them interact. *Man…They're really hittin' it off.* John went outside again and, now careful to wipe his feet, returned with another can of M, popped it open, and the three of them clinked cans. *You've had enough John. You can't. Please. Please. I am begging you.*

"Here's to those who are about to die."

John took a long pull.

"He's been saying that lately."

"Well…it *is* kind of gladiatorial," she said. *And please don't let us be eaten by the lions tonight.* John took another pull.

"Ri? Huh…Ri? She knows James. Listen to thswomn. She knows. Blood for the rich vampires in the luzhry boxes and penhouses…I wou' curse here but…."

Oh God…I can't stop him. Her mind was working feverishly.

"Her father pretty much thinks the same thing. Right, Lace?"

Oh God, I have to. I have to. "Worse. He thinks the people who…um… sanction…that's the word he uses…sanction this…he says they're all criminals. They should be locked up."

I feel sick. All this saliva…Don't throw up. She rose to go to the bathroom.

"Yes! They shou.' Crimnals! You're speakin' truth. He souns like someone I'd like to meet!"

Oh God. She moved quickly.

"Where you goin, Lace?"

"The bathroom. Be right back." *He's starting to grind and slur. Stop drinking John…Please stop drinking.* No sooner did she close the bathroom's accordion door behind her did she retch. *Oh Christ.* She stood up and—*Do it!*—rinsed her mouth with the brown water. She returned to the kitchen sink where she rinsed her mouth again with what was left of the boiled water. John was in full flight.

"Can' wait tmeet im. People jus' take it…Jus' accept it. Yr fathr's 's ri… lock 'em up."

He took another swig, rose, lurched outside, returned with three cans of M, and set them down on the table.

"Not for me, Pop. But I think you have to slow down."

Tell him James. Take one. It'll be one less for him—if it's not too late already.

"I'll take one." *I have to…even if it looks suspicious.*

John got up, picked up the other can of M and headed for the door.

"I'm puttn this back in thfridge."

John placed the can in the snow and returned—each time careful to wipe his feet.

"Man, iss cold."

"My father also says that too many of us are too accepting."

"An' too mineless."

"James and I joked that you two should have a beer together."

"I think I wou' enjoy that. Seitup."

"I'm thinking about when would be a good time."

"Lacey thinks you parents should *definitely* get together. I mean, since…"

"Since I'm crazy about your son."

John downed the rest of his M-POW!-r, went outside and quickly returned with one more.

"Well, I thin you two may a smashn couple."

He chugged half of the can. *She took a small sip of hers. Still two left.*

"Luh this shit. Luh! 'Scuse me for my coarse lange, Lace."

I don't know. He really hasn't said too much that might get daddy nervous. And he knows how much I love James and want this to turn out alright.

"Pop, please slow down with the M."

Make him James. Please make him...Because I can't.

"Mgood...Don' worr. Sometimes I jus' can't help it. I can't blieve how good I feel. It has...I hope I'm not em—embrassing my son...buss all to do with you...joining our famly."

James quickly jumped up out of his seat pumping his fist in the air.

"Wow! They just *destroyed* that guy."

Lacey laughed. It was half-hearted. *Please, let there be no more. Get him off the insults.*

"Did you bet this game, Dad?"

Dad again. This girl is gold. Gold! I couldn't have picked a more agreeable daughter-in-law if I tried.

"I wou *love* to mee your father."

You're being watched Alex. "My mom would like you too."

"I haven't met them yet myself but I know I will soon, right hon?"

Play it out. "They're dying to meet you James."

"The KneeKabbers 'r startin' t'geh serus."

John took another pull on his can.

"He thinks that the guys playing BashBall are the same as the soldiers who are just...Pop, what do you call them?"

"Iss not wha I callm, iss wha they're. Cann'n forr."

You have to. "You're kidding...My father actually used that exact expression during the Destroyers game the other night."

"My man! Here's to gray mines. Cann'n forr. Gray mines thick a li." John raised his can in a toast.

John…stop! It's enough!

"Gray mines."

Lacey and James both took sips, John took another long pull on his M-POW!-r, drained the can, and crushed the empty. Another player was down on the ground convulsing. The crowd was booing.

"They're fricking booing thisspoor schmuck who'll prolly ner walk again. These peop're nothin buh ghoulish scum. I'd li tsee the thresisance tosssome bombsin those luzhry bahsses. Lace…cyou geme nother."

No…Dear God John! What are you doing? You are destroying us. But she knew she had to get him the M. She couldn't be seen to impede the man's headlong rush to wherever this was going. Her own father's head was also on the line. She was hoping it was going towards John's passing out as soon as immediately. As she reluctantly went outside to get him the can of M she knew that her father had already made up his mind to want to see more and that the offer he'd made was a hair away from being taken off the table. She returned with the next to last can and handed one to John. John immediately popped it open and took a long pull. *Fuck! It's all fucked!* This from a girl who hardly ever cursed. On the screen another player was on the ground writhing in agony. His leg at an angle no human leg should ever be at. James was pumping his fist.

"Holy…Could the Bloodlust win this?"

"The Kneekabb…the KneeKabb…the Nyrkrs'll comeback."

"Pop, really! You have to stop drinking!"

Tell him James. Insist.

"Mgood. Mgood. Njoyin thgame."

"Okay, but just slow down. Yeah?"

"Lace...Lace, lemmee ask ya...freal...whayou think of a siety that couwatchthis...an'...an'somethinlige...lige RME?"

"You're right. It is barbaric."

"Pop, I'm going to insist that you slow down."

Yes, James! Yes. Take the damn can out of his hand!

"Yeahissbarbrig. Killm. Killm. Thass wha theywan!'"

"Pop...Pop...Come on man... please...ugh!"

"ThasswhimsayinwhothefugcouinventsuchbarbrigshitHuhLaceiss-barbrig.

Through his grinding jaws John took another deep swig.

"Killm. Thass whatheywan."

"Pop, that's it! You've had enough."

James reached for the can in his father's hand. John quickly pulled it away.

Take it, James! Take it!

"Iworghard...deservetogedalilshifaced. RighLace?"

Don't ask me...Fuck!

"James, he's just letting off a little steam. My father does it too."

"Like that? I say he should slow down."

John began to cough. It went on for a good minute.

"Pop, you're sweating like crazy. That shit is not helping."

"Yeahslowdown...slowwwwdowwwn...ManIfeelgoodYEOW!"

"Maybe I *should* take this."

He grabbed for his father's can of M-POW!-r. Again John easily pulled it back out of James' reach.

"I'mgooI'mgoodonworrymokay."

There was a time-out in the game as another player was being carried off on a stretcher. At that precise moment the face of Ransom B. Conover Sr. filled the screen. It was a holo-vid created for this special occasion to see whether or not it would set John off. It was supposedly an old holo-vid of Conover bragging about his great prowess in football.

"I hope you're enjoying this great game. I used to love playing and I still hold the all-time rushing, passing, and touchdown records. Believe me. The all-time records!"

John was on his feet *screaming* at the top of his lungs at the TV.

"FAHFUGGNEVPLAYEDFOOBALLINHISWHOLE FUGGIN-COWARLYDRAFFDODGIN'LIFE...EIFUGGIN'HADETHIS-FAHFUG!"

Lacey watched in horror. John fell back onto his seat. James took the can from his hand.

"Mutha fuggascumbaganallthese richfucks... Iwdshootemallbetwee theeyesinasecon."

James stared at him.

"Pop! What are you saying?"

"Iwdshootemall."

"What? Nobody's shooting anybody."

"Blammblammkillemall."

Oh God. It's done. Lacey was close to tears. *Keep it together.*

"Pop! Stop it! You're not killing anybody, okay?"

"I'mnah?Mnah?Whahareyoutheeggsperdonwhocnshoosomeone?"

"Pop, please. You wouldn't do such a thing. Lacey tell him to stop it… please. He'll listen to you."

"John, James is right. You wouldn't shoot anyone. *It's done. It doesn't matter now.* And I think you've had enough M- POW!-r too."

"I don't know why he's saying these things. He doesn't even have a gun."

John got up quickly, almost falling, and began to stagger to the back of the trailer.

"Pop, you alright? Where are you going?"

"Berighbahwannshowyoubowsomethin."

He lurched to the back, opened the closet, reached into the hidden compartment and took his gun from its chamois wrapping. Waving the gun wildly, he quickly reeled back to the table and practically dove onto his seat, sweating profusely and alternatively speaking between almost completely locked jaws and a lip-licking tongue.

"Donhaveagunhuhdonhaveaguh?"

"Holy father in heaven, Pop! What the heck? Where did you get that? Please put that thing away!"

Lacey, besides being destroyed, was now officially scared. This was a horror show. And it was all on the TV. Was it pity she was feeling for James? For John? For herself? For a life together ended? Was it guilt? It was one big knot of all of it.

"John, is that thing loaded?"

"Damnrighissload!"

"Alright, now you're scaring us pop. Please…give me the gun."

"John…please give your son that thing…or at least lay it on the table. Please."

"FicouevergeclosetathichairfugJeffersI'dshoohimbetweehisfuggineyes."

"John, what are you saying? You wouldn't shoot anyone. Look at me. You would not shoot anyone…let alone the Chairman."

"Iwoudnhuh? IwdkillJeffersnallofeminasecnd."

"Please…Pop…stop it. Pop, you're scaring me."

"Ligeidroppeddoseguysthuthernigh."

They stared at him.

"Thuthernighdroppedemallblamblam!"

"Huh? What are you talking about? Dropped what guys? He's babbling Lace."

"Othernighoffedfivethesessnotsthahassledmeonthetrainbrogemymedcine."

"What? What did you say?

"Something about the train and broke his medicine?"

"Shotfiveof'emmuthafuggersnersawitcominmesswime."

"You what? Pop, stop it! Stop saying these things. And stop waving that thing around."

"OusideabaronJagsonfivefugghezzbambambambambamfuggmearounbraymymedcine."

"Okay…You're hallucinating. He's hallucinating. What are you talking about? You didn't shoot anyone pop. Stop it! You're scaring me."

Lacey rose from her seat and headed for the back of the trailer. *I need to get out of here.*

"LaceLaceLacewhereyougoinhon'? Comebaggsiddownwewatchinthgame."

"You're scaring the hell out of her. Out of both of us, Pop!"

"TheserichfuggsshouallbeshotIwouldlovetokillthissassholechairman."

Oh my God! He is dangerous! She knew it was all over. She grabbed her coat off the bed and came back up front where James was holding the can of M-Pow!-r out to her.

"It's…It's *this*…crap! I'm sorry about this…he's never been like this. Never."

She quickly put on her coat. "James, I'm kind of frightened."

"He's never been like this. I swear I had no idea he had a gun."

"LaceLace…siddownlesshaveanother.

"Sweetheart, I know you didn't. But I think I should go and you should let him sleep it off. I think he's…you know…projecting. And, I get it. He's got a lot to be worked up about."

"Lacemysonizcrazyfryounmetoo."

"Look. I'll see you at work tomorrow."

She turned towards the front door.

"Youdonhavetoleaveissearlythegame."

"Lacey, wait—I'll walk you to the el."

"No. take care of your dad. It's only two blocks. I'll be fine. I promise. I'll see you tomorrow."

Just get him to bed and let him sober up. And, hide that *gun* from him."

James was totally deflated—*and* in a state of shock. "No...I'm walking you to the el."

He threw on his coat and together they walked through the snow to the elevated train. He watched her as she blindly climbed the stairs. As soon as she was out of his sight he turned and headed back. She waited of couple of minutes, came back down the stairs and stood in a doorway and called for a Heli-Vee to airlift her home. *It's all gone. Everything. And I've just left him with this mess. And there's no way...*She stood there crushed and in shock, waiting in the snow, or hail, or snain—or whatever it was that she had no idea was coming down on her—until the Heli-Vee came to carry her away.

His

father was now pretty much passed out face down. James carefully took the gun out of his hand and struggled to get him onto his feet. Even though he was quite thin he was dead weight. *What the heck just happened?* His father was a mess. James had never seen him this bad. Close, but not this far gone. *He said he shot and killed five men? No! Was he serious? Was he hallucinating? Was it wishful thinking? He does have a gun though - that part's true.*

It hadn't been easy getting him to the back of the trailer and onto his bed, but after much stumbling he finally managed it. John was mumbling gibberish all the way to the back, though he could make out some words; "the fucks" this and the "cocksuckers" that, and "Lacey," and the unmistakable "motherfucking scumbag Conover." *Forgive him Father.* Finally, and with much difficulty, he was able to get his father to his bed. John fell onto it face down and had barely moved since. James had removed his shoes and with some effort rolled him to one side and pulled the blanket from under him. He'd rolled him to the other side until he could pull the blanket completely out from under him and cover him with it. Then he stood there, still in disbelief, and watched as his father quickly fell fast asleep. After a while he went back to the front of the trailer, stared at the TV without seeing what was on the screen and tried to decompress. About three minutes passed when he got up quickly as the realization hit him that he had to hide the gun. Looking around the space and seeing, perhaps for the first time how sparse it was, he finally put his father's gun in the pail under the sink and covered it with a rag. He wondered if he should take the bullets out of it and then decided that he had to. Taking the clip out of the pistol wasn't as easy as he thought it would be. He finally located the magazine release, pressed it, and was startled as gravity did the rest and the clip suddenly fell from the grip to the floor with a loud thud. The sudden noise broke the dead silence and shocked him. *HOLY…* He looked upward as he crossed himself, put the gun back under the sink, picked the clip up off of the floor and stood there. *Where the heck am I hiding this?* He decided somewhere in the rear of the trailer would work and he headed for the back. The only place he could see that would do was their old cardboard dresser. He opened the bottom drawer and placed it beneath his underwear. He closed the drawer and stood looking at his father who hadn't moved an inch and was sound asleep and snoring. *Sweet Lord.* Shaking his head, he went back up front and sat down on his beach chair. He tried to watch TV. The game was long over and he found it difficult to pay attention to what FAIR was now showing. Selfishly, all he could think about was what Lacey would say tomorrow about what happened tonight. *Of all the nights he could have chosen to get so s-faced this was the worst.* He wondered if it would affect his relationship with Lacey. *How* it would affect it. *She did say her father thinks the people who sanction BashBall are all criminals. They should be locked up. She gets it - she understands pop's got a lot to be pissed off about. But…* He was fairly certain her father didn't have a gun and hadn't gone and shot five people dead. Or even *claimed* to have done such a thing. He knew one thing for sure—he had to try and convince his father to cut back on the M-POW!-r. *Maybe I should too. And maybe I shouldn't buy it at all. It would save us some money too.* Money they could no doubt put to a good use. Money he could use to pay his share of their dates. Wait a minute! *I'm thinking of myself? Why am I thinking these kinds of things at all when my father just said he killed five people?* Now, he sat there trying to process that his father had said he'd done such a thing. *Had he really? And, if he actually did, how could he bring himself to do such an insane thing? And if he did do it when did he do it?* He knew his father was angry but *that* angry? He did mumble something about them breaking his medicine but...*Did he shoot them on the train? And, if he did, how many people saw him do this? And where did he get the gun? Was it from their connection? How could he even afford to buy a gun? Was he just imagining this...this massacre because it was something he thought about doing? Are the police going to come knocking at our door to arrest him? And, if I know about it, am I an accomplice? Is Lacey? Damn! I haven't seen anything on FAIR News about five men being gunned down so...I dunno...maybe...* These thoughts were flooding his brain as he sat there. And, try as he may, he selfishly couldn't help it that all these thoughts eventually came back around to; *is this going to change Lacey's opinion of me. Would she want her parents to meet my father now? A man who might be a murderer.*

His mind was racing and he wasn't the least bit tired. He began to make himself a cup of instant Kaw-Fee. He tried focusing on the TV. FAIR was showing a late night movie about a talking car. He wasn't even remotely in a laughing mood and for the first time in his life he thought that something on FAIR was really dumb. Flat out unredeemable. He measured the Kaw-Fee out, added the water and stood there waiting for it to boil. He would talk with his father tomorrow about all this. *What will he say about all of this when he's sober. Will he remember any of it? Will he still say he killed five men?* He wished he had a phone so he could call Lacey and apologize for what had occurred. For what she had to *see.* What she was probably thinking. *What is wrong with you? Why are you making this all about you?* He couldn't believe he could be so self-centered. When did *that* happen? He poured the coffee into his mug, left it on the table to cool and walked back to check on his father.

John was sound asleep and now he was talking, or rather mumbling, in his sleep. It sounded like he was saying "bloody" and "can't stop it" over and over again. And then "Jane." *That's Mom's name.* James stood there trying to make out what his father was saying. Then the mumbled words; "abortion," and "butcher," and then again "can't stop it." *Oh my L...did my mother die in a botched abortion?* He'd never heard his father talk in his sleep before.

Maybe he always did and he just never heard it because he was a sound sleeper. He stood there listening for more.

#

It was the same terrible dream he'd been having for fifteen years. His wife was laying there all bloody and he was unable to move a step in any direction. She moaned for him to please help her. He was now hovering over her and when he tried to close her wounds his hands went right through her. Off in a corner of the room a heavy-set man was sitting behind a large partner's desk eating well-done steak smothered in ketchup and potato chips. Now, he was looking for his car. He was sure this was where he parked it. He definitely parked it on this street—but it was gone. Again. This was the third car he'd bought and the third time someone had stolen it. Why only his cars? It was night and he was walking on a desolate road somewhere. He had no idea where he was. There was a signpost up ahead and, as he neared it, the writing on it began to blur. The more he tried to read it the more blurred it became. The landscape in every direction was treeless. He walked on and came to a red house. He entered it. It was dark. There was a basin of blood on a table and a woman stood over it washing her hands. She looked up at him, smiled, and held out her hands for him to smell. He looked through all the rooms in the house. They were empty. Then his wife entered the room and he went to embrace her but could not reach her. The closer he got to her the further away she was. He tried to say her name and couldn't speak. He was on a staircase. At the top it ended and there was nothing below. He gripped the rail tightly as he tried to backtrack down. He tried to play the guitar in his hands but it had no strings. The heavy-set man was laughing at him as he held out a package of guitar strings to him. He tried to take them and the heavy-set man threw them into the abyss. He was trying on jackets in a men's store. Every jacket he tried on was either too big or too small. Nothing fit. He was in a panic clinging to a railing in a howling wind with the city far, far below.

#

His father had stopped talking and James was now wondering if the car accident story was a lie. *But why would he lie about it?* He made up his mind he would ask him about his mother tomorrow night when he came home after work. And about the five men he said he'd killed. This had turned out to be quite a night. He went back up front, sat down and drank his Kaw-Fee. After a while he realized he was tired enough to go to bed himself. More to the point, he was wrung out.

#

It's done. This phrase was playing on a loop in her mind since she left James' trailer. It was there as she waited huddled in a dirty doorway on a smelly Bronx street for her HeliVee to transport her back to her world. And it was interspersed among her other thoughts up until she finally fell asleep. She was now a part of the TV holo-vid record her father would soon look at, if he hadn't already done this, and it was now stored among the endless rows of digi-files in the vast sub-basement of that nondescript windowless building—along with the millions of daily entries all to be accessed upon formal request. A request that was merely an empty formality which existed solely as a pretense to further the myth of Democracy. The people who were the stewards of these formalities themselves believed the myth. In truth there were no fetters left on The State. *And I'm one of them.* All she could feel was the terrible guilt that was now full blown. She had successfully "played" an innocent boy—*I played him…both of them…that's exactly what I did*—in order to get to his father and now she was about to, in effect, make this boy, who she was now hopelessly in love with, an orphan.

The unease she felt was profound. However her father would be feeling about what she did could never fill what was now a deep hole in her center. She had been hollowed out. Telling herself it was her duty made her laugh hysterically.

This society, this country, the world is far too complicated to be let loose to govern itself. We have to do it. The educated ones. We must. We do what we do for the benefit of all of society everywhere. Those early century factions like The PEEPS, their insistence on vague notions like "individuality," "freedom." All that did was leave most of the population, who needed guidance, out in the cold. It's up to us to lead, to keep order. What I'm doing, we are doing, what I did is right. What my father does serves to protect us all. "Dissent Equals Descent."

"The. Third. Time's. The. Charm."

She stopped laughing when she started crying.

Of

course the ten years of holo-vids from the TV in their mobile home
showed that the son James Bedloe was a model A Class Associate and
the father John Bedloe was clearly dangerous and, as such, an enemy
of the state. She had called in sick as the CyScenSec people reviewed
them the next night. Per Arthur Winstead, they found the salient ones
by pre-programming their TV to bring up the vids that contained the
words "Conover," "Conover Jr.," "Conniver," "Conjob," "Conoverallofus."
"Conovereveryone," "Jeffers," "Jeffers Jr." and "jerk-off." There were
plenty. Naturally, what sealed John Bedloe's fate was the last, and most
incriminating holo-vid of the lot. James' father's rant in which he revealed
not only his hatred for all the Chairmen but that he'd had a gun and had
used it to kill five Socee men, which didn't matter in the least to them, but
did mean he could conceivably shoot someone important one day. Didn't
he say he would shoot Jeffers? They saw him passing out, she leaving, and
James hiding the gun under the kitchen sink. And, just for kicks, they
viewed the Klown Bar massacre, which was captured on all of that block's
ninety-six heat-seeking surveillance cameras—out of the eighteen hundred
and forty two of those cameras in that South Bronx neighborhood alone.
Bets were made on the elapsed time between the first and last victim of the
shooting, which all the assembled CyScenSec agents admired for its cold

efficiency. After the viewing, they called to congratulate Alexandra on a job thoroughly well done and to invite her for a well-deserved caviar, steak, lobster and champagne dinner celebration at the best, most expensive, steak house in town. She respectfully declined saying she was "under the weather." Her father had come to her bedroom to tell her how sad it all made him and to try to comfort her. He also was effusive in his praise for the way she handled a very difficult situation and mentioned there was an important appointment to be had if she wanted it. She told him she would let him know and not to be sad, that she would be alright. He held her for a while and then left for CyScenSec.

Meanwhile, neither James the son, or John the father, had even an inkling of what the ramifications of her visits to them would be and what was about to take place.

At work the next day she was near tears as she did her best to soothe James saying that his father's outburst in no way reflected on him. It was the most she could manage without more outright lying. They held hands over lunch at the auto-cafe and he was starting to feel a little better. She tried her best to ease his mind saying that his father had every right to do what he did to those men in light of what they'd done to him—breaking his medicine and all that. And she truly believed this.

#

At the same time they were in the auto-cafe John Bedloe was staggering out of bed where he had slept for twelve straight hours. He had to take a mighty piss. His head was killing him and he wondered why—having only a partial recollection of what had transpired the night before. His son's girlfriend had been there. She'd brought soup, which was so kind of her. They had the soup, opened some cans of M-POW!-r and watched most of the first half of a BashBall game. The rest was a complete blank. He remembered nothing more of the night or having his recurring nightmare. He hoped he hadn't embarrassed himself—or his son. He brushed his teeth, got dressed and brewed up a cup of Kaw-Fee. Actually, he wasn't brewing anything, it was instant Kaw-Fee, since after spending the money for the clip he couldn't afford to buy real Kaw-Fee—which, of course, was fake to begin with. He smiled wryly at the thought as he sat drinking his breakfast, his head still pounding. He rinsed his cup in the tan water and then began to get ready to go to work when he heard a very loud and persistent knocking up front at the trailer's door.

"Who the hell…"

"Open up! Now!"

A voice yelled. He was puzzled - why would his neighbor be pounding on the door? Has the hose sprung a leak again? Then another voice:

"Open this door!"

"Hold your horses, I'm coming."

"MAKE IT QUICK!" the voice bellowed from outside. "Hurry up, we don't have all day!"

We? What the fuck is this? He moved to the door, opened it, and as he did, one of the men at the door forcefully pushed it open the rest of the way. He saw two large men, both wearing long black leather trench coats.

"Get your coat and let's go," the bigger of the two large men growled.

"Why…I don't understand. Go where? Why are--"

"Get your coat! Now! Let's go!"

"But…What the hell's going on?"

One of the men went under the kitchen sink and took his gun from where James had stashed it. The burlier of the two burly men said:

"Where did he put the clip?

What? What the—Where did who put what? Is this about the five men? Shit.

"He went to the back."

Who went to the back? What are they talking about? The man walked to the back of the trailer and quickly found the clip in the drawer beneath the underwear. He returned to the front of the trailer.

"If you'd rather go without your coat it's okay by us."

"No…no. I - I'll get it."

John went to the rear of the trailer, the other of the men following, got his coat from off the door hook and put it on as he was being hustled out the door. He would later be as glad as he could be, under the circumstances, that he did.

"Why are you doing this?"

This has to be about the five men I shot. What else could it be? Do they care after all?

"What have I done?"

"Shut up. Get in the car."

He was shoved into the back of a black sedan with dark windows. One of the men slid in beside him. The door slammed shut.

"W-where are we going?"

Am I being arrested? He was starting to be frightened with the realization of what was happening. There was no answer. He was breaking out in a cold sweat.

"My son…I have to let my son know where I am…please…PLEASE! Let me leave him a note…at least let me do that…please."

The car took off.

"TELL ME WHAT I'VE DONE! WHAT HAVE I FUCKING DONE? You fucking robot fascist freaks."

No sooner were the words out of his mouth then he regretted saying them.

"Please...I'm sorry...I'm...Please, just tell me what I've done?"

Still no answer as the car sped through the streets.

"You have children, right? My son's going to be frantic when I don't come home."

"What makes you think you won't be going home?"

The man behind the wheel finally spoke.

"Have you done something bad? Maybe you have eh?"

This is...It's some kind of a fucking sport to these goons

"I haven't done anything. I was just getting ready to go to work....I work in a diner on Simpson Str—you already know that, don't you? Right? That's all I do. Don't do this...please."

Silence. The car sped through the snainy, snowy, trash-lined Bronx streets, onto the East River Drive, under all the bridges, and off of the Drive somewhere way downtown. *Jane... Jane...I'm in the back seat of a car being carried off by strangers to something that...I don't know...I...* He had given up beseeching the two men up front to tell him what he had done and why he was in the backseat of their car. The car had finally turned into a dark industrial looking street way downtown. It stopped...In an alley. They were getting out. Getting him out. *Where the hell are we? What is this building?* He was quickly manhandled out of the back seat and shoved through a knobless unmarked sliding steel door in an unmarked nondescript windowless building and hustled down a long narrow dimly lit hallway and into a bare concrete room with a single glaring lightbulb hanging from the ceiling. *I'm in a fucking B movie.* A man dragging a hose entered. *We're animals? We should be so lucky...We're not fucking good enough to be animals.*

"Take off your clothes and pile them in the corner."

He hesitated...

"Take off your clothes! Don't make me say it again!"

He did as the man said.

"Why am I here? I haven't *done* anything!"

"Turn around!"

"But what d—"

"TURN AROUND!"

Bedloe slowly turned to face the concrete wall as a stream of very cold water hit him in the back of his head—*What the fucking shit!*—and traveled down over his back down to his buttocks and to his feet. He had tried with every ounce of his will to think of anything other than what was happening at the moment - what he was almost certain *was* going to happen to him. The sweat was rolling down his back... *Jane...Jane...What are they going to do to me? Torture? Stop it! Stop! Deep breath... Again...Breathe...That night; Fire Island. Magical... Remember sweetheart? We all ate mushrooms... went off down different wooden paths...Glorious...moonlight on the rushes and paths...The sound of the ocean...Star-strung night sky... Miraculously, the paths converged...You in my arms... Gardenias...Jasmine. This sweet kiss... Jane...my Jane...The taste of you...so sweet...keep on...Don't---What will happen to James?* The jet of water traveled up and down his body. *No, no, maybe it won't end badly. Don't get ahead. Maybe. Breathe. Keep the faith. Keep strong...Concentrate. I can't take torture... Kill me. Just kill me. Jane, Jane, stay with me. I love you so much...your scent on the pillows...hold me close... your laugh...I am the luckiest man on the face of--- This has to be about---this is about the killing of those men...It must be...What else can it be?...They just want to question me...They have to...It's their job. They don't care...This is pro forma... Calm...Stay calm...That's all it is Jane.* The terrible jet of water finally stopped. He stood there shaking. He heard the man replace the hose and leave. Slowly, he turned around. *Don't worry, we'll be okay. James is a good boy...He can't help it...All the propaganda Jane... Brainwashing... Disinformation...Not his fault Jane...Calm Johnny...Calm...*

Now the two men re-entered, grabbed him roughly and dragged him, soaking wet, out of the room and down the long dim hallway.

"Can I have my clothes? A towel? Say something! Anything. Just fucking speak."

Nothing. They pushed him into a small eight by eight room containing one chair and also lit by a single harsh bulb hanging from the ceiling. It was truly like a scene out of any bad movie he ever saw. The man with the hose who had made him strip and directed that strong stream of cold water at him entered and threw a rough grey jumpsuit at him ordering John to put it on. He told him to sit down and then left. John was shaking with fright. The sweat rolled down his back and into the crack of his buttocks. What seemed like hours went by as he sat afraid to even get up. *I have to piss.* Finally, he got up and started to move towards the corner of the room intending to relieve himself when a voice over a speaker said;

"Sit down!"

"But I...I need to urinate."

"SIT. DOWN!"

He did so - and finally, unable to hold his bladder back any longer, wet himself. He sat there terrified, humiliated, wet, and after a while feeling cold as his urine-soaked jumpsuit bottom chilled. More hours went by - or, what seemed like hours.

He was at the very top of that very high stairs that was in the middle of nothing. He had to continue climbing but there was an empty space in front of him where the steps were missing and he had to get over the space to the next landing. He was terrified and held tightly to the rail afraid to look down at what he knew was an abyss. He was frozen. It was night. He was on a vaguely familiar street peering into all the stores looking for a certain market. It was a street he thought he'd been on many times before. He passed the movie theater. Then he was in the market looking through the meat department. All the meat was piled on a table near the paper towels. The floor was slippery with viscera. He and Jane were sitting on a park bench eating pizza. She laughed, got up and walked behind him. He turned to see her and she wasn't there. He was on the train going to work. The heavy-set man sat opposite him eating a raw steak with his bare hands. His mouth and chin were smeared with blood. He was---

"Get up!"

Someone wearing a heavy steel-tipped boot kicked him sharply in his leg.

"GET UP! Hurry!"

He stood, glistening with sweat, his crotch and legs still damp. The man grabbed his arm and hustled him out of the room and down another long dimly-lit corridor - or was it the same corridor? He was quite disoriented...confused. *Why am I here? This has to be about the five men.* He had always believed they didn't care about Socee on Socee violence. *I can't believe I was wrong. But... if it isn't the shooting then what is it? Is our connection a government spy? Is that it?* He was shoved into another room and pushed down onto another chair. The man left. He looked around him.

Five floors above the room where he was seated, two of Alex's CyScenSec colleagues stood watching John Bedloe's interrogation on the monitors. A man carrying a chair entered the room.

"That's Erickson." One of them said, "He's one of our new guys. This'll be good for his training."

They watched as Erickson planted the chair squarely in front of Bedloe, then walked around behind him and stood there. Bedloe felt his heart pounding.

"Do you own a gun?"

"A gun?"

"Do. You. Own. A. Gun? Yes or no? Simple."

This is about the five men. He almost felt relieved. *Should I admit it?* He knew that an Associate owning a gun would be dealt with harshly. *But, what if it isn't? What if this has nothing to do with the five men? I can't say anything.*

"No."

"You do *not* own a gun?"

"I do not. No."

"Have you ever shot a gun?"

"A long time ago in the Iraq war."

"And recently?"

Was it someone at the Klown?

"Recently?"

Do I admit it? They must know about the shooting… That's why I'm here. But, should I admit it? Will they go easier on me if I do? I'm sure they don't give a shit about Socee on Socee violence. It's an everyday occurrence and they never do anything about it. But a gun…

Of course Alexandra's colleagues knew about the incident at the Klown Bar and they couldn't have cared less about the people John shot. However, the fact that he hated the authorities passionately, had a gun, and wasn't above using it—*that* they did care about. Five floors above him they peered intently at the giant holo cube. One of the twenty within the vast room. They had already seen all they needed to see; the ten years of holo-vids from his TV and last night's shitshow. This, however, was SOP *and,* since they had him, why not give him over to this new agent as a valuable part of his on-the-job training.

"I said, recently?"

He decided to stonewall it. "No."

"Did you tell your son that filling the rosters with the Socees who played BashBall was the equivalent of getting soldiers to enlist in a brutal clash with the high probability of being maimed, paralyzed, and even killed?"

What? What?? How…Where did this come from? He managed a bewildered shrug.

"Why…why would I ever *say* such a thing?"

"And that our brave soldiers are nothing but cannon fodder and the administration was as cruel as gladiatorial Rome?"

Silence. *Why are they asking these things? How could they know these things?*

"Did you say that?"

"Of course not."

"And, you'd like to see the resistance toss some bombs in the luxury boxes." *When did I say that? I never said that. Is this not about the five men?* His mind careened from bad thought to worse. *Am I going to be tortured? I am. No…No, You don't know that. Keep it together. Jane, let's meet for a drink later. Wear that lovely pale yellow, blue and white sundress.* He felt the sweat now rolling down his legs. *Is it the girl? He told her things he shouldn't have. But, she's just not the type.*

"Did you call our esteemed ex-Chairman Ransom B. Conover Conovereveryone?"

This he knew he could not admit to. And now his mind was beginning to formulate the one horrendous thought that, try as he might, he could *not* hold back from running him over.

"Did you say Conovomics was Conovomit?"

Oh my fucking bloody Christ! It can't be James! It can't! I mentioned that word to him alone. Once – and that was only in passing. No one else could've possibly known I'd said that. My son. My own son turned me in to the authorities! Told them all these things. How could James have done this to me? His already destroyed heart now broke anew with the realization that his impossible fear was realized; he had indeed raised a Nazi youth. *Kill me. Kill me. Please kill me.*

"Do you harbor a hatred for the wealthiest among us?"

"No."

"Didn't you say you would kill Jeffers and all of them in a second?"

"No."

"You never said you'd like to kill him?"

"Never."

"That somebody ought to bomb FAIR?"

Oh God…My own son who I love. Who I thought loved me. How could he have done this? He couldn't process it. The realization was crushing. The rest of the interrogation went pretty much the same way. He denied everything, and in the end they threw his coat to him and he was hustled out of the room, down the long dimly lit corridor, out of the building, into a waiting black van and taken to a railway station where, under armed guard, along with twenty others, he was hustled onto a train and taken to an airport. The word among them was that they would all be imprisoned somewhere for life. The sick joke to him about this whole thing was; he'd always said to anyone who glibly remarked "life is short," that one could never appreciate how long life *really* was until one got sentenced to it. *The joke's on you, Einstein.*

And, as FAIR-TV's all across the land were trumpeting the "incredible new free tabloid publication The Daily Fare," the New Populist Servers were announcing the roll-out of an "awesomely fabulous" new National Constitution guaranteed to soon make everything "unbelievably great again." One which will "insure the liberty of every citizen in this great country." One which was drawn up by the most "tremendous and incredible minds" in The Chairman's inner circle acting in conjunction with The Evangelical Thought Group for America. "A fantastic group, the very best people. Believe me. Many people have said it. They are the very best."

#

As this was happening, John Bedloe's plane was banking eastward out of LaGuardia, Down below him through the snainy mist he could see The Statue of Liberty. He was being flown to Eurasia, then transported by another far less comfortable train to an isolated prison in Oymyakon, Russia, the coldest inhabited place on Earth, never to be seen again by his son or anyone he ever knew. Along with the other 2,582 inmates, considered to be the most dangerous enemies of the United Oligarchy, he was allowed one hour of freezing cold daylight each day, nothing to read, and no contact with anyone but his taciturn guards for the other twenty-three hours. The frequency of his recurring nightmare increased. There was no talking allowed in the twice a week supervised communal showers. His head and beard were inspected and shaved once every six weeks for lice and his nails were clipped every week to prevent him from gashing his wrists. His meals, eaten without utensils, were provided to him through a small revolving opening in his cell door. This was his new existence.

His ongoing ranting led to his becoming known as the "Madman of Oymyakon." At long last, with the bitter heartbreaking abiding thought that his son had betrayed him, he mercifully died of acute respiratory failure nine long hard lonely years later—with his wife's name on his lips.

#

The evening after John, the father, was shipped off to this miserable fate she, code name Lacey, went with he, real name James Bedloe, to the trailer. Her guilt, and the achingly undeniable fact that she *was* in love with him, compelled her to try to comfort him in some small measure while he waited hopefully, anxiously, and in vain, for his father to come home. He hoped that maybe his father was with that waitress. She agreed that he probably was. He finally fell asleep in her arms, and she spent the entire night next to him awake—intermittently and uncontrollably sobbing quietly.

By late morning his father still hadn't come home and the son was beginning to panic wondering where he could be. She tried to calm him, telling him his father would probably soon be home. She made him breakfast and sat with him while he ate what little he could; a cup of instant Kaw-Fee and one and a half Twin-keez Pluss cakes. Finally, she told him she had to get home before she went to work and promised she'd see him at work later—and at the auto-cafe—and not to worry, his father would soon be home...*And*, that what*ever* happened she'd *always* be with him. As she said this she knew what a terrible lie she was telling him. Even if her father gave James the position he spoke of, the mountain of guilt she felt now made being with him impossible. Had she been able to think of it she would have, at the very least, made certain he could never be fired from his job. She thought of this later in her bedroom—when later was far too late.

The

Heli-Vee landed on the roof of her building. She got out and made her
way to the maglevator for the four flight descent to the first floor of their
penthouse. She looked into the iris scanner that unlocked the maglevator
door. It slid open, she stepped in and descended to their penthouse. The
door of the maglevator opened onto PH-A. She entered her huge four
story home. It was eleven AM and the apartment was empty, her mother
having gone to the Mayor's office, her father to the nondescript building
downtown, and her brother to private school. She took off her coat and
scarf, hung them in the hall's triple wide walk-in closet, removed her
scuffed boots and placed them neatly in the basket on the mat beside the
maglevator door. She padded some twenty steps, stopped—and stood
and looked around her at the beautiful home in which she grew up. She
went into the large kitchen, took a drinking glass from the cabinet, and
then padded up the stairs to her parent's bedroom and into her mother's
bathroom. She went to the sink and looked at herself in the medicine chest
mirror. Her eyes were swollen and red. She opened the medicine chest and
stood reading the information on the vials on the shelf. She found the one
she was looking for.

She poured a glass of water from the bathroom faucet and emptied the entire full vial of her mother's sleeping pills into her palm. She returned the vial to the shelf, closed the medicine chest door and once again stared at her image in the mirror. After some thirty seconds she popped all the pills into her mouth and swallowed them with the entire glass of water. She put the glass down on the sink, turned, padded to her own bedroom and very slowly laid down on her bed.

EPILOGUE

James was heartbroken by the terrible realization that his father had been "disappeared," and that "Lacey" the girl he loved, the girl who loved him, was indeed gone. Disappeared.

He went repeatedly to her building in Chinatown where no one had ever seen her—nor was there a family living only four in an apartment rent free—which elicited some laughter from all the tenants he asked.

It took only two weeks, but since James was unable to concentrate on his job he was let go. It was impossible for him to find a roommate who wanted to live in the Bronx, in that neighborhood, and in that freezing-cold rusted out mobile home. With no way to meet his rent obligation he was evicted. After living on the street for three months, during which time he became unkempt and so lost his side job, he was then left with no other choice but to join the armed forces. He requested a deployment with the Special Elite Troops. And, since he had reached the age of sixteen, was old enough to be accepted for that special force. At age eighteen, uncaring if he lived or died, he was killed in a search and destroy mission against entrenched rebel forces in the Gobi desert foothills of the Tian Shan, or

"Celestial," mountain range.

In the wake of Alexandra Barnes Winstead's suicide, her mother divorced Arthur Winstead and took her ten-year-old son with her to live in Paris.

The Honorable Arthur B. Winstead III, Bureau Chief of State Cyber Security from 2033 to 2042, completely shattered by his guilt over his daughter's suicide, left Cyber Security and lived as a haunted recluse in one cluttered room of the large, otherwise empty, PH-A until the age of ninety-seven.

Made in the USA
Las Vegas, NV
29 August 2021

28970209R00173